Praise for the novels of B.J. Daniels

"Great start of a new series featuring rival ranching families."
—*Fresh Fiction* on *Dark Side of the River*

"Daniels always nails it with her well-developed plot..."
—*A Midlife Wife* on *River Justice*

"Daniels is a perennial favorite, and I might go as far as to label her the cowboy whisperer."
—*BookPage*

"Another ingenious plot from a grand author who deftly takes us along for the ride."
—*Fresh Fiction* on *Under a Killer Moon*

"I highly recommend this novel to readers who enjoy contemporary romantic suspense with great characters."
—*One Book More* on *Out of the Storm*

"Super read by an excellent writer. Recommended!"
—Linda Lael Miller, #1 *New York Times* bestselling author, on *Renegade's Pride*

"The action will set you on edge... Daniels has created a story that has suspense to spare."
—*Fresh Fiction* on *Redemption*

"Will keep readers on the edge of their chairs from beginning to end."
—*Booklist* on *Forsaken*

Also by B.J. Daniels

Powder River

Dark Side of the River
River Strong
River Justice
River Wild

Buckhorn, Montana

Out of the Storm
From the Shadows
At the Crossroads
Before Buckhorn
Under a Killer Moon
When Justice Rides
Out of the Blue
Before Memories Fade

Harlequin Intrigue

A Colt Brothers Investigation

Murder Gone Cold
Sticking to Her Guns

Look for B.J. Daniels's next novel
River Legacy
available soon.

B.J. DANIELS

NEW YORK TIMES BESTSELLING AUTHOR

RIVER WILD

First Published 2025
First Australian Paperback Edition 2025
ISBN 978 1 038 94076 6

Published by
Mills & Boon
An imprint of Harlequin Enterprises (Australia) Pty Limited (ABN 47 001 180 918), a subsidiary of HarperCollins Publishers Australia Pty Limited (ABN 36 009 913 517)
Level 19, 201 Elizabeth Street
SYDNEY NSW 2000
AUSTRALIA

Printed and bound in Australia by McPherson's Printing Group

River Wild

B.J. Daniels

This book is dedicated to my father, Harry Burton Johnson.
A born ambitious dreamer himself,
he told me I could be whatever I wanted.
All I wanted was to tell stories. Thanks, Dad,
for giving me so many of your genes. I'm doing what I want.

CHAPTER ONE

HE HAD THE nightmare again last night. The faceless woman, her mouth opening and closing, the primal sounds a deafening shriek, his fear and pain visceral. He knew it wasn't real, just a bad dream, yet he couldn't wake up, as hard as he tried. It was like being caught in an eddy on the river, his fear rising as his thoughts whirled, and the current took him out deeper with only one clear thought. *This time, you're going to die.*

"Still having the nightmares, Stuart?" the psychiatrist asked as she looked up from the notes she'd been taking.

"Nope," Sheriff Stuart Layton said with a shake of his head. He adjusted his Stetson balanced on his crossed knee and lied. He'd been coming here once a month since the "incident," as they called it, seven months ago. As an officer of the law who'd fired his weapon, killing a person in the line of duty, he had been required to have counseling until it was determined he could still do his job.

"How would you say you're dealing with the trauma of the incident?" she asked, pen poised above the paper.

His near-death *incident* was being attacked by a knife-wielding woman who'd left scars over his arms and torso, and even worse, invisible wounds that made him question his sanity—let alone why he was fighting so hard to keep his job.

Seeing that the doctor was waiting for a reply, he shrugged and said, "As well as can be expected. Life goes on. I have a job to do." She didn't like his comment, he noticed at once. "Keeping busy helps. I just had a kidnapping case, a thirteen-year-old." He didn't add that ultimately, he hadn't saved the girl himself. He certainly couldn't take credit for that. He had saved one life, though, and had done his job to the best of his ability, which he didn't feel was saying much.

"Do you ever question that you might be in the wrong profession?" the doctor asked.

He almost laughed out loud. When he fought his way out of the same recurring nightmare at three in the morning, he told himself he was done. He couldn't do this anymore. But with daylight, he could breathe again, forcing the darkness and his fear back for another day on the job—the only job he knew.

His father had been the sheriff before him. He'd grown up with the law living in his house. Going to the police academy out of high school had made sense after living in the small, isolated town of Powder Crossing, Montana, where there weren't a lot of opportunities. When his father retired, Stuart had stepped into the position that no one else really wanted. It seemed like a no-brainer.

"Who wouldn't question going into law enforcement?" he said, more to himself than to the doctor. His strict, distant father had used his silver star like a shield, a stoic, hard-nosed hero. Because of that, Stuart had thought he knew what he was getting into. He'd been wrong. "You start off thinking it's a higher calling only to realize that it's really just a thankless job—one that can get you killed. Pull over the wrong car, try to break up a domestic argument, step out of your office and look down the barrel of a loaded gun in the hand of someone with a grudge against you."

He saw her expression and cursed himself. He'd said too much. This wasn't the way he wanted to go out, failing his psych evaluation. All he'd had to do was get through this last required session of six. It didn't matter that he'd decided he had no business being sheriff anymore. He just needed her to sign off and let him hang up his star and gun on his own terms. Now he feared that he'd blown it.

"Given all of that, why have you stayed?"

He'd been too honest, so why stop now? "Because it's what I do to the best of my ability." Growing up, Stuart had wanted to be just like his father. Now that he had a better idea of who his father really had been, he feared that he had become him.

"Have you been depressed?"

She thought he was merely depressed? "Everyone gets down sometimes," he said, reminded of those nights alone in the house he'd grown up in, thinking about his life as he cleaned his gun. But then there were the nights when Bailey McKenna would stop by at all hours and, fool that he was, he would happily open his door to her, knowing the danger.

He'd definitely been down in the dumps before she'd started coming by. Often, he was depressed after she left hours later, the two of them having talked over a beer or two. Only talking. That's all they ever did, sitting out on the porch when it was warm. Otherwise curled up at each end of the couch while a fire crackled in the woodstove in the corner. He knew she wanted something from him, but he had no idea what. He'd just known that whatever it was, it could get him killed.

"Is there anything that might keep you from continuing to do your job, Stuart?"

Boy howdy, he thought. The last woman he'd gotten involved with had tried to kill him, nearly had. *So, yes, doctor, I have the unfortunate habit of getting tangled up with dangerous women.* It wasn't like he didn't know that Bailey was damaged, and yet she drew him like gawkers to a car crash. But how could he admit to the doctor that Bailey McKenna might prove to be the most dangerous of them all, yet he'd never wanted any woman more in his life?

"Actually," he said to the psychiatrist, "I think this introspection has been good for me. I see things more clearly. Maybe I'm maturing. It's possible, isn't it?"

She smiled, and he saw in her smile that she was going to sign his paperwork. He smiled back, pretending he wasn't worried about anything, not his future, not his growing feelings for Bailey. The last time he saw her, she'd been running scared, confirming what he'd already suspected. Bailey McKenna was in trouble up to her pretty little neck.

He feared what he was going to do about that, especially since things had been too quiet in the Powder River Basin. It gave him an eerie feeling he couldn't shake, like the lull before the storm. As he headed home, the signed psych evaluation form folded into his shirt pocket, it felt as if the storm clouds were already gathering for what would be one hell of a maelstrom.

This time, you're going to die.

BAILEY MCKENNA HADN'T realized it was so late. She looked up from her laptop, surprised to find that some of the library's lights had already been turned off, leaving pockets of darkness. She loved libraries, their smell, their solitude, the silence as heavy as the books lining the walls. And it wasn't just the libraries that she loved. She loved the books that opened doors into other worlds, cracked open other people's lives and shed a blinding and often insightful light on them.

Libraries and books had saved her growing up. Now they still provided her a place to escape. She always found a corner on the least used floor and settled in for hours.

Tonight, though, she'd stayed too long, and now she feared she might have gotten locked in. Closing her laptop, she gathered her things into the large bag she carried everywhere. She didn't let the bag or laptop out of her sight, not after all the months, years that she'd been working on her secret project.

It didn't matter that she'd backed up everything on the cloud. She didn't trust it. She needed to hold her project close. If anyone found out about it, they would try to stop her. She feared it might already be too late.

As she reached the third-floor stairs, she stopped to peer down. Darkness creeped up the steps from the pitch blackness below. What if she was locked in? It wouldn't be the first time she'd slept in a library since she started this. But lately, she'd felt as if she wasn't safe anywhere. She couldn't shake the feeling that she was always being watched. For all she knew, she had been followed here tonight. If so, they understood what she'd been up to.

The real boogeyman was who scared her the most. *He* was out there, had been for a long time. It was just a matter of time before he came for her again. That's why she'd been working desperately to find him before then. As her heart rate kicked up, she told herself she still had time. He'd waited this long. Why would he make his move now?

Starting down the stairs, though, she wasn't so sure about that. She stopped on a step to listen. The quiet she usually loved now felt ominous. She couldn't shake the feeling that while the library appeared empty, she wasn't alone.

On the second-floor landing, she turned the corner, then moved fast down the stairs, eager to reach street level. If she'd been accidentally locked in, she would call the emergency number. Someone would come get her out before long. But with each step, she found herself getting more nervous.

At the first floor, she had started toward the front of the huge building when she heard a scuffling sound, shoe soles moving across the library floor. She'd been right. She wasn't alone. She stopped again, listening even as her hand snaked into her bag for her pepper spray.

She'd been carrying the spray since being attacked outside the Wild Horse Bar in Powder Crossing. Her attacker had tried to take her bag with her computer in it. She'd fought him and gotten the bag away from him. Unfortunately, it had been too dark that night to see his face. He'd worn a hoodie and had run away when the female bartender had stuck her head out the door to see what was going on.

Bailey hadn't realized that she'd been screaming before that. Maybe the attacker just wanted money from her purse, also in her bag. Our maybe he'd wanted her laptop with what she'd been working on. She'd told herself it had been random since no one knew what she'd been up to, but she feared she was wrong.

She heard the scuffling sound again as she moved cautiously toward the front of the library. Maybe she'd been wrong and they weren't closed yet. Which meant the doors would still be open. Or maybe she was only hearing the janitor cleaning after hours.

Bailey rushed to the front door and hit it, expecting it to fly open. Instead, alarms began to go off. She leaned against the glass, clutching her can of pepper spray, expecting whoever she'd heard in the building to appear. If it had been the janitor or a librarian working late, they would come to see what was going on, right? But no one appeared from the darkness inside.

Instead, a police car roared up, siren and lights flashing. She stood, her back to the door, and stared into the darkness. It wasn't *Him*. Not here, not like this. No, but someone knew. She was no longer safe anywhere.

AFTER SHE'D BEEN QUESTIONED, scolded and made the subject of a police report—procedure, she was told—the young deputy offered to walk her to her car. Her answer surprised her.

"Please," she said, a quaver in her voice. She felt vulnerable, something she hated. But she wasn't sure at this moment that she was capable of taking care of herself. She'd had a scare tonight in the library. She hadn't been alone. The library had closed, but hadn't she heard someone else in the building? Where had they gone? Maybe more importantly, where were they now?

The back door opened onto the parking area—now empty except for her car. As she and the cop walked along the side of the building to the back, she saw her SUV sitting like an island in the middle of the blacktop sea. Beyond it were darkness and shadows that seemed to grow and fade with the passing traffic along 6th Street.

"You sure you're all right?" the deputy asked as she slowed, her eyes darting around the parking area—and the night beyond. She could only nod, knowing whoever it was hadn't left. They were somewhere in the dark, waiting for her. Her heart raced. What if it was *Him*? What if he was through waiting? But why now?

She and the officer continued toward her car. Her ears were tuned for the sound of a heel scraping over blacktop. She wasn't even sure the deputy would be able to protect her if the man attacked. Hurriedly she fumbled in her bag for her keys.

For a moment, she panicked. What if the cop left her before she found her keys? Her fingers trembled as she felt warm metal and pulled the keys from her bag—only to fumble and immediately drop them. They fell into the shadowy darkness at her feet, making a ringing sound as they struck the blacktop. For a moment she felt so helpless, so alone, so afraid that she thought she would start to cry and not be able to stop.

"Let me do that," the deputy said, scooping up her keys and opening her SUV's door. The overhead light came on inside it. She saw him look into the back before he handed over her keys.

She took them, fighting to pull herself together. This wasn't her. She was a fighter; it was the only reason she was still alive.

But lately, she'd been feeling as if she was constantly being watched—like now. Watched and followed. If she was right, *He* could be here watching her. Which meant he'd followed her to the library. He'd wanted her to know he was there. He wanted her to be afraid so he could watch her fear grow until he made his move.

Clutching the keys in her fist, she tried not to stop searching the darkness at the edge of the parking lot as she slid behind the wheel.

"You sure you're up to driving?" the deputy asked, studying her in the dim light spilling out of her vehicle.

"I'll be fine," she said, hoping it was true. "I'll stop and get some coffee and a bite to eat. I haven't had anything since breakfast. I'm a little shaky."

He took her answer at face value. "All right then, drive safely." For a moment, he studied her again as if he wanted to say more. Instead, he nodded and stepped back to close her door firmly. For a moment, their gazes met through the glass. She tried a smile as she reached to start the motor. "I'll be fine," she said as the engine throbbed to life. The deputy seemed to hesitate before he turned his back and walked away.

The moment she'd driven out of the semidarkness of the parking lot and caught her first stoplight, she saw it—something small and white stuck under her driver's side windshield wiper.

Her pulse jumped, her gaze flying up to the rearview mirror. She expected to see a face, smell sweat, feel something close around her throat. But there was no one hiding in the back of her vehicle. The officer had checked. Still, she felt jumpy.

Bailey drove a few blocks before she found a busy fast-food restaurant with a well-lit parking lot. She pulled in and, leaving the engine running, jumped out to lift the wiper and free what she now saw was a piece of paper folded tightly.

She didn't unfold it until she was back safely behind the

wheel, the doors all locked. Logic argued that it could be an advertising flyer stuffed under the wiper at any time while she was in the library.

Or it could be what she knew in her heart. The note had been left for her by the person who'd been hiding in the library, watching her.

Carefully unfolding the paper, her hands began to shake as she held up the note to the light. The words were written in a hurried scrawl. *You got lucky tonight. Won't next time.*

She balled it up and lowered her window, ready to throw it out. But she was a Montanan raised by Holden McKenna. You didn't litter. She threw the note to the floorboard.

Cars pulled into the drive-through. Others sped past behind her on the street. There seemed to be people everywhere. Life going on around her, *without* her. Her sudden desperation to get to Powder Crossing verged on panic. All she could think about was getting home. Home. Too bad she no longer felt safe on the ranch that had always been her home. Too bad she didn't feel safe anywhere but one place—the last place she should go.

Pulling out on the street at the first break in the traffic, she checked her rearview mirror again but saw only dozens of headlights. *He* could be in any of the vehicles behind her. The stoplight changed. The driver behind her honked and she hit the gas, telling herself not to look back. But how could she do that? She'd been looking back for twelve years. She couldn't stop now.

SHERIFF STUART LAYTON didn't hear about what had happened at the Billings Public Library until the next morning when the police report crossed his desk via computer. He'd been updated because the woman in question was a local.

> Bailey McKenna of Powder Crossing, Montana, was released with only a warning after setting off after-hours alarms at the library. She claimed she'd been listening to music on her headphones and hadn't heard the announcement that the library was closing.

"Well, that explains my visitor last night," Stuart said to himself with a shake of his head. Actually, it had been late when Bailey had shown up at his door. He hadn't known what had happened—just that something had the moment he saw her face in his porch light. He'd been sound asleep when he'd been dragged abruptly awake by her knock. He'd scrubbed his eyes with the heels of his hands, taken off guard not by seeing her at any hour of the night, but by seeing her this upset.

Wordlessly he'd motioned her in. It was too close to daylight for beer. Yet too early for coffee. Still caught in the remnants of one of his nightmares, he'd been taken by surprise when she'd thrown herself into his arms.

He'd held her for a few moments before she'd quickly pulled away. Having grown up with Bailey in the small ranch community, he could count on one hand the times he'd seen her scared. Mad? That was another story. She'd always come out fighting, usually more than capable of taking care of herself.

"Bailey," he'd said, startled and worried. It wasn't like her to throw herself into his arms, though he'd dreamed of her doing just that. She had to know how he felt about her. Terrified, yet tempted by her. It's why, he figured, she kept him at arm's length. But seeing her this scared… "What's going on?"

She'd stepped back, shaking her head as tears swam in

her blue eyes. "I'm fine." Her voice had cracked. "I'm just really tired. Everything is going to be fine." She'd taken another step back, widening the distance between them. For the first time, she'd seemed to notice that all he was wearing was his jeans, his chest bare, his scars showing.

"Let me put something on," he said, uncomfortable around people without a long-sleeved shirt or jacket covering the remnants of the "incident."

"Don't leave." He'd started toward his bedroom, but then stopped, afraid she'd go back out into the darkness, afraid that whatever had her scared was waiting for her there.

He'd suspected there might be a man, a love affair gone wrong, though he couldn't remember seeing her with anyone. If she'd been dating, the gossip would have stretched across the Powder River Basin with lightning speed. He hadn't heard a thing about her and a man. To most people she was a mystery, apparently friendless, coming and going at all hours of the night, alone and secretive.

Turning back, he'd looked at her, so pretty and yet always so skittish. He'd desperately wanted her to open up to him and let him in. But he'd seen that wasn't happening, not then, maybe not ever.

"I just need..." She'd looked around as if almost surprised that she'd come there and didn't remember why she had. She looked exhausted and lost, and it broke his heart. He'd desperately wanted to comfort her but had known instinctively that wasn't why she'd come to him.

He'd pointed to the spare bedroom. "Get some rest. You're safe here. Stay for breakfast."

Her eyes had filled again with tears. "Thank you."

He'd shrugged and padded back to his own bed. He'd only had a few hours before he needed to get up and go to work. He'd thought he wouldn't be able to get back to sleep knowing she was just in the next room, but he'd been wrong. After he'd heard the creak of the bed in the next room as she'd lain down on it, he'd slept hard, awakened by his alarm.

When he'd gotten up, no surprise, Bailey had been gone. There was a slight impression in the mattress where she'd slept on one side of the spare bed. But other than that, there was no sign that she'd stopped by, let alone stayed long.

Sitting in his office now with a mug of hot coffee, he wondered what she'd been doing so late at the Billings library that she'd gotten locked in. At least now he had some idea why she'd come by his place last night and maybe why she'd stayed. But he couldn't imagine that was why she'd been so scared.

Remembering the fear in her eyes only made his concern for her escalate. What was it she'd said? *I'm fine. I'm just really tired. Everything is going to be fine.*

He had no idea what she'd been talking about. But he had a bad feeling it wasn't going to be fine any more than he suspected she did.

CHAPTER TWO

THE CALL CAME into the sheriff's department midmorning. Stuart hadn't been able to get Bailey's visit last night and his one-sided feelings for her out of his mind. Those feelings were complicated to say the least. He wasn't even sure exactly what he wanted from her—let alone what she might want from him.

All he knew was that she had secrets he feared were dangerous. He couldn't help but worry about her, even while admitting that she was a dark path he knew he shouldn't take.

He accepted the call as if he'd been waiting all morning for bad news.

"Ralph Jones is on the line," the dispatcher said. "He says it's urgent. Wouldn't say more than that."

"Put him through." Stuart leaned forward in his chair. Along with an ongoing feud with his closest neighbor, Ralph Jones was the head of a so-called secret local organization called Dirty Business. Jones had organized some area residents against coalbed methane drilling. But from what the sheriff had heard, the group hadn't been meeting much lately after a guard from the gas company had been killed and another injured. Drilling seemed to have slowed down.

Stuart assumed the call had something to do either with CH4, the gas company that had been operating in the area, or Jay Erickson, the feuding neighbor, and braced himself. All morning he'd had a familiar itch on the back of his neck. He blamed Bailey's visit for leaving him on edge and anticipating the worst.

"Ralph," he said into the phone. "What can I do for you?"

"I'm by the river. Stopped on my way back from taking a horse down to Wyoming." The rancher's voice sounded strained. "I was taking a piss in the trees when I saw...a body in the water. A woman's body."

Stuart felt all the air rush from his lungs. His first thought was the woman who'd left his place before daylight this morning. "Do you recognize the woman?" It was a small community where most everyone knew each other. *Everyone* knew Bailey McKenna. She was the daughter of Holden McKenna, a wealthy, powerful rancher who probably had the governor's cell phone number, he was so well-connected.

"She's lying face down in the water. She's completely naked and..." Jones said, voice hoarse with emotion. Before Stuart could ask if he had checked to see who it was, the rancher said, "I thought it was Bailey McKenna, the dark, curly hair... But when I checked, I saw it was Willow Branson, the young woman who works...worked at the hotel. Then I saw...someone did something awful to her."

"Okay, Ralph." The rancher's words were still echoing in his ears, making his heart pound, his stomach roil. *I thought it was Bailey McKenna.* "Where exactly are you?" Jones told him. "Stay there. Don't talk to anyone about this, and don't touch the body again. I'm on my way." He disconnected and called the coroner.

Twelve minutes later, he was securing the crime scene site with one of his deputies keeping everyone away from the spot next to the county road along the Powder River. After taking photographs of the overall scene, Stuart jumped from rock to rock down the river to the body, hoping not to disturb any more evidence than had already been lost.

As he neared the body, he slowed, his stomach doing a roll. Jones was right. At first glance, the young woman lying dead in the creek could have been Bailey. They were close to the same size and shape, both with a head of dark, curly hair, both attractive young women, although Willow was about ten years younger.

Even though he knew it wasn't Bailey, the knot in his stomach tightened, the pressure on his chest making breathing unbearable. She lay face down in about six inches of water, just as Jones had said. She was naked, her long hair floating in the water around her head.

Crouching down next to her, he swallowed back the sudden nausea, hating what he was about to see. Gently, he lifted her head so he could see her face. It wasn't Bailey. He felt a guilty stab of relief even though Jones had said it wasn't her. But the resemblance was uncanny—and startling since the last time he'd seen Willow, she'd been blonde.

His relief was followed by a heart-pounding need for justice. Wasn't that why he'd talked himself into taking the sheriff job? This was someone's daughter, a young woman in the prime of her life, murdered. He thought about how he'd feel if the woman in the river had been Bailey. He'd never condoned vigilante justice, but he'd never understood the need until right now. Someone hurts the person you love, you hurt them back. Another reason he shouldn't be sheriff, he thought.

As if moving on rote, he lifted the victim's shoulder to see the damage done to her left breast. His stomach lurched, and for a moment, he thought he'd be sick.

Stuart fought it back as he let go of her shoulder and stood awkwardly, balancing on the rocks, legs weak. This woman deserved the best criminal investigator around. It wasn't him, he told himself. He couldn't keep lying to himself. The "incident" had scared the hell out of him. He'd no longer been sure he could do the job. As he looked at the river water washing past her body, he feared he wasn't the one to get her justice.

To make it worse, the river had washed away any evidence by now, which was why he suspected her body had been dumped here. Feeling as if he was sleepwalking, he took out his phone and photographed the scene, documenting it and the wounds on Willow's body. But he couldn't blot out the pain he saw on the young woman's body. The ligature marks on her wrists and ankles and neck.

Forcing himself, he lifted her shoulder high enough that he could photograph what the killer had done to her. Bile rushed up his throat, filling his mouth, as he carefully lowered her back down and stood again.

His stomach cramped as he straightened and tried to breathe. The cool breeze coming down the river steadied him, allowing him to fight back the spasms as everything in his stomach fought to get out. *Think like the law that you are.*

Or walk away.

It was an option that had been in the back of his mind for weeks. He could quit. There was no shame in admitting that he couldn't take it anymore. Hell, better men than him had walked away. He'd lied to the doctor. He wasn't up to this. Not anymore.

Phone still in his hand, he made the call to the state boys in Billings.

BAILEY REALIZED THAT the news of her run-in with the law at the Billings Public Library had gotten out. She just hadn't expected it to reach the McKenna Ranch so quickly. This morning, just before daylight, she'd left Stuart's house and driven out to the ranch where she still technically lived. She'd gone to her wing of the new larger-than-ever ranch house her father had built after a fire had destroyed the old one.

She was almost thirty and still lived at home, but she hadn't been able to force herself to move out. She had a love-hate relationship with the ranch. Also, she could come and go without seeing anyone, thanks to the private entrance she had insisted on during construction.

The huge ranch house was mostly empty. Her brother Cooper lived in the home he'd built on the ranch with his new wife, Tilly. Her older brother, Treyton, had his own place, so she never saw him, which was fine given his bad-tempered disposition, worse than her own. Her youngest brother, Duffy, was down in Wyoming, working in the oil fields. That left only her father, his teenaged ward, Holly Jo Robinson, and their housekeeper and cook, Elaine.

Since Holden McKenna had brought the then twelve-year-old Holly Jo home, Bailey had stayed clear of the girl. She tried to stay clear of her father as well, unable to explain even to herself her no-doubt unwarranted anger toward him. Knowing that he always took an early morning horseback ride, she left her wing to see if Elaine had made her usual blueberry coffee cake this morning.

"Bailey?"

She slowed to a stop at the sound of her father's voice as she was passing the dining room. Why wasn't he on his morning ride? Having no choice, she turned to face him. Holden sat at the head of the table. She wasn't surprised to see Elaine sitting in the chair where her mother had once sat. At least, that's what she'd been told. Bailey had been too young when her mother died to remember her now.

"Good morning," Bailey said pleasantly enough, she hoped. "I was just on my way to the kitchen." She started to leave, but her father stopped her.

"Bailey, wait. I need to talk to you."

She tried not to sigh loudly and start an argument. She wasn't in the mood for a lecture—let alone an inquisition as to why she had stayed so late at the library that she'd gotten locked inside. She assumed that was what this was about. It would be just like someone from the police station to call her father. But she especially didn't want to get into what she'd been doing at the library—not just last night but for years.

When she turned, Elaine, also her father's faithful co-conspirator, was on her feet. "I'll get you some coffee cake. Would you like anything else?"

"Just coffee and a piece of the cake to go," she said, hating her own discomfort. For so long, she'd felt apart from everyone—her family, but mostly her father and even Elaine, who was as nice as anyone could be. Much of the time, Bailey wished she was invisible and could just go through life not being seen at all.

"Come sit down," her father said, and pulled out the chair next to him.

Feeling trapped, she walked into the dining room and sat down. When she looked at her father, she felt a shock. He'd aged. His usual salt-and-pepper head of dark hair was more salt now. His blue eyes were still bright, his skin tanned from his morning horseback rides now that the doctor had okayed them again. There were lines around his eyes and his mouth. She was reminded that he'd almost died not all that long ago after being shot several times.

There was no doubt that almost dying had taken something out of him. Yet he had the bearing of a man who was still strong and powerful. When she looked into his face, she realized how handsome he still was.

She felt a kindness toward him that she hadn't felt in a very long time.

"I've missed you," he said, reaching over to place one of his large, weathered hands over hers. "You know how important family is to me."

She nodded, relieved when Elaine returned with several plates of food, fresh coffee and an extra place setting. But sensing that Holden wanted to talk to his daughter alone, Elaine excused herself. "I'll leave you two alone. There's fresh fruit and coffee cake, but I'd be glad to fix you something else."

"Thank you," Bailey said. "This is more than I need." She could never understand why her father hadn't married Elaine. The woman had been like a mother to them for years. Elaine's own mother had been their original housekeeper and had been raised here on the ranch. She'd often said that it was the only home she'd ever known.

Bailey helped herself to a cup of coffee from the carafe on the table and waited for her father to tell her why he'd wanted to talk to her. She'd learned from an early age not to confess to anything before hearing what he already knew.

"I was worried about you after I got the call this morning from Ralph Jones," Holden said.

She looked at him, trying to make sense out his words. Local rancher Ralph Jones? How would he have heard about the fiasco at the Billings library? Or was this about something else entirely?

"A woman's body was found in the river," he said. "Apparently, she'd been murdered. Ralph said he had a scare because when he first saw her lying there, face down in the river with her dark, curly hair floating around her head…" Her father's voice broke. "He'd thought it was you."

Bailey couldn't inhale. "Who was it?" The question came out on a ragged breath.

"Willow Branson."

She had an immediate mental image of the young woman who worked at the local hotel. Bailey had noticed Willow's resemblance to her the first time she'd seen her. Willow was young and trusting, and she looked enough like Bailey to be her little sister.

Except that Willow was blonde.

"No, it can't be her," Bailey said. "Her hair isn't dark."

"It was when I saw her last week," her father said.

"Why would she change it?" she demanded too loudly.

Her father was looking at her strangely. "I guess she got tired of being blonde. I don't think it was her natural color. Bailey, are you all right?"

HOLDEN STARED AT his daughter with growing concern. All the color had leached from her face. Her blue eyes, so like his own, were wide with a fear that alarmed him. "Bailey?"

Her hand trembled as she put down the cup of coffee she'd picked up. "I have to go." She rose unsteadily. He reached for her even as she pulled away. He couldn't remember the last time she'd let him touch her more than a few seconds, let alone hug her.

When he'd mention being worried about her, Elaine always pointed out how independent Bailey was. He knew how stubborn she'd been as a child and wild as a teenager. But he couldn't remember her being so distant. When had she become like this? He couldn't recall. He told himself that they'd been close when she was younger. He recalled little gestures, like homemade presents and Father's Day cards as well a hug or an arm around him, a kiss on his cheek. When had all that stopped?

He felt as if there was so much he'd missed because he hadn't been paying attention. He'd been so wrapped up in his own problems.

Bailey had been difficult during her teen years, rebellious, often in trouble. But she'd outgrown that at college, apparently, because she'd obviously studied hard, graduating at the top of her class. After college, when she'd come home… He frowned. She'd graduated early, smart as a whip. He'd thought maybe she would go back to school, become a lawyer. She'd talked about it when she was younger.

Frowning, he wondered what had changed her mind. Not just about being an attorney. She hadn't found a career after college. He honestly didn't know what she did every day. He hadn't thought too much about it until she'd become so angry. Angry at him, he thought as he watched her leave.

Pushing to his feet, he called after her. "Bailey, I'm worried about you coming and going at all hours of the night. You're scaring me."

She had reached the front door and turned to look back at him. For a moment, she was his little girl. Something replaced the anger that so often burned in her blue eyes. He recognized the emotion with a start. Pain. Regret. Remorse. It hurt him to see it so blatant in her expression. Worse, he saw something else. Blame, as if he was the one who'd caused all that naked anguish behind the shine of tears.

And then she was gone out the door.

He slowly lowered himself into his chair, stricken by what he'd seen. What had he done to his little girl?

THE SHERIFF MADE himself go through the motions as he waited for the state crime team to drive over from Billings. He'd made the necessary calls and taken the necessary photos, looking, he hoped, as if he knew what he was doing even when he no longer trusted himself.

Now, as he stood on a rock in the river and looked upstream, he noticed with a start what a beautiful Montana fall day it was. The blinding blue of the sky overhead. The crisp air scented with the pungent smells of fall, from the dried grasses and leaves to the faint hint of smoke from someone's early morning fire. He could feel winter's breath on the back of his neck, and something darker as he realized the killer might have stood in this very spot not all that long ago.

He felt a chill as if the killer might be watching them from the thick stand of cottonwoods along the river that was the heart of this basin. It began in Wyoming and traveled more than one hundred fifty miles to empty into the Yellowstone.

It was not like any other river in the state. Many claimed that the Powder River was a mile wide, an inch deep and ran uphill. The running joke was that it was too thick to drink and too thin to plow. Captain Clark of the Lewis and Clark expedition had named it Redstone River. But the Native Americans called it Powder River because the black shores reminded them of gunpowder, and that had stuck.

"Okay to take her?" the coroner called to him, dragging him out of his reverie.

Stuart nodded and moved to help the coroner and EMTs retrieve the body and transport it to the waiting coroner's van that would take Willow to the local hospital morgue for the autopsy.

As the coroner slammed the van's back doors, Stuart asked, "Any idea how long she's been in the water?" He was still the sheriff, still in charge of this case—until the state team arrived.

"Once I get her on the table, I'll check her temperature, but from the color of her skin, I'd say she was dropped in the river early this morning. She hasn't been in the water long."

"Cause of death?"

"Will depend on if there is any of the river water in her lungs," the coroner said. "I suspect strangulation given the ligature marks on her neck. I'll call when I have more."

With that he left, leaving Stuart to glance back at the river through the trees and bushes next to the county road. The deputy he'd called in was searching the area along the river and road for any possible footprints or evidence that might have been dropped.

The grass along the side of the river had dried as summer faded into fall. He could see where the fallen, dried leaves from the cottonwoods had been crushed into the ground where someone had stepped. No drag marks that he could see. Which meant he'd carried her out into the river and laid her face down in the water, which felt odd. Dead weight wasn't that easy to carry—especially over the boulders in the river.

Why not just dump her out beside the road or into the water at the edge of the river? It seemed almost…caring to carry her out there. But why put her face down? Because the killer couldn't bear to look into her face?

He turned to gaze back at the distance from the river's edge to where she'd been left in the water. The victim was about five-five and weighed about a hundred twenty pounds. Dead weight like that would have required some strength to carry that far out into the river. Stuart felt there was little doubt that her killer had been a man.

After Willow Branson was in a body bag on her way to the morgue, Stuart pushed away the ominous feeling that had overcome him and went to work searching the area with his deputy. He told himself this would be the last time. By afternoon, he would no longer be sheriff. He was stepping down. He didn't feel as relieved as he thought he would. Nor did he feel guilty. He felt numb and had for a very long time.

But for now… The county road was gravel and well-used. The weather had been clear. The killer hadn't left any tire marks at the edge of the river.

But his deputy had found one boot print that didn't match Ralph Jones's near the edge of the water. Stuart took photos of the print and called his other deputy to come out with materials to make a plaster mold of it.

Some paper and other garbage had blown into the weeds

at the base of several nearby trees along the river's edge. He had his deputy bag everything they could find in the vicinity, even though it was doubtful the killer had left them a clue.

As soon as a couple of the state boys arrived, Stuart headed into town with only one clear thought. *I can't do this anymore. I don't have to. I'm done.*

CHAPTER THREE

THE SHERIFF HAD just gotten a call from the coroner when Bailey walked into his office. He hadn't changed his mind about quitting. The first thing he'd done when he reached his office was type up his resignation, but he hadn't had a chance since then to turn it in—or let anyone else know.

"Sheriff?"

He'd missed what assistant coroner Ronald Danbury had said on the phone because he'd been surprised to see Bailey charge into his office, her face pale, her blue eyes wide. "I'm sorry—"

"I was saying the small horseshoe on her left breast appears to have been made with something hot that seared the skin and left a definite scar, as if the killer had wanted to brand his victim," the coroner continued. "The position and placement of the U-shaped brand on her breast must mean something to him. Also, I have the cause of death. She drowned, which means she was alive when she went into the water, but probably not conscious."

Stuart closed his eyes for a moment. Why the brand, he

wondered in horror. It wasn't uncommon for cowboys to have the brand of the ranch they worked for emblazoned on their clothing and tack. Brands, especially in Montana, had meaning and stayed registered to the family often even if the ranch was sold. Along with showing livestock ownership, brands had historically represented the cowboy, his work, his ideals and his hopes.

In the case of the woman this man had tortured and branded, it could also be a sign of ownership or at least possession. He became physically ill as he thought of what this monster had done.

"Ronald, I'm going to have to call you back," he said as Bailey closed and locked his office door behind her. She seemed to vibrate with tension, practically wringing her hands as she paced his small office. He had no idea why she was here, but she was clearly agitated. He tried to remember if she'd ever been to his office before. He didn't think so. He quickly disconnected.

"Bailey—"

"I need to ask you something," she said, stopping in front of his desk. "About Willow." So, she'd already heard about the young woman's body being found in the river. No surprise given how quickly information was disseminated through the Powder River Basin grapevine.

Her gaze met his, holding it. He could see the tautness in her face, but it was the bright fear in her eyes that scared him, a more brilliant shade of fear than even last night. He'd never seen her like this. "How was she killed?"

"Why do you want to—"

"*Just tell me.* Please."

He heard the desperation in her voice. He went with

the partial truth, the less painful truth, since she seemed so upset about Willow's death. He was surprised since he hadn't known that they were friends. Bailey and Willow resembled each other, but they were about a decade apart in age and were nothing alike. Willow was all rainbows and sunshine, while Bailey was… Bailey. To see her this upset…

"She drowned."

Bailey stepped back, breaking eye contact. He saw her immediate relief as her body seemed to slump with the weight of it. "So, she wasn't…" Her voice broke. Turning abruptly, she started for the door.

"Wait," he said as he rose from his chair, but she had already unlocked the door and was halfway out when she said over her shoulder, "That's all I needed to know."

He started to go after her when his phone rang. He'd been expecting a call from the crime team. He needed to let the leader know about his resignation as sheriff. He had to take this. Swearing, he picked up. A tech was calling with information about the boot print that had been found at the edge of the river.

"Size ten and a half." The lab tech went on to explain that cowboy boots usually come in three common heel heights. "A walking heel is about one inch, and a riding heel is up to two inches. A walking or roper heel is usually flat and blocklike, while a riding heel is underslung or tapered."

"Right," he said, hoping to move him along as he looked after Bailey, trying to make sense of what had just happened in his office. Until he turned in his resignation, he was still assisting the state crime team on a local level.

"The leather soles of cowboy boots are smooth for safety while riding. If you fall from the saddle, the smooth soles will slip from the stirrup irons easier, keeping you from getting stuck. What makes this boot print unusual is that it is worn to the point that the soles are no longer smooth, and it has a buckaroo heel."

"What's a buckaroo heel?" the sheriff asked. He'd worn cowboy boots since he was a boy, but this was a new one on him.

"It's high and tapered in the back and leaves a distinct print." The tech sounded excited about this. "Also, buckaroo-type cowboy boots are higher up the calf. The leather is thicker to protect the horseback rider."

"So all we have to do is find the man wearing these boots," Stuart said.

"He might only wear them when he kills."

That caught him off guard. "You think this isn't his first?" He felt that glimmer of excitement he used to feel about solving a case, but it quickly waned. He could no longer do this in good conscience. He no longer trusted his judgment.

"Hard to say if he's done this before. I'll run the boot prints and the mark left on the body from the photo the coroner sent through our system. If he's done this before, I'm betting the disfigurement is his signature. Maybe we'll get a hit."

Stuart disconnected and swore as he looked out his window to see Bailey driving away from the sheriff's department. Her words kept coming back to him. *So she wasn't...*

Gooseflesh rippled over the bare skin of his arms. So she wasn't what? Raped, bound, disfigured and then left in the river to drown? Why had Bailey asked that? He knew why he'd lied to her about what had been done to the victim. He was still the law. He couldn't share details about an ongoing investigation.

Yet he couldn't shake the feeling that Bailey knew something. He'd been afraid for her before this, but now he was terrified. He tried her number. It went straight to voicemail.

"We need to talk. It's urgent. About Willow...there's more that I couldn't tell you."

He disconnected, his mind racing. Bailey had been afraid that more was done to Willow. Because she knew someone it had happened to? Or... He wouldn't let himself go there. If Bailey had crossed paths with this killer at some point, why wouldn't she have come forward? He knew women often didn't go to the law for a lot of reasons. Fear, embarrassment, a need to forget.

But not Bailey. She wouldn't have kept silent. Yet...

Stuart tried her number again. Voicemail. "Call me, Bailey."

He recalled how nervous she'd been in his office. How afraid she'd been. Grabbing his Stetson, he headed for his patrol SUV to look for her. He couldn't depend on her to come to him.

But when he hadn't found her hours later, he was forced to return to his office to do what he had to, knowing that even if he could have found her, he couldn't make her talk to him if she didn't want to. His resignation letter was still on his desk, but it was too late to do anything with it today.

He told himself that there was nothing more he could do tonight. Tomorrow he would officially resign. The state crime team would find Willow Branson's killer since Stuart knew he wasn't up to it. The young woman deserved better than him, he told himself.

He tried Bailey's number again. It went directly to voicemail. He didn't bother to leave another message.

BAILEY DIDN'T KNOW where she was going—just that she needed to drive after listening to Stuart's message. *We need to talk. It's urgent. Willow...there's more that I couldn't tell you.*

She gripped the wheel, her fingers going numb. She should have left years ago. At least, she shouldn't have come back after college—not after knowing what she was coming home to. There was still time. It wasn't too late. She could leave and never look back. It didn't matter that she had no idea where she would go—just away. Somewhere safe.

But even as she thought it, she knew that there was only one way she would feel safe. That's why she'd come back to the ranch. That's why she couldn't leave, especially now.

More that I couldn't tell you. She almost called Stuart, but the pit in her stomach already told her what he would say. She'd known the moment her father had told her Willow had been murdered that she'd changed her hair color, that she looked so much like Bailey that Ralph Jones had thought at first it was her. Bailey had known.

Yet she'd wanted so desperately to believe she was wrong that she'd accepted Stuart's simple cause of death. Drowning.

There's more that I couldn't tell you.

At the quick, sharp burp of a siren, her gaze shot to her rearview mirror. A patrol SUV? Stuart? She started to slam her foot down on the gas pedal, needing to run, but stopped herself. She couldn't outrun him. Even if she got away tonight, he'd come looking for her tomorrow.

She slowed and pulled over, realizing where she was. On an empty road miles from town. Frowning, she glanced in her rearview mirror, but could see little because of the flashing lights.

Stuart? How had the sheriff found her? Had he followed her out of town? She hadn't been paying attention, a mistake on her part that could have been much worse if the person in that car had been someone else.

The sheriff was the one person in this town she felt she could trust, and yet she knew Stuart wanted much more than her trust, which complicated things.

As he pulled behind her rig, she cut her engine and lay over the steering wheel, suddenly exhausted and afraid that once she looked into Stuart's face, she would tell him everything. She'd been running from this for years, but she'd never been running more scared than she was now.

Bailey looked up as she heard the patrol SUV driver's side door open. In her side mirror, she saw with a start that it wasn't the sheriff but a middle-aged female patrol officer who stepped out and approached.

There were no women on the county force, which meant this officer was out of her jurisdiction. That thought zipped past as she noticed something disturbing. The female officer had dropped one hand to the weapon at her hip.

As Bailey reached toward her glove box for her registration, she told herself this was just a standard stop. Maybe she'd been going over the speed limit. Maybe she had a taillight out. Maybe… The hard tap at her side window made her jump.

She looked over to see the name on the officer's uniform. R. Durham. She felt a chill. Everything about this, including the dark night, had her nerves on edge. Her instincts screamed that something was wrong.

Bailey swallowed the lump that had risen in her throat,

fighting the instinct to make a run for it as common sense told her running could get her thrown in jail—if not killed. She put down her window. "I have my license and car registration right—"

"Get out of the car. *Now!*"

Bailey turned to see that R. Durham had stepped back, the gun now in her hand.

"Get out of the car!"

She was still trying to convince herself this was some kind of mistake as she stepped out of the car. She barely got her door closed before she was struck. The woman slammed into her, shoving her face-first into the side of the SUV and pressing the gun to the side of her head.

"What is this about?" Bailey cried, fearing this was no mistake after all.

R. Durham leaned closer, holding her face crushed against the side of the car, the barrel of the gun pressed even harder against her temple. "You've messed with the wrong family. I know what you've been doing, going around digging into things that are none of your business."

"I don't know who you are."

"Oh, you'll remember me, though," the woman said, and slammed a fist into the small of Bailey's back.

The blow knocked the air from her lungs and seemed to paralyze her legs. She slumped to the ground as the woman stepped back to tower over her.

"You leave my family alone," the officer said, grabbing a handful of Bailey's long hair and dragging her to her feet, all the while keeping the weapon trained on her. "I always heard you were tough. Don't seem so tough right now."

"You have a gun to my head. Put down the gun and badge and we'll see who's tougher. But you're not looking for a fair fight, are you?" Bailey said through gritted teeth as her hands fisted at her sides.

The woman dragged her to the rear of the SUV, then shoved her hard. Bailey tumbled down into the deep, weed-filled barrow pit. As she rolled, dried weed stalks tore at her face, at her bare arms, ripping her shirt until she finally came to a stop at the bottom.

Officer R. Durham stood on the edge of the road, silhouetted in the lights from the patrol car, her weapon dangling from her hand. She raised the gun slowly. Bailey didn't move. Couldn't. If this was where it ended, fine. She almost welcomed it. In her nightmares, her death had been much worse.

"Leave the Durhams alone. Next time, you won't be getting out of that ditch." She holstered the gun and walked back to her patrol SUV. A few moments later, her engine revved. She sped off in a hail of dirt and gravel.

Bailey lay in the dried earth and weeds at the bottom of the barrow pit, listening to the patrol car drive away. She didn't have to ask how she'd gotten here or why. Slowly rising, her body aching, her skin bleeding where it had been scraped raw, she crawled her way back up onto the road.

The dark night closed in around her, the silence deafening, as she stood in the middle of the road. R. Durham had believed that she'd scared her. The thought made her laugh as she reminded herself what was out there in the darkness coming for her.

But her laugh ended abruptly as she let out a howl of frustration that turned into a scream. The sound filled the night, chasing back the darkness and the fear before she pulled herself together. She wasn't going down without a fight.

STUART HADN'T REALIZED how late it was. He'd been tying up loose ends, preparing to step away from the office for good. But when he saw the time, he knew he needed to go home and try to get some rest.

He wondered if he'd see Bailey, doubting it. She knew he was going to demand answers, so she'd probably stay away. Maybe it was better that way.

As he got up to leave, he was notified that someone wanted to talk to him about Willow.

"Did you get a name?" he asked.

"Aaron Branson." Before he could ask, "He's Willow's brother."

"Send him back," Stuart said, even though it was way after hours. Until it was official, he was still the only law in this part of the Powder River Basin.

A few moments later, a tall, nice-looking dark-haired man with a cleft chin was at his door. He motioned him in as he stood to shake the man's hand. "I'm Sheriff Stuart Layton. I'm sorry about your sister."

"Have you caught the person who did this?" he demanded.

Stuart sat down behind his desk again, motioning to a chair for his visitor, but Aaron Branson didn't sit. "Maybe you can help me do that."

"I don't see how. My uncle called. I had to hear it from him. I don't understand why no one called me. My number is in her phone as a contact."

"Her phone hasn't been found."

Branson seemed to take that information like a blow. He stumbled to a chair and sat, dropping his elbows to his knees, then dropping his face into his hands as he cried silently, his body heaving.

"Your uncle was listed as next of kin at the hotel where your sister was employed."

"He raised us." Lifting his head and wiping away tears, he said, "How could this have happened to Willow?"

"Were you in contact with her since she moved to Powder Crossing and took the job at the hotel?" Stuart asked.

"We talked all the time."

"Then you might know why she changed her hair color recently."

Branson stared at him. "Seriously? That's what you want to know?"

"We think the man who killed her was looking for a certain…type."

"If you're insinuating—"

"That's not what I'm saying. He might not have even noticed her before she changed her hair color."

Branson seemed to give that some thought for a moment. "A few weeks ago, she said some guy at the bar made a crack about her hair."

The sheriff felt his pulse quicken. "What exactly did he say?"

"That he didn't like her blonde. He said it wasn't her natural color and he would love to see it natural."

"Did she mention who this man was?" Stuart asked, his heart in his throat.

Branson shook his head. "I said the guy was a jerk, and she should have told him where to get off."

"Did she?"

He sighed. "Doubtful since a few days later, she said he was right. She looked better with it closer to her natural color."

"What else did she tell you about the man?

"Nothing, except… I know she changed it for him. The only reason she would do that was because she liked him. Are you telling me he's the one who…" He broke down, his face in his hands again.

The sheriff gave him some time before he asked, "She said she met him in the hotel bar? I know she worked behind the hotel registration desk."

"Sometimes she filled in for one of the bartenders, usually a young guy she called Luke."

Willow wasn't legally old enough to bartender, but this wasn't the time to get into that. "Luke Graves?" Stuart said. He remembered the name from the list of employees that had been sent over from the hotel. "Was Willow dating anyone?"

Branson shook his head. "There was one guy, but they'd broken up."

"Who—"

"It wasn't serious—at least for him. A rancher. He broke it off. Said she was too young."

"How long—"

"A couple of months off and on. Willow was falling for him. She didn't care that he was a decade older than her."

An older rancher. It wasn't much to go on. "Can you think of anything else?"

Branson shook his head, tears in his eyes. "Willow was careful. She'd already had her heart broken. She had her whole life ahead of her."

"Why did she come to Powder Crossing?" Stuart asked.

"To put the past behind her. Her fiancé from college had just gotten engaged. She needed to go to a place where no one knew her. I think she said she found the job posted on a bulletin board at a gas station in Miles City."

"Are you going to be in town for a while?" the sheriff asked. "I know the state crime team will want to talk to you."

CHAPTER FOUR

THE SHERIFF WOKE to the sound of knocking on his front door. He glanced at his phone. Three a.m. Startled awake, then remembering the body at the river and realizing a killer was still out there, he hesitated. Pulling on his jeans, he grabbed his service weapon from the end table next to his bed before padding barefoot to the door.

To his relief, he found Bailey McKenna standing on his back step, facing away from him. He felt some of the fear dissipate and knew he'd had the dream again, because his body ached as if he'd been fighting off the stabbing. He took a breath, let it out and felt his heart rate drop a little. It was Bailey, not his almost-killer.

So why did his chest still ache? She seemed to be staring out into the darkness, but he could feel the tension coming off her body, smell the panic.

He thought about all the other times she'd shown up at his door, apparently just to visit. The night before had been different, and so was tonight. He remembered why he'd been so determined to find her earlier. It came back to him like a swift kick to the gut as she turned to gaze at him.

She looked as if she'd been in a fight with a mountain lion. "Bailey, what the hell?" he said on a ragged breath when he saw the scratches on her face, the black eye. He drew her into the house and into the light.

"It's nothing," she said. "You should have seen the other woman."

He let out a curse. "Come on." She protested as he closed the door and led her down the hall to the bathroom. "Sit." He put down the toilet seat and nudged her onto it. "What happened to you?"

"I fell down."

He shook his head. "Right. Before or after you were dragged through the dirt?"

She was silent as he got out the first aid kit and went to work. As he did, he took in her injuries, glad to see that they all appeared minor. She didn't flinch as he cleaned the wounds and applied antiseptic to them. Most were scratches, some deeper than others, but there were bruises on her face as if she'd run into something hard.

He brushed back her long, curly, dark hair, his fingers grazing her cheek and making her flinch. "That should do it," he said drawing his hand back. "Now tell me what really happened." He busied himself by closing the first aid kit and putting it back into the cabinet.

While he'd been patching her up, he'd been concentrating on her injuries. But now the close confines of the small bathroom felt too intimate.

She looked up at him, her blue eyes luminous. The pain he saw there nearly dropped him to his knees. "Bailey—"

Rising abruptly, she shoved past him and out of the bathroom. He took a breath, his chest aching again, the memory of the dream hanging around like a bad smell. Being around her like this was killing him. He wasn't sure how much more of it he could take. Once he resigned as sheriff, there would be nothing keeping him in Powder Crossing, he told himself. A bald-faced lie.

He turned to find her standing in the doorway and felt his heart break at the thought of walking away. But if he didn't—

Her voice sounded strange as she reminded him, "You said you didn't tell me everything about Willow."

Stuart shook his head. "Bailey—"

"Just tell me."

He met her gaze and felt his stomach drop. She already knew, but if she did… "She was assaulted." He swallowed, fear running an icy finger down his spine as he saw that she was waiting for more. "She was raped, choked, tied up, and her body was disfigured." The moment the words were out of his mouth he saw her reaction.

Tears filled her eyes as she nodded. "I have to go." She rushed toward the door.

But she wasn't fast enough this time. He grabbed for her arm and pulled her around to face him. "You aren't going anywhere until you start telling me the truth," he said, locking eyes with her as he tightened his hold. He told himself that there was no way he was letting her go back out into the darkness alone, not tonight, maybe not ever. But even as he thought it, he knew he couldn't keep her here with him against her will—any more than he could force her to talk to him. She would do as she pleased, and there was nothing he could do to stop her. There had never been.

He tried a different approach. "Bailey, you wouldn't have kept coming back here unless you needed my help."

Her gaze softened. Her whole face did. "You think that's the only reason I come here?" She took a step toward him, rocking up on tiptoe to press her mouth to his.

He wanted the kiss, had dreamed of kissing this woman, just the touch of her lips, the scent of her… Laying his gun aside, he grasped her shoulders and pushed her back to hold her at arm's length. Shaking his head, he said, "You ever want to do that again, you let me know. But it's not what you want from me, not tonight."

Her smile was sad as she shook off his hold, turned and opened the door to leave.

"If you know something about Willow's murder, you have to tell me, Bailey," he said to her retreating back.

She stopped to look around at him. He'd never seen her appear more lost than at that moment. "Why would I tell *you*? I saw your resignation on your desk. Are you even still sheriff?"

Before he could answer, she was gone. Not that he knew what he would have said. She'd caught him by surprise. But it was what he heard in her voice that stole any chance of sleep the rest of the night.

For years he'd disappointed himself, but to disappoint Bailey? He wasn't sure he could live with that. Worse, he kept seeing her face when he told her how Willow had died. Just as he'd feared, she'd known.

HOLDEN MCKENNA SADDLED his horse earlier than usual and rode out across his ranch toward the Stafford Ranch. The sun hadn't yet scaled the mountains to the east but had set the sky aglow in pale pinks. He'd ridden every morning since his doctor had said he could after his gunshot wounds had healed. Each day he told himself Charlotte Stafford would be at the creek where they used to meet to make love.

Those days were apparently long behind them, leaving him both brokenhearted and filled with a deep, aching sorrow. Charlotte had been the love of his life, still was. They'd both made mistakes, but his, he'd come to realize, were the worst. He'd pushed her away—and now she was gone.

He had no idea where she'd gone or if she would ever come back. Still, he rode to a stop along the creek in a place that held the happiest memories of his life. A slight breeze stirred the tall fall dried grasses and golden leaves on the cottonwoods as he dismounted and walked to the large rock where he and his Lottie, as he'd always called her, had last embraced.

Sitting down, he stared into the water that in a matter of yards would join the Powder River. He listened to the breeze for a moment, then whispered, "Come back, Lottie. Please, come back to me." After a few minutes, he rose and walked back to where he'd ground-tied his horse. He told himself that she was still alive, wherever she was. If she'd died, he would know it in his heart.

For years after he'd betrayed Lottie, she'd been unable to forgive him. They'd become mortal enemies, dragging their children as well as their hired hands into the feud. It broke his heart, all the years they'd wasted. Before she'd left, it seemed they might reconcile their differences. They might find their way back to each other. But he'd pushed her away when he'd learned of the secret she'd been keeping from him for years.

He deeply regretted that soon after, but it had been too

late. She'd left town, and no one seemed to know how to reach her. The pain of it had almost laid him out for good.

"I've heard of people dying of a broken heart," Elaine had said recently. More than a housekeeper and head cook, she was his confidant as well as his friend. She knew him better than anyone. He loved her in his way. Elaine was dating his ranch manager, Deacon Yates. Deacon was a good man, and Elaine deserved to have a man in her life—other than him.

Elaine had sighed. "I'm worried about you, Holden. Charlotte will come back. She loves you."

He'd smiled, grateful that she cared and hoping she was right.

"It breaks my heart to see you like this," Elaine had said.

"I'm fine," he'd promised. "I don't mean to make you worry. It's just that my kids are all grown, living their own lives. I'm at loose ends."

She gave him a look that told him she knew better. It had always been about Lottie. No wonder his adult children didn't need him. He'd spent his life obsessing over a woman he'd lost and feared he would never have again.

"She'll come back," Elaine had said. "Stop looking as if you have one foot in the grave. It's morbid."

He'd chuckled. "That bad?" She'd nodded, and he'd seen the worry in her expression. He definitely thought he could die of a broken heart if Lottie didn't come back.

Mounting his horse now, he rode back home, promising his aching heart that one of these mornings, he would find Lottie there, and nothing could keep them apart ever again.

In the meantime, as the daylight peeked through the cottonwoods, he worried about Bailey. It was high time he found out what was going on with his daughter—whether she liked it or not.

THE SHERIFF GLANCED at the clock. Too late to go back to bed. After Bailey's visit, he knew he wouldn't be able to sleep anyway. He felt as lost as she had looked. Startled by the sudden pounding at his door, he hurried to it, thinking that Bailey had returned. He was already rehearsing what he'd say to her when he opened the door to find Holden McKenna standing there, face flushed.

Panic filled him. Had something happened to her? "Bailey—"

He'd barely gotten the word out when Holden pushed past him, storming into the living room before swinging around to face him. Holden was a big man who was in good shape for his age, but it was the air of authority the wealthy rancher wore that made most men give him a wide berth.

"What the hell is going on?" Holden demanded.

"What—" He stared at him, confused and terrified that Bailey had been hurt again.

"What are you doing with my daughter?"

Stuart blinked. "I..." He was going to say that he didn't understand but realized with a wave of relief that Bailey was okay. This was something else. "If you're asking where she is—"

"I don't need to. I just saw her leave your house before it was hardly daylight," the rancher said. "How long has this been going on?"

Stuart almost laughed. He didn't even know what "this" was. "Coffee?" he asked as he turned and headed into the kitchen, realizing he couldn't carry on this particular conversation without the caffeine jolt.

"I don't want coffee," Holden bellowed, but followed him into the small kitchen.

"I do." He began to put on a pot, knowing that he was

stalling. How could he possibly explain his relationship with Bailey—if he could even call it that—when he didn't understand it himself?

"I asked you what's going on with you and my daughter," Holden said behind him in the kitchen doorway.

The coffee on, he turned to the rancher. "Bailey and I are friends."

"*Friends?* Stuart, I've known you since you were born, and you understand damned well how worried I've been about my daughter. Is this where she goes at all hours of the night? Are the two of you—"

"We're *friends*. She stops by to talk occasionally. Sometimes she stays over—in my spare bedroom. I can't tell you any more than that."

"*Can't* or *won't*? If you know what's going on with Bailey, you have to tell me."

"Maybe you should talk to your daughter."

Holden let out a curse. "I can't get more than two words out of her. It's like she's...angry about something I must have done. Or didn't do. I have no idea."

Surprised at the rancher's candor, Stuart's heart went out to the man. Holden was right. He'd known Stuart his whole life. He'd known Stuart's parents. He realized there was something he'd wanted to ask him for a very long time but hadn't found an opening.

"You knew my mother." The rancher stared at him as if blindsided by the question asked so out of context. "What really happened to her?" Holden blinked and took a step back as he raised a hand to rub the back of his neck.

"You're right. You've known me since I was born. You knew my mother. You knew my father," Stuart said, realizing that he couldn't leave Powder Crossing without knowing the truth about his mother. He'd heard whispers. The few people he had asked about her hadn't wanted to talk about it. All he knew was that there was some mystery about her leaving. "I've never gotten a straight answer about what happened to her. If anyone knows the truth, I figure it's you."

"We're talking about my daughter." When the sheriff said nothing, the rancher shook his head. "Son, that deal with your mother was long ago."

"Not so long ago that you don't remember. How about you be truthful with me, and I'll be the same with you about your daughter."

Holden's eyes narrowed. "So, you do know what's going on with Bailey." Stuart said nothing. "Fine. Your mother left town in the middle of the night and was never seen again."

He shook his head as he turned back to the coffeepot and poured them both a cup. He motioned to the table as he set a cup down in front of his chair and another across the table in front of the only other chair. "Seems like quite a few people leave here in the middle of the night and are never seen again." He pulled out his chair and sat before picking up his cup and taking a sip of his coffee, watching Holden over the brim of his cup. "Like Charlotte Stafford's second husband. No, that's right, he was found in that large old abandoned well on the property next to her ranch."

"She didn't have anything to do with his death," the rancher snapped.

"You're missing the point. People don't just leave in the middle of the night, never to be seen again, unless they're dead. Be honest with me. Is my mother dead?"

"Did you ask your father?"

"He lied too," Stuart said. "I had hoped you would be more honest." He'd never been this candid, but since he was quitting his job and leaving town, he had nothing to lose, right?

Holden pulled out the other chair and sat, but he didn't reach for the coffee. "I don't know if she's still alive. I do know that she had some…emotional problems, and that your father did the best he could with her, taking her to doctors to try to get her help. I don't think I have to tell you that she wasn't cut out for motherhood. Your father worried about you constantly. Other than that, all I know is what he told me. That she left in the middle of the night and never came back. Now it's your turn."

It was and wasn't what Stuart had hoped to hear. He'd known there was something very wrong with his mother. Holden had just confirmed it, now making him wonder how many people knew about her. And why Holden McKenna, a local rancher, had been asking his father about her. He'd never gotten the impression that the rancher and his father had been friends.

"You asked about me and Bailey. I'm in love with her, have been for a long time. Can't tell you how she feels about me because I don't know. Right now we're friends. Sometimes she just needs someone to talk to so she stops by, often in the wee hours of the morning. Eventually, I fall asleep. When I wake up, she's always gone. We aren't lovers, but I hope like hell that someday we are. I want a marriage and even—why not—kids."

Holden looked at him in surprise. "You and Bailey, married with kids?"

"Do you have a problem with that?"

The rancher shook his head, but it was clear he had a problem with it.

"Is it because of my mother?"

Holden looked confused for a moment before he waved that off. "If I hesitated, it was because I can't see Bailey settled down being a wife—let alone a mother. She's hardly dated that I know of. I was beginning to think—"

"I can see her as a wife and mother," Stuart said, wondering if that was true or just his wishful thinking. "Right now, she just needs time and space to figure out a few things on her own." He hoped to hell that was all that was wrong with her. He was still worried, especially after telling her about Willow. Bailey knew something. He wasn't sure how, and maybe that worried him the most.

"I've been giving that girl space for years," Holden snapped.

"Try doing it a while longer. I think she's working some things out."

"About me?"

"Space," Stuart repeated and glanced at the time. "I need to get to work, so if that's all..." Today he was resigning. He felt lighter having confessed how he felt about Bailey. But mostly because while he might wish he and Bailey had a future, he didn't believe it. He would be leaving town, leaving all this behind. He'd go to a place where no one knew him, knew his father or his mother or anything about the mistakes he'd made in life. Unfortunately, his scars and probably his nightmares would be going with him. Nothing he could do about that.

"Fine," the rancher said as he readjusted his Stetson before looking at Stuart again. "Take care of my daughter." His words were so filled with emotion that Stuart could only nod as Holden showed himself to the door.

Take care of my daughter. That's exactly what he'd been trying to do, he told himself as he showered, dressed and headed to the office, determined to turn in his resignation and get it over with.

After that, Bailey would have to take care of herself. That worried him, but he'd come to realize that he'd been kidding himself thinking he was the answer to her problems.

CJ STAFFORD NEEDED money bad. Even the lousy attorney he'd managed to hire from prison was refusing to work his case unless he paid him. And not unlike the world outside his barred cell, he required money to operate.

The moment he got his turn to use the hall phone, he made a call to the one man who could make that happen. For a moment, CJ thought Treyton McKenna wasn't going to take his collect call. He balled his fists, a litany of swear words rising in him like hot water about to erupt out of Old Faithful. He'd seen the famous geyser a couple of times when their mother had taken him and his siblings to Yellowstone Park.

He'd been of the age that he hadn't seen himself in the famous geyser. Instead, he'd been thinking about taking the wallet of a woman whose purse was right next him—wide open. He couldn't believe that anyone could be so careless as to leave her purse open with a kid like him standing right by her. Clearly, she deserved to lose her money. Probably had too much of it to worry about what was in her wallet.

Turned out, there wasn't all that much in the purse, but it had taught him a valuable lesson. CJ had been taking advantage of trusting souls ever since. He'd also learned that he could take what he wanted and often not get caught.

"What?" Treyton demanded after he'd finally accepted the charges from his least favorite felon.

"You'd better always take my calls," CJ said, trying to

rein in his earlier fury. He knew the cops would be listening to all his phone calls, so he had to be careful.

"Or what are you going to do about it?"

He laughed. "You really want to find out?" Silence. "Do you have something to write on? Take down this address. I need you to get two grand to my lawyer until I can afford someone better."

Treyton swore. "You're a ballsy son of a—"

"I don't have much time. There's a line waiting for this phone. Here's the address." He gave it to his so-called partner in crime. "You owe me, remember? You came to me, not the other way around, old buddy."

"The worst day of my life, and you're not my buddy."

CJ laughed. The Staffords and McKennas had been at war for years because of their parents, making him and Treyton strange business partners. "Thanks to me, you're doing quite well."

"If you expect me to thank you—"

"*You're* not in jail, *I* am, and if you want to stay that way—"

"Don't threaten me, CJ. I'll get your lawyer money, but we both know no one can get you out of all the felonies you're facing."

"We'll see about that."

"Don't call me again," Treyton said, and disconnected.

CJ squeezed the phone so hard it cracked. The inmate behind him grabbed it and shoved him out of the way. He let the shove go. He had bigger fish to fry, he told himself, knowing who he would call the next time he got to use the phone.

Treyton needed to be reminded who was in charge—and what happened if he screwed with CJ. He hated ingratitude the most. He had let Treyton in on his operation. It wasn't his fault it went south. It was his sister's. Admittedly, trying to kill her had been a mistake, one he was already paying dearly for.

He'd lost the family ranch when his mother had turned on him, and now he was facing life in prison unless this new lawyer could spring him. He thought of the ranch he loved, that he'd fought to keep thriving, that he'd given his life to, and how his dear mother, Charlotte Stafford, now ignored his calls.

CJ had heard that she'd left not just the ranch, but the county, and possibly the state. Where had she gone? He didn't have to guess why. That damned Holden McKenna. It had always been about him.

Yet he held out hope that she would return, forgive him, and get him the best lawyer that money could buy. He needed out of here. He had things to do.

BAILEY HAD PASSED her father's SUV as she was leaving Stuart's house this morning. She didn't have to guess where he was going. The road dead-ended at the sheriff's house. She told herself Holden McKenna might have business with the sheriff that had nothing to do with her.

But she'd seen him brake when he recognized her SUV. She'd sped away, definitely not in the mood to see him, especially the way her face looked with all the scratches. She'd turned and parked to wait next to an old shed at the back of a resident's property, telling herself that if he had been looking for her, he would be coming down the street right away.

But he didn't appear. That's when she'd realized that he hadn't known she was at Stuart's—until he'd passed her. But now that he'd seen her leaving the sheriff's house early in the morning…she had no idea what he would say, let alone do. Angrily, she reminded herself that she was a grown woman. There wasn't anything he could do or say to her. Or Stuart.

But she wondered what the sheriff would say to her father. She didn't like the two of them discussing her, but she knew that wasn't what had her so upset. Stuart was resigning. He was giving up not just on his job, but on her. He would leave Powder Crossing like anyone with any sense would do. He would not look back. He must feel as if there was nothing here for him.

That she felt rejected almost made her laugh. How could she blame him? She'd pushed him away for years even as she couldn't stay away from him. He must be horribly confused about her. He'd been more than patient with her, putting up with her visits, keeping his distance, waiting for her to make the first move—not knowing what was going on with her because she'd kept it from him. Yet it broke her heart and made her angry, the thought of him resigning, leaving, when she needed him more than ever.

When her father still hadn't driven past, she glanced at the time. Throwing her SUV into gear, she sped off toward the ranch. She needed to get changed. She had a drive ahead of her. As much as she didn't want to make her appointment in Billings, she had to, even if it was the last thing on her mind right now.

Since Willow's murder, she'd felt as if a clock were ticking. It terrified her to think about what would happen when it stopped.

CHAPTER FIVE

AFTER HOLDEN LEFT, Stuart tried to phone Bailey. The call went straight to voicemail again. He didn't leave a message because he wasn't sure what to say. She was right. Why tell him anything? He no longer felt he could do his job. Better to let people more qualified solve Willow's murder and get her justice.

Yet he kept thinking about Bailey and what would happen to her after he quit and left town. That look on her face. She'd understood what had happened to Willow. But how? The cop in him needed to know the truth–even as he feared what she might tell him.

At his office, he picked up his resignation from his desk and stuffed it into a drawer. He hated the sight of it, knowing that he'd let Bailey down. He swore. The woman expected too much of him. Did he really think he could keep playing this cat and mouse game with her? He didn't just want to be her friend. He loved her. He wanted her. If he couldn't have her, then he had no choice but to leave town.

Not that he didn't try calling her again. This time, he

left a message. "I'm still the sheriff. I need to talk to you. I need the truth, and damn it to hell…" He disconnected. He wouldn't turn in his resignation yet. What was a few more days? Meanwhile, he'd do his job. He checked in with the state crime team. Nothing on the boot print or the trash picked up along the river where the body was found.

So far, they had no idea where Willow was abducted. He called her boss at the hotel, got her schedule. Willow had worked that day until four, when she'd left, her boss assumed, to go home. She rented a small house outside of town, lived alone, and had been an exceptional employee. Stuart got the address, thanked her distraught boss, and hung up.

He called the state crime boys, passed along that information, and tried Bailey again without any luck. Opening his desk drawer, he took out his resignation for a moment, but quickly put it back as Bailey's brother Cooper filled his office doorway.

"Buy you an early lunch?" Cooper had been his best friend, off and on, over the years. They'd had their problems but had managed to stay friends. Stuart realized how much he was going to miss him.

His stomach growled, reminding him how little he'd eaten in the past few days. "You bet," he said, and reached for his Stetson.

"To what do I owe this honor?" he asked later when they were seated in a booth at the café. They'd ordered, not bothering to look at their menus. After all this time, they knew the menu at the Cattleman Café by heart since it hadn't changed in years.

"Haven't seen you for a while," Cooper said, studying him openly. "How are you doing?"

Sometimes it slipped his mind, nearly dying from all the stab wounds. Not often, but the past few days, it had. "I'm doing okay." It was almost true.

His best friend shook his head. "You don't look okay."

"What do you expect?" Stuart snapped. "I have a murder on my hands and—" He almost voiced his concern about Bailey but stopped himself as he raised his gaze to Cooper's. He lowered his voice even though there was no one sitting close by. He swallowed. "I'm thinking about quitting."

"You've been thinking about that for years," his friend said. "Why now?"

He shook his head and looked away. "I'm not sure I'm up to it anymore."

Cooper sat back. "No one would blame you after what you've been through."

Someone would, he thought as he remembered Bailey's reaction.

The waitress brought their burgers, fries and colas. They ate in silence for a few minutes.

"Would you leave town?" Cooper finally asked between bites.

Stuart nodded without looking at him.

Putting down his burger, his friend asked, "Does this have anything to do with my sister?"

He thought about pretending he didn't know what Cooper was talking about but saved his breath. "It might."

Cooper shook his head and let out a curse. "Why do you always pick the wrong woman?"

The sheriff laughed since this had become a running joke between them. "You know me."

"Yeah, I do," his friend said, suddenly serious. "You've had a crush on Bailey from as far back as I can remember."

"Sad, isn't it," Stuart joked as he picked up a fry and popped it into his mouth. He could see where he'd tried to substitute other women for her, and look how that had turned out.

"What's sad about it is my sister. Bailey's messed up." Stuart nodded, unable to argue that. He feared it was much worse than anyone knew. "I don't want you to leave, but it's slim pickin's in the Powder River Basin. Any woman with a brain gets out of here as quickly as she can. If you're serious about quitting..."

"I've already written up my resignation. I just haven't turned it in."

Cooper looked surprised. "I suppose you told Bailey how you feel?"

"She knows I'm resigning."

His friend shook his head. "Not about you resigning, about how you feel about her. You haven't, have you." He let out a curse. "I'm sorry, but there is no way you should leave town without telling her. You owe it to yourself and to her. She might surprise you. Or not." His laugh was sad. "You do realize that no one would wish Bailey on you, including me as your friend."

Stuart smiled and nodded.

"I left for two years, but I had to come back," Cooper said.

"Your father owns one of the larger ranches in Montana."

"That wasn't why I came back, and you know it. Maybe you just need a change of scenery, and you'll come back like I did."

Stuart chuckled at that. "Seriously, you had a ranch and family to come back to. If I leave, I won't have anything to come back to."

"Except your best friend."

He nodded. "I will miss you." As he said it, he realized Cooper was about all he would miss—other than Bailey. Powder Crossing had some bad memories he'd gladly leave behind.

TILLY STAFFORD MCKENNA stood in front of the hall mirror, her hand over her baby bump. She wanted to pinch herself, but it would probably make her throw up. *She was having a baby!* She should have been jumping up and down with excitement. *She and Cooper, the love of her life, were having a baby!*

If not for the almost constant nausea—*morning* sickness my foot!—she would have been working on the baby's nursery or going to Billings with friends to ooh and ahh over cute baby clothes. Instead, she kept waiting for this part to end.

And feeling sorry for herself, as her younger sister had pointed out when she'd shown up on her doorstep.

"I can't believe Mother hasn't come back," Oakley said, her gaze going to the baby bump. "She wouldn't want to miss this."

Tilly's throat tightened, and all she could do was nod and invite her sister inside. When she was being truthful, she knew it wasn't only the nausea that had her feeling bad. This wasn't the way she'd pictured being married, pregnant and about to have her first child. Had she not fallen in love with Cooper McKenna, the son of her mother's worst enemy, maybe things would have been different.

"So, you're telling me you haven't heard from Mother?" Oakley asked as Tilly followed her into the kitchen and watched her check the cookie jar. Oakley was always hungry.

"I haven't seen her since my wedding." Their mother, Charlotte Stafford, matriarch of the Stafford Ranch, had at least attended the wedding. Coming in at the last minute and leaving the moment the pastor had declared her and Cooper man and wife. The Stafford and McKenna families had been at war for years because of her mother's and Holden's long-ago love affair that had ended badly.

"But you talked to Mother before she left," Oakley prodded, opening the refrigerator to look inside.

"Just to thank her for trying to help when Holly Jo was missing." Holly Jo Robinson was Holden McKenna's thirteen-year-old ward. "I thought Mother would want to be here for this," Tilly said.

"Well, you have me," Oakley said, closing the refrigerator with a sigh.

Right, she had her sister, who didn't want to hear anything about babies. Oakley had recently gotten married and was more interested in long horseback rides with her husband, Pickett Hanson. The whole pregnancy thing with its bodily issues grossed her out, she said.

Just then, Tilly had to run to the closest bathroom to throw up.

"Don't you bake anymore?" Oakley called from the other room. "All you think and talk about is babies. Have I told you how not fun you are anymore?"

Had she ever really been fun? Tilly wondered as she rinsed her mouth with mouthwash. She had thought that she'd be sharing all of this with her sister and mother.

"Where do you think Mother went?" Oakley asked as she came out of the bathroom. "Do you think she's ever coming back?"

"I have no idea. I've tried calling her cell phone number.

It goes straight to voicemail. I'm worried about her. What if something has happened to her?"

"Charlotte Stafford? Seriously?" Oakley laughed. "If it was anyone else, maybe you would worry. But not about our mother. I'm sure she's fine, though she was acting strange before she left. Can you believe she left the house for Holden and family to live in after the fire destroyed the one at McKenna Ranch? The man she has despised all of our lives? Something must have happened to make her do that. Maybe a heart transplant."

"Ha," Tilly said. "Maybe she was tired of being bitter about Holden breaking her heart."

"Or maybe she was running away from all her lies," Oakley said. "Do I have to remind you of even half the things our mother has done—not to mention our brother CJ?"

"No, please don't. I'll admit, it's been a lot more peaceful without either of them around." Tilly's hand went to her stomach again. She felt the flutter of movement and smiled through tears she hadn't realized she'd cried. "But I'm pregnant. Why wouldn't she want to be here for me?"

"Not the waterworks again," Oakley said with a groan. "Really, sis, you're convincing me to put off baby making as long as possible."

"Doesn't Pickett want children?"

"We both do, but not yet. I want more time alone with my husband."

Tilly realized with a start that her sister always avoided her gaze when she talked about her and Pickett having children. Had they been trying and failing? Was there more going on than she'd realized?

"Wasn't that awful about Willow?" Oakley said, changing the subject. "I suppose you heard that Ralph Jones thought at first it was Bailey."

Yes, Tilly had heard that. "They did resemble each other, especially after Willow went back to her natural color hair." She thought about asking her sister about her suspicions, but let it go. Oakley would eventually tell her what was going on with her and Pickett if there was anything to tell. Maybe.

"And Bailey is like an alley cat prowling around at night," Oakley said of Tilly's sister-in-law. "What is the deal with her anyway?"

She shook her head. Oakley was still living on the McKenna Ranch in Pickett's cabin until her and Pickett's house was finished. "I never saw much of her, especially after the fire, when all of us were living at the Stafford Ranch while the house was being rebuilt. Cooper says she's always been like that, but I know Holden worries about her. I've always suspected she has a secret lover. Does she even date?" Oakley walked over to gaze out the large picture window overlooking the McKenna Ranch land.

"Not that I know of." Tilly wanted to change the subject, feeling uncomfortable talking about her sister-in-law.

"I always thought she and Stuart would get together," Oakley said dreamily.

"What? Why?" Not that long ago, Tilly had dated Stuart. She definitely didn't want to talk about Bailey and Stuart. "If you aren't really worried about Mother, there must be another reason you stopped by?"

"Oh yeah," Oakley said, turning to look at her again. "I want to throw you a baby shower. If that doesn't get Mother home, at least it will make her aware you're pregnant."

Tilly felt that sharp pinch of pain that brought tears to her eyes. "I wish she wasn't the way she is."

Oakley laughed. "Don't we all. Are you sure Elaine doesn't know where she is?" As the McKenna housekeeper and head cook, and Holden's confidant, she always seemed to know what was going on—at least at the ranch.

"Why would she know?" Tilly asked in surprise. "Elaine got Mother to help her one time, but that was all."

"Well, I saw Elaine and Mother down by the creek before Mother left town. I think they're actually friends."

Tilly rolled her eyes. "I can't imagine that." Nor could she imagine Stuart with Bailey. "You've always had an overactive imagination."

Oakley shrugged. "I know what I saw, and one time I saw the sheriff with Bailey." She nodded her head, smiling. "When you think about it, those two might just be made for each other."

Tilly shook her head, remembering Stuart's reaction when she'd broken things off and started hanging out with his best friend, Cooper McKenna, her now-husband. She'd reminded Cooper once about how strange the sheriff had behaved. The two best friends had almost come to blows, their friendship nearly lost forever.

"Stu was in a bad place back then," Cooper had said, brushing it off. "A lot has happened since then. I heard he's been seeing a therapist. He seems better, more like his old self."

Tilly remembered the darkness she'd glimpsed in the sheriff—along with the anger. It had frightened her. She thought of the darkness and anger in her sister-in-law, Bailey. Is that why Oakley thought they were perfect for each other?

Tilly couldn't help but wonder what those two kinds of powerful dark energy could become if brought together. Sounded dangerous to her.

ON HER WAY to Billings, Bailey hadn't gotten far out of Powder Crossing when she picked up the tail. A gray SUV had pulled in behind her as she'd left town, but it hadn't tried to catch her. Instead, it hung back, matching her speed a quarter mile or so behind her.

After what had happened with the female officer the last time she'd tried to leave town, she felt a sliver of fear pierce her already pounding heart. She glanced at the road ahead, seeing no other vehicles and knowing that she might not for miles. She began to drive faster. So did the vehicle behind her. The driver kept the same distance between them—at least for now.

Call Stuart. She balked at the idea. By now he would have resigned, she told herself. Unfortunately, she'd learned the hard way she couldn't always take care of herself. The fact that she needed Stuart rankled. But she also knew he was one of the few people she could trust.

The call went to voicemail. She had no choice but to leave a message, hoping he checked it soon. Unfortunately, from experience she knew that she might lose cell service soon. Once she topped the upcoming hill, she wouldn't be able to get coverage until she was closer to Billings.

She'd taken the shortcut road as she always did to get to Montana's largest city. So she knew that for miles there was nothing but open country, badlands and little to no traffic. It was why she always came this way.

Except today she regretted it as she looked back to see the car still behind her. She called and left another message. "I'm being followed on the shortcut road to Billings. I'm going to drop back and see if I can get a license plate number." She disconnected. —if she could get it.

She still held out hope that the car following her was only someone else from the Powder River Basin headed for Billings on the same road. Except that this wasn't the first time she'd been followed.

But it might be the last, she thought as she waited until the vehicle behind her disappeared around a curve. She hit her brakes, pulling quickly off the road behind a large stack of hay. She would be able to see the car that had been following her when it went past, but the driver wouldn't be able to see her. At least until he realized he'd lost her.

Bailey waited, heart in her throat. She didn't have to wait long.

AFTER HIS MEAL with his good friend, Stuart returned to his office more determined than before to give his notice. He sat down behind his desk and pulled out his resignation. That's when he realized that he'd turned off his phone. As soon as he turned it back on, he saw that he had two messages from Bailey. He swore as he listened to her voicemails, especially the last one.

He checked the time of the calls. Not that long ago. He stood, reached for his Stetson and headed for the door. A text from Bailey came through on his phone. A Montana license plate number.

At his computer, he quickly ran the plate. "What the hell?" he said, shocked to see that the SUV was owned by Ralph Jones—the rancher who'd found Willow's body in the river.

Why would Ralph be following Bailey?

PICKETT HANSON WALKED through the open doorway of their home under construction and stopped short. Shoving back his Stetson, he leaned against one of the wood studs to study his wife. He would never get tired of looking at this woman or counting his blessings. The surge of love he felt for her almost dropped him to his knees.

Oakley must have sensed him watching her, because she turned and broke into a smile. "What are you doing, cowboy?"

"Admiring the most beautiful thing I've ever seen," he said truthfully.

"You're talking about our house, aren't you," she joked. "Wait until it has walls."

"I like it just fine this way." He could see the entire open stud structure. He didn't need to imagine what it would look like when finished. He enjoyed taking it a step at a time, savoring the slow progress the same way he enjoyed each new day in this new life with his bride. He didn't want to rush a thing.

Oakley moved to him, shaking her head with each step. "You aren't tough enough on the contractor. At this rate, they aren't going to get it done before winter."

"Then I guess we'll just have to keep bunking together in my small cabin, where you can't get away from me." She laughed as he pulled her into his arms.

"Doesn't anything bother you?" she asked, backing up a little to meet his eyes. She'd touched a nerve.

He knew he'd often moved too slow, while she tore through life as if it were a race. "I don't like you being here alone," he chided her. "It's dangerous." He saw her bristle, this independent woman who had proven she could take care of herself in most every circumstance. He didn't want to remind her that she'd almost died because of her stubbornness about doing things at her own pace alone. "A woman's been murdered."

She pulled free. "Don't you think I know that?" She turned away for a moment before spinning toward him again. "Pickett, I know you feel you have to rein me in sometimes, but do not try to corral me."

"I wouldn't dream of it," he said, wishing he hadn't mentioned anything. He wanted her in his arms. "You know we have the perfect opportunity right now to try out every room in the house."

That's what he loved about her; she didn't stay angry long. "I wish we could," she said wistfully, "but I have to plan a baby shower for Tilly."

He knew Oakley was disappointed that she hadn't gotten pregnant yet. He could tell it was why she'd been complaining about her sister, saying babies and pregnancy were the only things Tilly now talked about. He'd even overheard her saying that the two of them didn't want children for a while, just wanted to spend time together.

"I'm sure Tilly would love to help with the shower," he said.

She let out a bark of a laugh. "Take over, you mean. No, I have this. I just wanted to check our house before I head into town to see what they have at the general store for decorations. We'll hold it at Tilly and Cooper's house since ours is so…airy."

He smiled at that and pulled her to him again to kiss her before sending her on her way. He fought the need to follow her into town to make sure she made it. Willow Branson's murder had shaken him to his core. He couldn't bear the thought of anything happening to his beautiful, headstrong wife. He hoped the killer was caught—and soon. One less thing to worry about, he told himself.

Just as he hoped his wife would soon be pregnant with the baby they both so desperately wanted. He couldn't stand seeing Oakley unhappy—let alone afraid it might never happen.

He glanced at the time, reminding himself that he'd promised Holly Jo a trick riding practice after school. Maybe he'd surprise her and pick her up at the bus stop on the county road so she wouldn't have to walk the quarter mile or so to the ranch house. He liked spending time with her and had from when she'd arrived at the ranch, hating everything but horses.

Pickett smiled to himself at the memory. He told himself it wouldn't be that long before he and Oakley would be picking up their own kids from the bus stop.

BAILEY HAD BEEN ready with her phone camera when the SUV following her went past. She had managed to get a decent shot of the back of the rig, capturing the license plate number.

She'd texted it to Stuart and nothing more. Afterward, she'd wondered why she'd bothered. If he was no longer sheriff, he couldn't even run the plate.

She'd told herself that it was just a matter of time before the driver of the SUV realized he'd lost her. Would he double back? Should she stay hidden?

She checked the time. She was going to miss her appointment if she didn't get moving soon. She knew this two-lane highway after driving it for years. If she left now, she would catch up with the SUV. And then what?

Her run-in with R. Durham had left her feeling vulnerable. It was a feeling she hated and yet had become used to. When someone wanted you dead, feeling vulnerable came with it.

She couldn't keep hiding here, she thought angrily. She didn't want to get caught here when the SUV doubled back. If he doubled back.

Looking up the highway, she had to make a decision. Cancel her appointment and drive back to Powder Crossing? Or take her chances and try to make it to Billings alive?

She pulled out, not sure which way she would go until she turned back toward Powder Crossing. The truth was that she wasn't up to taking her chances. Not after R. Durham. She glanced in her rearview mirror. Still no sign of the SUV. But she caught her reflection, her scratched, damaged face that Stuart had patched up.

Bailey called and changed her appointment to the next day. When she looked back, she saw the SUV some distance behind her. No question about it. The vehicle was the same one.

She sped up. Her best chance was to make a run for it, she told herself as she jammed the gas pedal to the floor. She looked back, not at all surprised that the vehicle following her also sped up. Her heart pounded as she realized it was gaining on her. Maybe she couldn't outrun the larger SUV, but she was damned well going to give it her best try.

As she topped a hill, scrub pine trees blurring past on each side of the highway, she looked up in surprise to see a patrol SUV. Instantly its flashing lights came on. Her heart thudded in her chest until she recognized the cowboy behind the wheel. She let out a shaky breath.

Looking in her rearview mirror, she saw the driver of the SUV following her then hit the brakes and turn off the road.

As Bailey sped past the patrol SUV, she heard the siren. She looked back to see him make a U-turn in the highway and come after her. She could no longer see the dark SUV as she pulled over and stopped, lying over her steering wheel, fighting tears. She was sure the person would make a run for it—not knowing that Bailey had gotten a plate number.

Not that she felt that jubilant. Being scared all the time was exhausting, she thought as Stuart pulled in behind her. She smiled at the sight of his handsome face as she finally admitted the truth. She couldn't keep doing this alone.

Stuart walked up to her window. She put it down without looking at him. "We need to talk. Can I trust you to follow me back to my office?"

She finally looked at him. "You're still sheriff?"

"Yes." There was a lot in that one word, but she told herself it didn't matter. Even if he resigned, she needed him. "Not your office. I'll meet you at your house."

His expression seemed to question if he could trust her. She didn't blame him. "Did you get the plate number I sent you on the car that was following me?"

He nodded. "I'll tell you when I see you at the house."

She watched him in her rearview mirror as he walked back to his patrol SUV before she put up her window.

It was time she told the truth.

CHAPTER SIX

STUART HADN'T KNOWN if Bailey would go to his house or not. He had no idea what she'd been doing on this road, where she'd been going, or what she planned to do now. But he'd come this far with her, trusting that at some point she'd be honest with him. Clearly something was going on with her and had been for a while.

Why did he think he could save Bailey when he doubted he could even save himself? As flawed and messed up as he was right now, what could he possibly give Bailey to help her?

He let her drive off first. As the back of her SUV disappeared around a curve, he started his patrol car and headed toward Powder Crossing. He was still sheriff. But he hadn't changed his mind about resigning. He promised himself he'd take care of it first thing in the morning.

His radio squawked. The dispatcher told him that there had been a wreck on the highway to Miles City, a semi and a couple of cars involved. She'd been able to reach one deputy, and a wrecker and trooper were coming from the other side of the mountain, but more help was needed.

Stuart texted Bailey. Let yourself in. You know where the key is. Wait for me.

He doubted she would, but there was nothing he could do about that as he turned on his lights and siren and raced to the first road he came to across the valley to the highway.

Stuart found himself questioning whether he should have told her the name of the driver of the SUV that had been following her. He just hoped she went straight to his house and would be waiting for him, because he had no idea when he'd get there. From what he was hearing on his scanner, it was going to be hours before the highway would be open again.

HOLLY JO ROBINSON couldn't believe how different this school year was from the last. She wasn't even sure exactly how it had happened, but she was suddenly popular and hanging out with popular girls. She felt a little bad because she used to make fun of them when Gus Montgomery was her only friend.

But a lot had changed over the summer. Not only did she have friends, she had a *boyfriend.* Buck Savage was sixteen and adorable. He told her that he wanted to be a bull rider and make lots of money. Right now he was one of the most popular boys in school because he was really good at every sport, just not great at school subjects, especially math. He was also really cute, and he liked horses almost as much as Holly Jo did.

Her guardian, Holden McKenna, or HH, as she called him, wouldn't approve. She was sure of that. So she kept that part of school to herself even though she felt a little guilty about it. Only months ago, she'd promised herself that she was going to be the perfect ward. Not only had HH taken her in after her mother had died, but also he had almost died trying to save her when she'd been kidnapped some months ago.

HH had also given her Honey, her very own horse, so she'd tried hard not to give him any trouble, eating the ranch beef even though she didn't like it all that much. Oh, and now he wanted to adopt her, make her a legal part of the McKenna Ranch family.

"I'm not calling you Dad," she'd said when he'd told her.

"You can still call me HH, if you like." But he'd sounded disappointed. She'd never had a dad, not one she remembered. Her mother had told her that he'd died before she was born. But calling Holden Dad seemed weird.

She tried not to think about it. Instead, she concentrated on her amazing new life. Holly Jo wasn't even sure how it had happened. Her bully and worst enemy, Tana Westlake, and her posse used to pick fights with her. But after the kidnapping, Tana had been nice, and now Holly Jo sat with her and her friends at lunch. Overnight, she'd become one of them, talking clothes and boys, movies and boys, music and boys.

When the boys had started coming around their table at lunch, joking and giving them a hard time, Tana had suggested Holly Jo help Buck with his math homework before he had to go to class. "She is a whiz at math," Tana boasted. Buck had sat down next to her and pulled out his math assignment, which he'd made an awkward attempt at completing. She'd had to try to write like he did, scratching out some numbers, adding others until it was finished.

Buck had smiled at her as he'd scooped up his homework, making her tingle. Most of the boys didn't pay any attention to her because she was so much taller than the other girls and even some of the boys. Teachers always said she seemed older than her age. Buck said she should go out for basketball. Wasn't the first time she'd heard that.

Holly Jo had never felt so happy—or so guilty. Along with keeping secrets from HH, she felt guilty about Gus Montgomery. They'd been friends before the kidnapping. She'd thought a lot about him while she'd been in captivity. But once Tana had taken her into her group, Gus kept his distance.

Holly Jo knew that she should say something to him. He'd been all she had at school last year, her only friend. But what was there to say? She liked hanging out with Tana and her posse more than she'd thought she would. She used to think they were stuck-up and silly. Maybe it was turning thirteen, but she felt more a part of them now, especially since she'd been spending more time with Buck.

As she moved toward her locker, she started at the sight of Gus standing next to it. She slowed. Clearly he was waiting for her. She didn't know what she was going to say. Or worse, what he would say. He didn't look happy, but then again, Gus seldom did.

"Hey," she said as she went straight for her locker and began to put in her combination—avoiding looking at him.

"I haven't hardly seen you since the beginning of school," he said. It sounded like an accusation, making her bristle.

"I've been busy."

"I've noticed. I was thinking maybe you and I could talk while we wait for the bus later."

"I'm not riding the bus today." She slipped off her backpack and quickly put away the books she didn't need. "Buck just got his license. He's going to give me a ride home." She slammed her locker.

"Oh. Buck, huh?"

Something in his tone made her turn toward him. She saw his downturned mouth, but it was the expression in his eyes that tore at her heart. He'd been all she had before this school year. "Gus, I'm sorry." He nodded. "Maybe we can—" But he didn't wait around to see what she came up with, because the bell rang.

She hadn't even known what she was going to say. While she hated hurting him, she was happier than she'd been since coming to the Powder River Basin. As she watched Gus scuff down the hall toward his class, Buck came up and put his arm around her. "I'm going to need your help for this math test," he whispered in her ear, making her giggle.

Smiling, she said, "You should have studied."

"Like that would help." He grinned at her and removed his arm. "You're the best, Holly Jo."

She felt as if she were glowing as they headed for class, even as she felt a tightness in her chest at the thought of Gus. She already felt anxious about HH finding out that she wasn't going to be riding the bus anymore.

But for now, it was her little special secret. She felt giddy with anticipation. She couldn't wait for school to let out.

"Maybe he'll kiss you," Tana had teased when she'd told her that Buck was giving her a ride home. "It's not like it's your first kiss, right?"

"Of course not," she'd said with a laugh.

But it would be her first kiss. Her stomach filled with butterflies at the thought even as she couldn't help grinning. Anything could happen on the way home in his pickup. He might even ask her to the dance.

PICKETT PARKED AT the edge of the road, the afternoon sun pouring in his open pickup window. He loved this time of year, the scent of fall in the air as the breeze rattled the drying leaves of the thick stand of cottonwoods along the river. His callused hands tapped out a beat. Sometimes he felt overwhelmed with gratitude.

He hadn't been born to this ranch life, far from it. He'd adopted it at a young age, just as Holden McKenna had pretty much adopted him. Pickett knew he would always be grateful to the man for giving him the chance. He loved being a ranch hand on this huge, magnificent place along the Powder River.

At the sound of the school bus coming up the road in a cloud of dust, he started to open his pickup door. He was already smiling, anxious to see Holly Jo and hear about her day. He knew there was a lot she didn't tell him, but he was okay with that. She still seemed to like hanging out with him.

The school bus slowed, then came to a noisy halt, the red stop sign coming out. Pickett was watching for Holly Jo to stand up and head for the door when the driver's window slid down.

"She didn't get on the bus," Edna Jacob, or Jake, as the kids called her, hollered through the open window.

He hurried over to the bus. Not all that long ago, this was the spot where Holly Jo had been kidnapped. "Does anyone know why she didn't get on the bus?" he asked.

Jake turned to ask the question to the other students. He couldn't hear their answer, but after a moment, she turned back to him.

"Gus says she told him her boyfriend was giving her a ride home," Jake said.

This was definitely something new. "Who's her boyfriend?" Pickett asked.

The driver turned back to the students for a moment. "Buck Savage. Guess he just got his driver's license," she said, her lips pursing.

"Thanks," Pickett said. As the bus pulled away, he looked down the road, wondering if the boyfriend had already dropped her off or not. Pulling out his cell phone, he called the ranch. Elaine answered.

"Holly Jo there?" he asked, explaining that they were supposed to practice a new horseback trick.

"Haven't seen her yet. The bus should be dropping her off any minute," Elaine said.

"Right," Pickett agreed. "If you see her before I do, tell her I'm looking for her." He tried not to worry as he hung up.

CHAPTER SEVEN

PICKETT WAITED IN his pickup, listening to the crickets in the cottonwoods, the breeze stirring the tall grass next to him, worry gnawing at him with each minute that ticked by. School had let out almost an hour earlier. Were they out joy riding? The thought terrified him, an inexperienced new driver showing off for a cute girl. He was just about ready to go look for them, wishing he knew what this Buck Savage was driving, when he saw a small gray pickup coming up the road.

Was this what being a parent was going to be like? Maybe they should put it off as long as they could, he thought as the rig slowed. The sun glinted off the windshield, but he caught a glimpse of Holly Jo in the passenger seat. She must have forgotten they were going to practice a new trick riding stunt after school.

He tried not to let that hurt his feelings. He knew what it was like to be young and infatuated with a girl. He figured it was the same for Holly Jo. "Her first big crush—a sixteen-year-old," he said between gritted teeth as he climbed out of his truck and stepped into the county road. If Buck tried making a run for it, it would be over Pickett's dead body.

The vehicle came to a stop a few yards from him. The passenger side door flew open, and Holly Jo jumped out, already making excuses.

Without a word, Pickett moved out of the road to let the boyfriend be on his way.

"I forgot," Holly Jo was saying as she hurried behind him to climb into the passenger side of his rig. "I planned on riding the school bus home, but then this friend of mine—"

"Buck Savage?" He'd gotten only a glimpse of the teenager behind the wheel.

"Y-yes," she stuttered, the look she gave him one of surprise. How did he know that? it said.

He didn't move to start the pickup, just sat looking straight ahead, wondering how to handle this. "Holden okayed you riding home with this boy instead of taking the bus?" he asked, not turning to her. Silence. "That's what I thought."

"It happened so fast. Buck just got his driver's license, and he offered, and I…" Her voice trailed off. "You can't tell on me. There's this dance coming up. I've got to go to it. Buck's already asked me. If you tell on me—"

"You're the one who's going to tell Holden," he said, turning toward her finally. She looked so grown-up and yet so young and naive and trusting. He remembered himself at sixteen and groaned inwardly. "Why did it take you so long to get home?"

She swallowed and looked away. "We had to stop because the truck seemed to be overheating."

He swore under his breath. "If that punk kid touched you—"

"He didn't!" she cried. "He didn't do anything. We just got out and walked around by the river for a little while. Then I said I had to get home, and he drove me here."

Pickett studied her. Something had happened at the river, he'd bet on that, but he suddenly felt so far out of his league. What did he know about raising a thirteen-year-old girl? He had been an only child who'd left home when he wasn't that much older that Holly Jo.

"When's this dance?" he asked, and saw her relax.

"Saturday. It's a Christmas formal. I get to help decorate the gym. I was going to ask HH if Buck could take me to the dance now that he has his driver's license."

Pickett started the engine and turned around to drive down the dirt road to the ranch house. "Go upstairs and change for your trick riding lesson. I need to talk to Holden."

"You aren't going to—"

"I'm not sure what I'm going to do other than teach you this new trick, okay? Later, you're going to tell Holden yourself and let the chips fall where they may." She started to argue, but he cut her off. "Actions have consequences. You should be aware of that."

"*But nothing happened*," she cried.

He didn't look at her, feeling afraid for her and this new world she was wading into. All of them had been more than a little protective of her since the kidnapping. She seemed to have put the whole nightmare behind her, but Pickett was glad that Holden had insisted she see a therapist.

Now she had a boyfriend.

Pickett had to remind himself that having a boyfriend at her age was probably normal. He expected her to be more wary and he was sure she was – just not of a cute boy from her school.

He told himself that she was dealing with what had happened to her. After that terrifying experience, she probably just wanted everything to be…normal. He couldn't definitely understand that.

The therapy sessions seemed to be going well. As the psychiatrist had said, children were reliant. He could certainly see that in Holly Jo.

But this was her first "boyfriend." She knew nothing about teenaged boys.

HOLDEN HAD SPENT much of the day trying to calm down after his run-in with the sheriff that morning. Bailey and Stuart? Could the sheriff handle his willful daughter? Could any man?

He'd gone into town to talk to the sheriff about the murder and how the investigation was going. He kept thinking about what Ralph Jones had said. *I thought it was Bailey at first.* His alley cat of a daughter, coming and going from the ranch at all hours, scared him.

What he hadn't expected was to see his daughter coming out of the sheriff's house at that hour of the morning. Stuart was in love with her? He almost felt sorry for the man and feared Bailey would never settle down. For a long time now, he'd feared that she would come to a bad end, and he'd have only himself to blame, because he hadn't been there for her when she needed him growing up.

After several meetings, lunch with an implement dealer, and then an afternoon taking care of other business in town, he headed home, tired and out of sorts. As he turned in to the ranch and drove to the house, he saw Elaine talking to Deacon Yates, his ranch manager, out in the yard, and felt a twinge of jealousy. For years, he and his housekeeper and cook had been as close as an old married couple. She'd been his most trusted friend, his rock, and now she was seeing Deacon.

He remembered the day Deacon had come to him, hat in hand literally, to make known that he wanted to date Elaine. He'd been looking for Holden's blessing. He'd had no choice but to give it when Deacon had showed where his heart lay.

It wasn't like he had any right to stand in Deacon's way. He loved Elaine—she was family—but he'd given away his heart years ago to Charlotte Stafford, his Lottie. He knew it, and so did Elaine, so he had to let her go even though he doubted he'd ever have Lottie. It felt as if everyone was leaving him.

With Charlotte gone and no one apparently knowing where she'd gone or if she would be coming back, he felt lost. Still he rode over to the creek almost every day—just in case she'd returned. What a damned fool he was.

As he drove up to the ranch and saw Pickett waiting for him in front of the house pacing and looking anxious, he swore. *Now what*, Holden thought as he parked and got out. He didn't feel like dealing with it after the day he'd had.

"What's wrong?" he demanded of the young man who'd become much more than a hired ranch hand. Pickett was like another son. If he was worried about something, then there was reason for concern.

"It's Holly Jo."

WHEN THE SHERIFF reached his house hours later, he was relieved and a little surprised to see Bailey waiting for him—not inside the house but on his porch in the dark. He parked, cutting his engine, afraid she was finally going to tell him something he now suspected.

After climbing out of his patrol SUV, he walked toward her in the darkest night he could remember. The blackness felt suffocating, the clouds low, not a breath of breeze. The stillness made his flesh crawl. He found himself watching for movement in the sleepy town of Powder Crossing as if every shadow could be dangerous. On the surface, it appeared to be just another night in the tiny eastern Montana town that was merely struggling to stay alive. But he'd learned as sheriff to look below the surface—even when he didn't want to.

Bailey rose as he approached. Their eyes met, and he saw naked fear and pain—both threatening to drop him to his knees. She was finally going to tell him. His chest tightened as he saw her face crumble. He reached for her, drawing her close and holding her. He could feel her heart pounding, her body trembling. He held her tighter, fearing why she'd been showing up at his door for months.

After a few minutes standing on his porch in the shadowy blackness of the night, he drew her inside and closed the door behind her, locking it. He knew what was out there in the dark, but what he was about to let inside terrified him more.

Whatever Bailey was going to tell him, it would change everything.

Why was he always drawn to women with secrets, women who lied to him, women who tempted him even when he sensed a strong undercurrent inside them that warned him how dangerous they could be?

This one had moved into the living room, taken off her jacket, tossed it on his couch and dropped her oversized satchel on the floor next to it, but she hadn't sat down.

She looked scared, but so was he. He wished like hell she

wasn't going to say what he knew she was. So he said it for her. "You already knew what happened to Willow. Bailey, I saw your expression in my office when you asked about her. You suspected what had really happened." He swallowed the lump that had risen in his throat. "You need to tell me. If you know who the killer is, if he's threatening you—"

"I knew because he did it to me."

CHAPTER EIGHT

"DID IT TO YOU?" Stuart repeated, as if trying to make sense out of this. "Are you saying—"

"He attacked me," Bailey said, her voice breaking. She could tell that he didn't want to hear this, didn't want to believe it had happened to her. She'd never told anyone, had hoped she'd never have to. There'd been a time when she'd denied to herself that it had even happened.

But when she met Stuart's gaze, she knew she was going to have to tell him everything. The thought made her sick to her stomach.

He stood, silhouetted against the kitchen light he'd turned on as if afraid to move. "I don't understand," he said keeping his voice soft, devoid of the one thing he knew would break her: sympathy. He was still the sheriff, the man she needed right now a lot more than the cowboy who'd been in love with her for years. But it was that lovesick cowboy who broke her heart. He thought he wanted to hear this, but he didn't. "If you know who he is—"

"How can you even ask me that?" She looked away for a

moment, hating the haunted look she'd seen in his eyes. He loved her. She'd never questioned that. Which made it so much harder to tell him, knowing how it would hurt him, because he loved her and always wanted to keep her safe—not knowing it was impossible.

He raked his fingers through his longish blond hair. "How is it you weren't killed?" he asked.

"I got away from him," she said, but could see he was still having trouble trying to understand why she hadn't come to the law for help. "Don't you think I would have told you if I knew who he was?"

She held his gaze with a defiant one of her own for a moment before she had to look away again. "I never saw his face. He wore a mask. He changed his voice. I don't know who he is." She sounded angry and frustrated and scared. That too was hard to admit. She was terrified. "If I knew who he was, he'd already be dead, and Willow..." Her voice cracked. "She'd still be alive."

STUART STARED AT HER. Hadn't this been his greatest fear? *Be what she needs right now. She needs the sheriff, not some lovesick cowboy.* "I'll take you down to the department, and we'll get it all on the record," he said.

She groaned. "I don't even want to tell *you*, because it won't help. Like I said, I don't know who he is."

"As much as I will hate hearing what happened, Bailey, I'm the sheriff—"

"But you're quitting," she snapped.

He swore, his gaze locking with hers. "There is no way I can quit now. Whoever hurt you... I have to find him." He shook his head.

Her eyes filled with tears. "I'll tell you. But not down there at your office. No… I can't."

"Okay, tell me here, now, just the two of us." She looked so skeptical. He hated to think that she'd lost faith in him—the way he'd lost it in himself.

She hesitated. Then the words began to pour out of her, tumbling over each other. "I was terrified at first that he could come for me again, and I wouldn't see him until it was too late. But he didn't," she said as she began to pace his small living room. "I thought since I'd gotten away, he'd never do it again. It was so long ago…" Her voice broke as she turned to look at him. "Then I heard about Willow."

"No one is blaming you," he said, still standing in the doorway.

Bailey shook her head. "*I* blame me." He could tell she was fighting breaking down. He'd only seen Bailey truly bawl once, years ago, when she'd fallen from a tree and broken her arm. Even then she'd stopped almost as quickly as she'd started, fighting the pain as if crying was a failing, a weakness she wouldn't allow herself.

"When Willow came to Powder Crossing, took the job at the hotel, I saw her resemblance to me when I was younger…" She breathed hard. "But she was *blonde*. How was I to know that she'd gone back to dark hair? With dark hair, she would have looked so much like me when I was that age that he…." She froze, her gaze slowly rising to his. "I didn't want to believe he would do it again, because that would mean he might still be coming for me. But when I heard it was Willow, I knew. Willow was his message. Unless you can tell me that he didn't do it again, that it was someone else… I need to know what he did to her."

Stuart thought about his resignation letter. He'd been

ready to walk away and never look back, but now… He cleared his voice. He'd been afraid that he could no longer do his job, and it was a disservice to the people he'd promised to protect. He'd handed Willow's case over to the state crime team, telling himself they would find her killer. But they hadn't yet.

He took a long breath and let it out as he watched her face. "Her wrists and ankles had been bound. She'd been choked with a cord or garrote. She'd been sexually assaulted." Bailey looked as if she had stopped breathing. He knew what she was waiting for, the one thing that might tie the two cases together. His heart pounded painfully. He could barely choke out the words. "She had a small horseshoe-shaped brand on her left breast."

Her hand went to her mouth, eyes filling again.

"Bailey?" He knew without her saying a word, and yet he was going to have to hear it all. Just as he knew that he was going to tear up his resignation letter first thing in the morning. He had to stay, knowing what the woman he loved had been through—that the man might be coming for her again.

As devastated as he felt, he fought not to show it. He didn't want to think about what the man had done to her. He fought to push away all his doubts and fears and just do the job he'd been hired to do. "When did it happen?"

"When I was seventeen, just before I left for college."

Oh, my God. He couldn't stand the thought that she'd been carrying this secret around all this time. The weight of it was enough to change her into the angry, secretive woman she'd become. His hands fisted at his sides. He had to remind himself that if he was going to stay on the job, he had to be the lawman he'd been trained to be. He had wanted the bastard found before. He just hadn't been sure he could make it happen. Now he had to.

But as angry and upset as he was, he ached to comfort this woman he had loved for so long. He desperately wanted to take her in his arms and promise that no one would ever hurt her again. But he couldn't make that promise. It was going to take a lot more than a hug and empty promises–two things she definitely wouldn't want right now. She needed him to be the law. She needed him to find this man.

"I'm sorry, but I'm going to need to know what happened to you, all of the details," he said. "It's the only way I can find him."

She gave him a disbelieving look. "What makes you think *you* can find him? I've been looking for him for years."

That surprised him. "You have?"

"He still lives around here. I can…feel him as if he's been watching me, waiting."

Stuart felt a chill encircle his neck like a garrote. Any other woman and he'd have thought this was only her fear talking. But this was Bailey McKenna.

"I've always known it was just a matter of time before he came for me again. I'd hoped to find him first." Her blue eyes gleamed with a hatred that couldn't dim the fear. "Willow was his message to me that the waiting is over. He's coming for me. If I don't find him before then…"

IT WAS GOING to be a long night. Stuart made a pot of coffee and finally got Bailey to sit down on one end of the couch. He took the other end—just as they'd done on so many other nights when they'd shared a beer or two. Only tonight all he'd offered her was coffee. "I need this on the record," he told her. "I need to video record it."

She recoiled. For a moment, he thought she might balk and walk out. He couldn't make her tell him. He could see how hard this was for her as she slowly nodded. "For Willow," she whispered.

He turned on his phone and recorded the date and who was present before he said, "I need to know everything you can remember about the attack."

"Don't you mean everything I can never forget?" Making an angry swipe at an errant tear, she took a ragged breath and let it out. He could see her drawing herself up, bracing herself to finally tell someone what had happened to her twelve years ago.

He recalled the young woman she'd been at seventeen and questioned why he hadn't seen a change in her before she left for college. Everyone had just assumed it had been the years away that had made her the way she was when she'd finally returned to the ranch. She hadn't even come home for holidays during college.

The woman who'd returned hadn't been the Bailey he'd known. Some people blamed an assumed bad love affair. Others thought it had been college, blaming higher education. Stuart only knew that she wasn't that wild, free spirit she'd been before that summer when she'd packed up and left for college.

Now she stared straight ahead. He could tell by her expression that she would have never told anyone, determined to handle it herself, if Willow hadn't been murdered.

"My father invited him to the ranch," she said, her blue eyes dulled by the memory. "Along with close to thirty other ranchers for some political maneuvering he called a barbecue."

Stuart heard the pain and anger in her words and felt a

start as he recalled the tension between her and her father all these years. Holden McKenna had invited the man who assaulted her to the ranch?

"I don't remember the exact reason for the barbecue," she continued. "Something about a bill he hoped to get passed to do with ranch land taxes." She shook her head. "He insisted I be there. Insisted I wear a dress and act the lady of the house." Stuart heard bitterness in every word she bit out. "He's the one who sent me down to the pasture after he said someone mentioned that one of the horses had gotten out. I questioned him after that. Why did he ask me to go to the stable? He said he could see how bored I was and wasn't surprised when I didn't come back. And no, he didn't recall who'd mentioned the horse being out."

Bailey fell silent for a moment, but he could hear her breathing. "I never saw the man's face, but I knew he'd been waiting for me and that he was from the group my father had invited to the ranch even before he grabbed me. I saw his boots, shiny dress boots, and his gray Western shirt when he grabbed me from behind, covering my mouth with his leather-gloved hand, his arm around my waist. He was large and very strong. My feet didn't touch the ground as he carried me away from the stable and into the woods to that old cabin no one had gotten around to tearing down."

"The one you tore down the summer you came home from college," Stuart said as everything began to make sense. Her brother Cooper, his best friend, had joked that his sister was taking out her aggression on an old building on the ranch. *She is one angry woman*, Cooper had said. *Dad has no idea what is going on with her but told us all to give her space. Not a problem given the mood she's been in.*

"I fought him until he pulled a syringe and stuck the needle into me. When I came to, I was lying on the floor of the cabin naked. I was gagged, my hands and ankles bound, and there was a rope around my neck. He was holding the other end, standing over me, wearing a mask that covered his entire head." She swallowed and looked away. "You don't want to hear this."

He didn't. Stuart knew it was going to break his heart—just as he knew he had to hear it. The two attacks, hers and Willow's, might be connected, even after all this time. If she was right, Willow had been the message that the man wasn't coming for her again.

"I'm the sheriff. It's my job. Help me catch the bastard."

She gave him a look that was easy to read. Bailey knew his interest in her was more than professional. He didn't bother to deny it. But right now, he had a rapist killer on the loose. He couldn't let his feelings for her muddy the waters. Nor could he turn this into more than his job—a sheriff bringing a criminal to justice. Even as he thought it, he honestly didn't know how he would be able to keep from killing the man when he found him. The idea that he might go rogue didn't scare him as much as he thought it should.

Bailey began to speak again. He listened, fighting not to show his heartbreak or his rage, as she told him in a monotone about the rape and how he'd cut the rope on her ankles but kept the rope around her neck to show her how easily he could kill her, taking her to the brink of consciousness and bringing her back.

"When he came at me with what looked like a miniature branding iron, I knew I would do whatever I had to, but I wasn't going to let him kill me."

HER WORDS CAME FASTER. "I was still suffering from whatever drug he'd injected me with, but not as much as he thought I was. He'd thought I was still docile like I'd been when he raped me." She shook her head. "The moment he started to touch my flesh with the branding iron, I saw my chance. He stood over me, the rope around my neck in his left hand, the branding iron in his right. He was smiling—excited, no doubt, to see my terrified expression as well as witness my pain."

She made a choking sound as if she was back there in that cabin, reliving all of it. "When the iron touched my skin, I brought my legs up and kicked him in the groin. He went down hard, dropping the rope attached to my neck as well as the branding iron. I picked up the still-hot branding iron and rolled toward him as he was trying to get up. I brought the iron down on his left shoulder, because that's all I could reach. It burned through his shirt, catching it on fire. He screamed, swung around and tried to take the iron from me. That's when I saw the knife he'd used to cut the cords he'd bound me with. I let him take the branding iron as I lunged for the knife. When I looked up, he had launched himself at me. I stabbed him in the side as he shoved the branding iron at my face. I stabbed him again, this time in the thigh as I rolled away. He howled in pain and tried to get away from me."

She sucked in a breath. "He was trying to staunch the flow of blood from his wounds. I saw the fear in his eyes, and it gave me strength. I knew what I must look like as I cut the rope that bound my ankles and went after him. He scrambled out of the cabin, bent over in pain and trying to stop the bleeding. I would have kept going until I caught up and killed him, but I was weak from the drug, from his choking the life out of me repeatedly. He got away."

This time her breath came out in a sob before she continued. "I went back into the cabin. There was blood everywhere, the floor slick with it." She paused. Her eyes were still dazed. "I think I was in shock. My chest was on fire from where he'd burned me. I remember going to the creek, washing myself, putting my dress back on and hurrying to my pickup. As you know, I keep a gun in my glove compartment for killing rattlesnakes. I pulled it out and started the pickup, and I went looking for him. I didn't know how badly I had injured him, but I knew he couldn't go back to the barbecue. I thought I might catch him on the road. I never found him. But I also never quit searching."

Bailey blinked as if coming back. When she looked at him, he stopped the recording and said, "My God, I've always known you were strong and determined, but Bailey, you are nothing short of amazing. I'm serious. You're alive because of your strength and grit."

She let out what could have been a chuckle. Or another sob.

"We're going to find him," Stuart said. "I promise you, I won't stop. We're going to get him." He looked into her eyes and saw them glint with both tears and a deadly hatred.

Something unspoken passed between them, making him feel a little sick to his stomach. A part of him thought it only fitting that she would get to kill the man who'd damaged her. The man was a killer. But Stuart was still the sheriff. He'd taken an oath. And until he quit, he had to behave like one.

Stuart also knew that killing him wouldn't give her the closure she so desperately needed. He promised himself that he'd find the man and see that he was punished under the law—and save Bailey from herself—if at all possible.

He still had his doubts about himself. Add to that how much harder this would be because of the way he felt about her. Not only would he have to find the man and bring him in, but also he'd have to fight Bailey to keep her from carrying out her vengeance. He wasn't sure he was up to either, but he knew he would die trying for Bailey.

WEAK AND SICK INSIDE, Bailey felt as if she'd fought the man off a second time. She told herself that she couldn't bear looking at Stuart. She'd feared that he'd never be able to see her the same way again.

But all she saw in his gaze was her pain and his love. He was right. He was the only person she could have bared her soul to because she'd known for a long time how he felt about her. How he still felt about her.

Tears in her eyes, she crawled down the couch and let him take her into his arms. He held her tightly as if never wanting to let her go. For so many years, she'd kept the horror of what had happened to herself, living with the memory, knowing she would someday come face-to-face with the man again—one way or the other.

"I know you have a lot more questions," she said, clearing her throat and extricating herself from his arms. "But not tonight." Rising, she went into his kitchen and opened the refrigerator. She stood letting the cold air soothe her burning skin. It would be daylight in a few hours. "Do you want a beer?" she called.

"Sure," he answered.

It would have been so easy to stay in Stuart's arms, so easy to give in to the desire that had beset her for so long for this man. But she couldn't, wouldn't, not until she'd put her past behind her. That meant finding the man who'd attacked her, the man who'd killed Willow, and ending this nightmare.

She didn't believe in happy endings, doubted she'd get one. But if they existed, she wanted that more than anything with Stuart.

CHAPTER NINE

HOLDEN WOKE THINKING about what his ranch hand had told him yesterday. He swore as he went downstairs to find Elaine setting the table for breakfast.

"You're not dressed for your morning ride," she said, looking concerned. "Is everything all right?"

He hated that seeing Elaine, he was reminded of how Deacon had touched her hand in passing yesterday. He'd been surprised by the intimacy of it. He wondered how far their relationship had gone and, worse, what might happen if it got serious. He couldn't bear losing Elaine, even to a good man like his ranch manager.

"Nothing is all right," he said miserably, realizing how true it was.

She smiled and sat down, patting his spot at the table. "Have a seat and tell me about it."

"I don't even know where to begin," Holden said truthfully.

"Why don't you let me get you some breakfast, and you

can tell me," Elaine said even as he told her he wasn't hungry. "I'll be right back."

He'd barely taken a seat before she returned with a carafe of hot coffee, slices of banana bread and a bowl of strawberries swimming in sweetened cream.

"I figured if you weren't hungry then you definitely didn't want eggs," she said. She'd always had a calming effect on him—and the rest of the family, for that matter. Except for Treyton and Bailey. "Why don't you start at the beginning. What are you doing up so early if not going for your usual ride?"

"Bailey," he said, taking a bite of the banana bread. It was moist and sweet and delicious. "Did you know she's been seeing the sheriff?"

"Seeing?"

He growled. "Whatever. All I know is that she came out of his house before sunrise. I passed her on the road."

"What were you doing on the road?"

"I wanted to see the sheriff before he left for the office, find out if there was anything new on the murder," Holden said, and shook his head. "Didn't even talk about that, as it turns out. Bailey was leaving his house. We passed each other, her just as brazen as daylight."

"Holden, she's not a teenager anymore. She's almost thirty. I'd expect her to have someone in her life. Or is the problem her seeing the sheriff?"

He growled under his breath. "Why Stuart? I mean, she has her pick of any rancher in the valley. Why the sheriff?"

Elaine shook her head at him. "You realize how you sound?"

"Is it wrong to want my daughter to marry well? She can

marry a man with a ranch and land and a good future just as easily as a…a sheriff."

Elaine's eyes widened. "You sound exactly like your father, and look where that's gotten you! I'd want my daughter to marry for love—not land or money—and I would think you, of all people, would know that marrying well doesn't mean happiness."

He felt as if she'd slapped him. His father had forced him to marry a woman he didn't love for what she could bring to the marriage—several ranches his father wanted to add to his holdings. It was how he'd lost Lottie.

"You're right, I'm a damned fool," he said, avoiding her gaze. "If she loves Stuart then I'll welcome him into the family."

"That's more like it, but it sounds as if your concerns are premature. Bailey hasn't been involved with anyone for so long, who knows what this might be between the two of them? Whatever you do, Holden McKenna, you don't say a word about this to your daughter. For the first time in your life, hold your tongue."

He had to smile. "What would I ever do without you?"

"Good thing you're never going to have to find out," she said with a chuckle as she pulled the bowl of strawberries toward her and picked up a spoon. "If you aren't going to eat these, then I am." She grinned.

"It's not just Bailey," he said gruffly as he recalled what Pickett Hanson had told him. "It's Holly Jo too."

"What about Holly Jo?' Elaine asked protectively.

"She has an older boyfriend who has his driver's license," Holden said pointedly.

"Oh," she said. "How much older?"

"Sixteen." He proceeded to tell her what Pickett had told

him. "He actually thinks I should let her go to this dance that's coming up at the school with this boy in his car—even after she didn't get permission when she ditched the bus to ride home with him. If Pickett hadn't been at the county road to surprise her with a ride, who knows when we would have found out about him."

Elaine chuckled again but quickly stopped when Holden added, "Pickett thinks someone needs to have the birds and bees talk with her. You're the logical person."

"*Me*?" she choked out.

"Who else is there?" he asked. "Bailey?" He guffawed at that.

"I think you should have a talk with her—" Elaine said before she was interrupted. "Not about the birds and bees, but about getting permission. I also think you should let her go to the dance—maybe drive her yourself until we know more about this boy. What's his name?"

"Buck Savage."

Elaine lifted a brow. "You know his father."

"Uh-huh," Holden said. "Why did I ever think I could raise this child?"

STUART HALF EXPECTED to wake up and find Bailey gone as usual. Last night they'd gone back out on the porch to drink their beers. The darkness had closed around them like a cocoon as they sat side by side in the wicker chairs he'd picked up at a garage sale. A breeze had come up, rustling the nearby trees.

For some reason, he hadn't been afraid of what was out there in the dark. They'd sat out there like two people who'd been together for a long time. Almost like married people, he'd thought.

He'd felt the same way this morning when he'd walked into his kitchen and found her there making coffee. Last night, he'd had her in his arms. He was still shaken by that brief embrace and what she'd told him. She'd come to him. *Finally.* His relief mixed with his horror and fear, a deadly concoction. He had to find the man and make sure that he never touched another woman again. That he never came back for Bailey.

She finished scooping the grounds and leaned against the cabinet next to him as the coffee brewed. As if on impulse, she reached over and took one of his hands in hers. "I've always loved your hands. Well-used hands, rough for a sheriff, tanned and scarred. I've often thought about these hands…" She let go of him and pushed off the counter. "Sorry. You probably don't want to hear that."

He grinned at her. "My hands on your naked body? I've dreamed of that."

"I want that," she said almost shyly. "Now you know what's holding me back."

Stuart nodded. "I'm going to find him so you can put the nightmare behind you. It will be harder since it's been twelve years."

"Go ahead, say it. I should have gone to the sheriff when it happened, but he was your *father*, and I couldn't because everyone would know. *He* would know. Since I never saw the man's face, I couldn't identify him. I was scared if I told anyone, he'd come back for me. The last thing he said as he stumbled out of the cabin was that he was going to kill me."

"It would have helped had you gone to my father right away," he agreed. "The man bled in that old cabin. My father would have gotten a sample of his blood, his DNA. It would have helped once we have a suspect." He looked over at her. "But mostly, you wouldn't have had to live with this alone all these years."

"I was *seventeen.* I was scared. I didn't want anyone to know because..."

"You felt you'd done something to make it happen," Stuart said.

"I can't believe how ridiculous that is, but at the time, I did."

He nodded. "Having his blood or even his DNA wouldn't have led us to him if he hadn't ever provided his DNA—unless he's done this before."

She nodded solemnly. "Did you get his DNA this time?"

"No, the river washed away any evidence he might have left. He was more careful." He rerouted the conversation once the coffee started dripping and they took a seat at the kitchen table. He pulled out his phone, set it up and hit Record. "Let's start with the rope he used. Can you describe it?"

"Clothesline cord, not rope. He had it cut in lengths, thus the knife he forgot."

"Was cord something that was kept in that old cabin?"

She shook her head. "The cabin was empty, half falling down. He must have put it there beforehand—just like the knife and the branding iron and the wood he'd used to make the small fire to heat the iron."

"He had everything he needed at the cabin and the syringe with the drug in his jacket pocket. Which means he'd been planning this for a while. All he needed to do was get you away from the house. You said your father sent you out to check the horse that had allegedly gotten out."

"It was a ruse. All the horses were fine," Bailey said. "It was him. He was waiting for me by the stable. All of the ranch hands were helping with the barbecue, so there was no one around."

"Any rancher would have known that," Stuart said. "He must have also known about that old cabin a good distance from the stable. He had already hidden the cord, knife and branding iron, which means that he'd been on the property prior to the barbecue—either hours or days."

"I've thought of that. I've asked myself who he could be. A close friend of my father's who often came over to the ranch to ride or pay for stud? Or someone who came to the ranch to see one of the ranch hands? Or a neighbor? That's just it. He could be anyone."

"It doesn't mean he's a friend of your father's," Stuart said as the coffee finished brewing and he poured them each a cup. "Even if he is, your father isn't to blame."

She took a sip of the coffee, saying nothing. He figured she knew she shouldn't have blamed her father all these years. But he could see that for so long, she'd told herself it wouldn't have happened if Holden McKenna hadn't held the barbecue and invited the man.

"Don't you think the man who attacked you would have figured out another way to get to you other than the day of the barbecue if he was that set on it?" Stuart asked. "Also, it would appear, given all the planning he did, that it was you he wanted. He didn't go after Willow until she changed her hair color."

"What are you getting at?"

"He must know you, have been interested in you for some time," Stuart said. "So, while there were people all over the ranch that day—"

"The actual barbecue of the pork and beef was prepared by the ranch hands and Deacon, but the sides were catered," she said, frowning. "There were strangers in and out all morning before the barbecue."

"But he wasn't a stranger, and if he wasn't...why are you so sure the man who attacked you was one of the ranchers your father had invited? There must have been something about him making you think that."

Bailey seemed to think for a moment, then shook her head. "Other than the way he was dressed, I don't know."

"What about his voice?"

"He only spoke in a hoarse whisper behind the mask—except when he cried out in pain."

"But you saw his body, all except his head covered in the mask, right?"

"He was big, over six feet, husky and very strong as if he worked the ranch himself, but there are a lot of ranchers like that."

He was still questioning why she was so sure he was a rancher. "He was dressed in Western attire," Stuart said.

"But that isn't the only reason I'm sure he's a rancher, someone from around here. He was so...confident. He didn't have any doubt that he could pull this off."

"Which leads me back to believing that he knew you. If he was a friend of your father's, he would have seen you at the ranch—and you him."

She shook her head. "I understand what you're getting at. If I'm right, why didn't I recognize him? I don't know."

He let it drop. "How old was he?"

"About my father's age at the time—early forties, maybe younger."

"So he might be a contemporary of your father's. Was there anything else about him?" She shook her head. "This barbecue, was there a guest list?"

OAKLEY STAFFORD HANSON knew when she was beat. With a sigh, she pulled out her phone and called her sister. "I need your help."

Tilly chuckled as if she'd been expecting this call and wondering why it had taken so long. "For what?"

"Don't play dumb."

"I have pregnancy brain."

"Pffft!" Oakley was already wishing she hadn't made the call. No matter what she said to her sister, Tilly always had to remind her that she was pregnant. Like her expanding belly wasn't enough, or that glow in her cheeks or all the baby clothes and paraphernalia all over the house weren't enough. "Are you going to help me with your shower or not?" she snapped.

"I thought you'd never ask. Where are you?"

Oakley looked around. "At the general store. There's nothing here to decorate with. Nothing."

"Don't be silly," her sister said cheerily. "It's fall, and we live on a ranch. There's something to decorate with *everywhere* if you know what to look for."

"Clearly, I don't," she groaned.

"I'll give you a list," Tilly said, quickly taking over, as expected. "It will be like a scavenger hunt. You can bring everything to my house. Then we can pick a date, put it in the *Tattler*, and decide who to invite personally, what to make for refreshments, and finally decorate together. How does that sound?"

"Just wonderful," Oakley said facetiously. Why had she suggested this? Because Tilly was pregnant and her sister, and because her brother Brand's fiancée, Birdie Malone, had asked if she was throwing a shower, like she should have already thought of that herself.

Things seemed to be happening too fast in some ways and too slow in others, Oakley thought. Brand had certainly fallen in love fast. Oakley was getting a sister-in-law she barely knew. Birdie would probably become pregnant right away—if she wasn't already.

In a lousy mood, Oakley tried to cut Birdie some slack. She seemed nice enough, but clearly she had no idea what she was in for, marrying into the Stafford family.

"When do I get to meet your mother?" Birdie had asked as she admired the diamond engagement ring on her own left hand. It had been their grandmother's. How Brand had gotten it, Oakley had no idea. Had she given the ring any thought at all, she would have assumed that their brother CJ had probably already pawned it. The ring was beautiful, and so was Birdie, Oakley had to admit. It was the long black hair, those big green eyes darker than Oakley's, and that innocent face.

"With luck, you'll never have to meet Mother," she'd told Birdie, who had looked like she might cry.

"Do you think she'll like me?" she'd asked.

"Birdie—"

"She'll love you," Oakley had said, even though she doubted her mother loved anyone. Except Holden McKenna, who she equally hated.

Climbing into the ranch truck she'd driven to town, she redialed her sister. "Let's not forget to invite Birdie to your shower. I feel sorry for her. She's afraid Mother won't like her."

Tilly laughed. "Birdie sure has you buffaloed. Trust me, Birdie can hold her own with our mother. She's going to be a great addition to the family. So, have you started on the list I gave you?"

"You mean what you were telling me on the phone just minutes ago?"

"You didn't write it down?" Tilly asked as if horrified.

"No, I'm on my way to your house. I thought we were doing all of this together. See you in a second." She hung up before her sister could comment.

BAILEY WASN'T SURE that telling Stuart how she felt had been a good idea. She felt safest when Stuart was in his sheriff mode. She could almost ignore the low-voltage sexual tension that vibrated between them. Actually, she liked the faint heated buzzing just under her skin when she got near him. It reminded her that she was still alive. That maybe one day…

Lately the tension had been stronger. She wondered how much longer she could fight it as she rubbed her arms and saw that he was still waiting for an answer to his question. It took her a moment to remember the question.

"The barbecue guest list," she said. "I have it." They both glanced at the large bag she always carried now lying on the floor next to the couch where she'd been sitting, but neither moved toward it.

"You say you've been looking for him all these years," Stuart said, his gaze intent on her. She felt the burn of it on her skin, the heat of it stirring a need she had thought she would never feel again. She hadn't dated in college, and what she'd done since she wouldn't call dating, because she hadn't been able to stand getting that close to any man.

"Is that what you've been doing when you come and go at all hours of the night?"

"I've been looking through the list."

"I don't know what that means," he said. "Earlier you said you've been searching for him."

Bailey sipped her coffee. She could feel his intent gaze on her. "I've narrowed it down to four ranchers," she said, not ready to tell him more.

He nodded. "But that's not everything, is it?" He stared hard at her. "Talk to me, Bailey. Don't shut me out like you always do when you're scared. What is it you aren't telling me?"

"I just bared my soul to you," Bailey snapped, pushing back on her chair and standing up. "That wasn't enough?"

The sheriff said nothing, clearly waiting as he got to his feet.

She let her gaze rise to meet his. She liked this man as much as she loved him. Wasn't that why she'd come close to confiding in him so many times over the past few years? He seemed to see her as no other man had. Like now. He knew there was more.

His eyes had sharpened. That glint in them told her he knew more than she thought he did. That was what scared her. That and whatever sizzled between them. She wanted this man, body and soul. He was handsome in a rangy way that made her pulse pound. She loved how he looked at her as if he wanted more than sex. He wanted her. All of her, and had for a long time.

Whenever she'd stopped by his house at all hours, she'd wanted him as badly as she knew he wanted her. But she'd been afraid to get too close. She didn't want him to see the ugly part of her. Not just on her body, but in her heart, the part that demanded vengeance. But her true fear was that she wouldn't be able to make love even with this man she desired almost more than her next breath.

"You don't have any idea how sexy you are when you're in sheriff mode," she said now.

He groaned, seeing what she was up to. "Bailey—"

"Be careful. You know what will happen if you and I get too close," she said, moving closer.

"I know what you're doing, but what do you think will happen if you and I get too close?" His gaze said that he knew exactly what would happen, that he'd been waiting for her to come to him, but it would mean surrendering all of her, including her secrets and her scarred body.

As much as her fingers itched to cup his strong, bristled jaw, to draw him to her, to kiss him, she didn't dare touch him right now because she knew he would reject her advances. He would see through her need to be pushed away rather than confide in him.

"I guess you'll tell me when you're ready," Stuart said, turning his back on her.

"It doesn't have anything to do with Willow's death or my assault," she said, fighting the urge to reach for him. She yearned to be in his strong arms. She yearned to bare her soul to him. No more secrets. No more regrets. But all she could do was let him walk away. Once she told him the rest, she was sure he would walk away for good.

STUART QUESTIONED WHAT he was doing. He knew how stubborn and independent Bailey was. Just as he knew that she was keeping something from him. She said it had nothing to do with her assault or Willow's murder? Something more personal?

Whatever it was, he told himself to let it go. Only hours earlier, he'd been ready to hang up his gun and star. Bailey had changed all of that. Now he had to find a rapist killer who, according to her, was one of them.

He turned back to her as he reached for his Stetson. "I'm going to need to see that guest list," he said, back in sheriff mode. He saw Bailey seem to relax as if she'd been worried that he might change his mind and resign rather than try to find the man who'd assaulted her. Didn't she know him better than that?

That was just it, he thought. Maybe she didn't know him any better than he did her. Through the window, he could see that the sun had crested the mountains and now painted the river bottom golden. He loved this time of year when the leaves on the cottonwoods began to turn, when summer heat waned and, with luck, winter was still a few months off.

He told himself that he'd find this man before the first snow and hoped he was right.

"Stuart—"

He cut her off. "My only concern right now is arresting the guy who assaulted you and killed Willow. How did you narrow it down to these four?"

Bailey looked as if she wanted to say more, but reached instead to open the large satchel-like bag she carried around as if it was full of gold. To her, it probably felt like that. This had been her life for so many of those years after the attack—trying to find the man who'd attacked her.

She pulled out her computer and then a notebook filled with papers. He could see her neat handwriting in the notes she'd made to herself. It only took her a moment to find a copy of the guest list.

As she handed it to him, he saw that most of the names had a line through them. All the ones she'd located who'd been at the barbecue that day and crossed off? He saw that it left only a half dozen. He looked up at her. She'd done most of his work for him. "These that are marked out—"

"Weren't him," she said. "But I didn't mark the name off until I'd checked to see if he had a son or nephew or someone visiting who could have been him."

He saw now why it had taken her years. She'd been thorough. "Why couldn't you scratch these last six off the guest list?"

She took the paper from him. "This one is dead. Died twelve years ago in a ranching accident. I've seen photos of him. I left him on the list because he could have been the man. But after Willow… It's not him." Pulling out a pen, she scratched off the name. "There's one more. He was injured in a car accident last year and is unable to walk." Bailey looked up at him. "He was a possibility, but not anymore."

He knew who she was referring to and nodded. "So that leaves four ranchers. What about the catering people?"

"I've vetted them all. It wasn't one of them. They were all women and were busy the whole time they were on the ranch."

"No one brought a brother or a boyfriend?" he asked.

"No. The man who attacked me had been on the ranch before. He knew about the old abandoned cabin. He knew me."

Stuart stared at her, knowing it was true. This wasn't random in any way. The man hadn't just planned the assault. He'd been after only one young woman—Bailey. It's why when Willow changed her long, curly hair from blond to almost black, the man had gone after her. She'd looked too much like the young Bailey who'd gotten away.

"There's one thing I don't understand," Stuart said. He knew criminals often followed a pattern. They normally didn't go twelve years before striking again, especially if

Bailey was right—it was only her he wanted—and killing Willow had been a message. "You came back five years after college. You said you knew he'd attack you again. I understand why you returned, but why did he wait?"

"Maybe I'm wrong and it isn't about me," she said. "I'm almost thirty. Willow was at least ten years younger, right? She looked like me when I was her age. Maybe he has a type. Maybe I wasn't even his first."

He met her gaze. "We're going to get him. We have you. You're an eyewitness."

She shook her head. "He knows I didn't see his face and can't identify him or he'd already be in jail. He knows I won't see him coming until it's too late."

That was Stuart's fear also. He looked at the list again. He didn't want to believe that Bailey was in imminent danger, yet his instincts told him that she was right. She was. This was about her and only her. This had been personal. The man had taken a huge chance doing what he'd done on the day of her father's big barbecue.

Had this started because it had always been about her father? Had this been a way to get back at Holden McKenna? It wouldn't be the first time someone had used one of Holden's family members to try to hurt him. But then, why Willow? No, the message had been sent to Bailey—not her father. This was about her.

Stuart looked up at her. He had to follow his gut and hers. The man was coming for her again, and they had to find him before that happened. "I want to know everything about these four ranchers left on your list. With luck, he's one of the four. I'm assuming you've seen each of these men."

She nodded. "Any one of them could be him."

"I'll check them out," Stuart said. "If he's one of them, then he wasn't home the night of the murder. Also, we have a boot print that was left at the scene. The print was fresh, but not enough to prove that he's our man. It could have been left by someone else who stopped by the river in the past few days." He frowned as he had a thought. "You don't happen to remember the type of boot your attacker wore, do you?"

"Black, crocodile, pointed toe."

"How about the heel?" he asked.

She frowned thoughtfully and shook her head no.

"A buckaroo-style boot by any chance, tapered at the heel?" Stuart asked. "Taller top with an extra layer of leather to protect the cowboy's legs from the thick brush and tapered heel in the back?"

"Sorry. All I can tell you was that they looked expensive."

Stuart nodded, though "expensive" could cover a lot of dress cowboy boots on ranchers in the area.

Bailey, he noticed, looked for the first time as if she believed the man could be found and stopped before he came for her. She reached into her bag and pulled out her computer. "I can send you everything I know about the four ranchers and their families. Everything but their boot size and style."

"Good, I'll see what I can find out." He glanced at the time. "I need to get to my office." The registration letter was still in his desk drawer. He didn't want anyone finding it before he could destroy it. Bailey was busy on her computer. He heard his phone announce that four emails had been delivered. "Bailey?"

She looked up as she finished and closed her computer.

"I was thinking it might be a good idea if you lie low in

the meantime," he said. "I'd recommend that you go out to the ranch… Maybe tell your father what's going on." She shook her head. "It's going to come out."

"I wasn't safe at the ranch when I was seventeen," she said. "What makes you think I would be now?"

She had a point. "Anyway, I have to go to Billings. If you need to get in touch with me, I'll be at the Northern for the night."

He couldn't hide his relief that she would be away from here. Not that the rancher couldn't follow her to the hotel. But he felt she should be safe in Billings since as far as they knew, the rancher wouldn't be as familiar with the city as he was with the Powder River Basin.

However, he had to wonder why she was going to Billings. She could be meeting a man at the hotel. She could be doing just about anything. If she wanted him to know, she would have told him, so he let it go. "Stay in touch."

She nodded, and they stood awkwardly for a few moments.

"I'm glad you told me." He said nothing as she turned and picked up her things. "You know I'll do whatever it takes to find him and bring him to justice."

Her smile told him how things would go. "You won't be doing this alone. You need me. Don't make me sorry I told you." With that, she swept past him.

He walked to the porch to watch her leave, even more worried about her than he had been. Whatever she was doing in Billings, it had to do with her assault, with the man who was coming for her. He just couldn't imagine how.

As she started to drive away, their gazes locked for a few seconds before she disappeared out of sight.

In those few seconds, he saw relief. She wasn't alone

in this anymore. The weight of it settled heavy on his shoulders, bringing with it all his doubts and his fears. He couldn't fail her.

CHAPTER TEN

STUART READ THROUGH the information that Bailey had texted him on each of the four ranchers before he checked in with the state crime team and the coroner. Ronald had little more to tell him after completing his autopsy and turning in the report. Willow had been sexually assaulted, choked repeatedly and finally branded before being dumped in the river, where she had drowned.

So where had the killer attacked and kept the victim? It couldn't have been too far from where he'd dumped her in the river, right? He sent two deputies to search the area near the drop site for any nearby abandoned buildings where the assault could have taken place.

In the meantime, he planned to talk to each rancher left on Bailey's list—beginning with the one closest to the drop site, Earl Hall. The sheriff felt a little more confident this morning as he picked up his Stetson and, settling it on his head, headed down the Powder River toward the Wyoming border.

All four of the men on Bailey's list were born and raised

in the area, attended country schools and inherited ranches from their families. The Hall Ranch, like many of those in the Powder River Basin, had been land claimed under the Homestead Act in 1905.

Stuart didn't call ahead. He took his chances that he'd find Earl Hall at home. Twelve years ago, Earl would have been thirty-six. He and his father, EW, had been invited to Holden McKenna's barbecue that day. If father and son had ridden to the barbecue together, Earl couldn't be Bailey's attacker. She had injured him badly enough that he would have had to leave at once.

But it was possible EW hadn't gone. Or that he'd taken his own pickup. Or that he'd helped his son. Now suffering from dementia, Earl's father lived in a rest home in Miles City. Bailey had crossed Earl's father off the list, the sheriff noted, because of a ranch injury to the man's right leg that had left it half the diameter of the other. But he could have been a co-conspirator, as horrible as that sounded.

Pulling into the ranch yard, Stuart parked in front of a two-story house that had fallen into disrepair over the years. Bailey's notes said that Earl and Iris Hall had three daughters. All three now married and living elsewhere. None of the three women's husbands were under suspicion, apparently.

As he climbed out of his patrol SUV in Earl's front yard, he glanced around. The ranch was a good sixteen miles from where Willow's body had been found. Still, he found himself looking around for any outbuildings that could have been used for the assault. None looked viable.

Also, the small house Willow Branson rented was on the other side of town, miles from here. But Earl could have picked her up at the hotel after her shift and brought her out here. Stuart had learned never try to make sense out of a psychopath's actions.

"Can I help you?"

He turned to see Earl Hall standing stocking-footed on the front porch of the house, squinting in his direction. Hall was a big man who'd gone to seed. His belly hung over his belt. From what Stuart could tell, little ranching was still done on the place. Just short of fifty, Earl looked at least ten years older than that. He hadn't shaved, his beard in disarray, and from the looks of his clothing, he hadn't changed in a while.

"Earl," the sheriff said as he walked toward him. "Just stopping by. Iris around?"

"At her sister's in Fargo."

Stuart suspected she'd been there for a while. "Suppose you heard about the murder," he said as he reached the man. Earl shook his head, appearing surprised. "The young woman who worked at the hotel? Found in the river?"

"Hadn't heard," the rancher said. "Haven't been to town."

The sheriff glanced toward Earl's pickup parked in front of the house a few feet away. The windshield was covered with dust, bird droppings and leaves. The truck didn't appear to have been moved for a while.

He took a few steps closer and glanced inside the cab. It was cluttered with junk on the passenger side floorboard, and the seat covers were torn and filthy. Nothing out of the ordinary. Same with the truck bed, which contained only a large toolbox, an assortment of rusty tractor parts and some trash. It looked like most of the old ranch pickups in the area.

His gaze returned to Earl as he stepped back to the foot of the porch steps. "Haven't seen anything suspicious down this way, have you?" Another head shake. "No more traffic headed for Wyoming than usual?"

"Nope." He shifted on his feet. "Not that I would have noticed. Been under the weather lately."

Stuart surveyed the man and his clothing. The sleeves of his dirty shirt were rolled up. No injuries showing on his arms or his hands, but then again, Bailey's attacker would have had marks on his left shoulder, side, and left thigh.

He would have liked to have seen the man's dress boots. But from the look of the once-white socks on Earl's feet, he'd been wearing them for a while and not dress boots. Not that the killer might have been wearing similar attire when he killed Willow, he reminded himself. But if the man had a pattern he was trying to duplicate, as Bailey suspected…

It was clear that Earl wasn't going to invite him in. Which was fine with Stuart. The smell that wafted out of the Hall house indicated a sink full of dirty dishes, last night's meal probably still sitting on the stove. He wondered if Iris would ever be coming back.

"Well, I'm just stopping by a few ranches to see if anyone noticed anything suspicious," the sheriff said, noting that Earl hadn't asked about Willow or where on the river she'd been found. "If you think of anything, give me a call." With that, he turned and walked to his rig. When he looked back at the house, Earl was still standing on the small porch, watching him go.

Past him, a curtain inside the house flapped open a little and closed. Either Earl hadn't been alone, or the breeze had made the worn fabric flutter.

CHARLOTTE STAFFORD HADN'T known how badly she would miss the ranch when she'd walked away from it. The pain had started like a dull ache in her chest. But it had gotten worse as the days and weeks had gone by. She'd yearned for the sight and scents of it, for the feel of the creek on her bare feet, for the sound of the birds high in the cottonwoods. She missed home desperately, but she'd promised herself she wouldn't look back, nor would she have any contact. She feared that if she knew what was happening back there, she wouldn't be able to stay away.

She missed her grown children, but she'd raised them to take care of themselves. Brand and Ryder would run the ranch. CJ…well, he was where he belonged. Tilly was married, and Oakley had been dating Pickett Hanson. By now they too could be married. Before she'd left, she'd heard rumors through the Powder River grapevine that Tilly was pregnant. Her first grandchild was on the way.

Still, as much as she ached to return, she couldn't. Not yet. Everyone was fine without her, she kept telling herself. Everyone but her. The ache in her chest was like a drum that woke her in the dead of night with a death march of a beat. *Go home. Go home. Go home before it's too late.*

She'd almost picked up her phone and called her only true friend back there, Elaine. But she knew what Holden's housekeeper would say. "Stop wasting time. You need to come back and settle things with Holden once and for all."

She'd always considered herself to be a strong, determined woman, but when it came to Holden—the man she'd loved her entire life—she fell short. She'd loved him and hated him in equal measure for breaking her heart. She'd never thought she could forgive him, yet she had before she'd left. But he'd made it clear how he felt about her after all the years she'd pushed him away, after she'd lied to him, betrayed him in a way worse than he had her.

She couldn't face him.

Even as she thought it, the pain almost doubled her over. Her heart ached to go back home. If there was even a chance for her and Holden, how could she not take it? They might not have that many years left.

STUART WAS DETERMINED to check out all four ranchers as quickly as possible while he waited for the crime lab's findings. The coroner had warned him not to get his hopes up. The river had washed away any obvious evidence.

Still, he hoped the state crime lab found something that would help. Every item, no matter how small, that had been retrieved along the edge of the river had also been sent to the lab.

He could feel the clock ticking as he drove out to AJ Plummer's ranch. If Willow's murder had been a message to Bailey, then the man might act quickly now. He would know that law enforcement was looking for him. But if he was as arrogant as Bailey seemed to think he was, he might enjoy watching the law miss finding him, confident he wouldn't be caught.

The sheriff found AJ saddling up his horse near the barn. The man's size fit Bailey's description of her attacker. Stuart was six-two, broad in the shoulders and slim at the hips. AJ was a good three inches taller and built like a brick outhouse, Stuart's father would have said. The rancher stood next to a horse that had to be at least seventeen hands tall, yet it looked average next to AJ.

As the sheriff approached, the rancher turned but didn't seem surprised to see him. Stuart noticed how the guy was dressed. He looked like a man going into town for a meeting with his banker, rather than one about to go for a ride.

The sheriff couldn't help but think about what Bailey had said about the confidence the man who assaulted her had exuded. AJ wasn't just good-looking. He'd excelled at everything he'd done, from high school and college football to raising prize-winning quarter horses.

"Have I caught you at a bad time?" the sheriff asked as he glanced down at AJ's boots. Not black crocodile, but definitely expensive boots. Not buckaroo-style either, he noted. Not that it proved anything.

"Just going for a ride," the rancher said cordially. "Want to join me? I could saddle up a horse for you." Strikingly handsome, AJ's smile transformed his face. It was no wonder he was considered a charmer—and the Powder River Basin's most eligible bachelor at the moment. He and his wife, Faith, were separated, so he was considered available.

Twelve years ago, AJ would have been twenty-six, younger than Bailey was now. His father had died in a small plane accident when AJ was nine. He'd been raised by his grandfather, who was now in his early eighties.

"Thanks, but I don't want to keep you," Stuart said. "I'm sure you've heard about the murder."

The smile disappeared in a heartbeat. AJ looked apologetic. "Of course. Hell of a thing. I don't understand it. It had to be someone passing through town."

That's what everyone always wanted to believe. Couldn't be anyone local. *Couldn't be one of us.* "I'm asking ranchers along this stretch of county road if they have seen anyone or anything suspicious."

AJ shook his head. "Truth is, I've been down in Wyoming for the past week. I just heard when I got back. Beautiful young woman. Damned shame."

"You knew Willow?" he had to ask, even though it

appeared AJ had an alibi for the time when she was assaulted and killed. "Date her?"

The rancher laughed. "She was too young for me, Sheriff." He raked his left hand through his hair.

Stuart noticed he was wearing his wedding ring again. A few months ago, he'd seen him in town and noticed he wasn't wearing it. The pale skin where it had been wasn't quite as tanned as the rest of his finger. At the time, the sheriff had heard that AJ and Faith were separated and had been for a while.

"I just knew Willow to say hello on the street," the rancher was saying. "I'd seen her a few times in the bar at the hotel."

"With anyone in particular?"

AJ frowned. "Usually she was with a female friend, but there was one time… Only reason I remember was because I was surprised to see her with him." He looked up, appearing to hate to tell on the dead woman. "She was with Treyton McKenna." He nodded at Stuart's surprise. "Surprised me too. Even more so because they seemed…" The sheriff waited, not wanting to put words into the man's mouth. "Close."

"Intimate?"

The rancher mugged a face. "Not exactly. But Treyton was definitely coming on to her, and she wasn't shutting him down."

"Thanks. I appreciate this."

"I just want to see whoever did this caught and behind bars."

As Stuart drove away, he thought about Bailey's brother. Treyton wasn't the man who'd attacked Bailey, but he might know something that could help find Willow's killer if he'd been hanging around the hotel, flirting with her. The problem was that the sheriff didn't have a good relationship with the obnoxious oldest son of Holden McKenna.

Still, he was anxious to talk to Treyton. Especially since he'd been wanting to see the property the man had bought recently out in the badlands away from town, away from the family ranch.

He'd been suspicious of Treyton for a long time, especially after discovering there had been a meth lab at one of the old homesteads that involved human trafficking. The lab was destroyed before Stuart could get any evidence against CJ Stafford. But the sheriff suspected he wasn't the only local ranch offspring involved, and Treyton McKenna definitely fit the criminal profile.

CHAPTER ELEVEN

TREYTON MCKENNA HAD been expecting a visitor since his last phone call from CJ Stafford. He regretted ever getting involved with the sick bastard. He'd thought that once CJ was behind bars, that would be the end of their so-called relationship. He'd been wrong.

At the sound of a vehicle coming up his road, he picked up the sawed-off shotgun he kept handy. He also had begun carrying a gun strapped to his ankle. The kind of men he dealt with on a daily basis made being armed a necessity.

But the kind of men he expected CJ would send to keep him in line would be the worst. His so-called partner in crime seemed to collect the lowest form of criminal, ones thirsty for blood.

He wasn't surprised to see the panel van roar up into his yard. He'd bought this property some time ago. It was badlands country incapable of growing a damned thing. But it had been cheap, had a building on it that he'd made into a home of sorts, and was far enough out that he didn't get visitors—normally.

The one time his father had paid him an unwelcome and unannounced visit, Holden had said he couldn't understand how he could live like this after growing up on the McKenna Ranch with everything.

"I want to be my own man," Treyton had said. "I can't do that standing in your shadow."

"You call this being your own man?" his father had demanded.

"I'm no longer under your roof or your thumb, so you damned betcha I do. Now get off my property, old man. You chose my brother over me a long time ago. You and I have nothing more to say to each other, so don't come back."

"I raised you and Cooper the same. Your problem with your brother is you, not him," Holden said, glancing around. "I don't know what you're doing out here, but I'm sure it isn't anything good."

Treyton had laughed. "You always had so little faith in me." He'd slammed the door in his father's face and never looked back.

But this wasn't his father who'd pulled in. The sun glinted off the windshield of the panel van, not allowing him to see who was driving or who was riding shotgun. But he wasn't surprised when he heard the side door roll open and saw two men come around the front of the van before the driver and passenger emerged.

Four men. It wasn't the first time Treyton had been outnumbered, but it could be the last. He scooped up two handfuls of shells and pushed them into his jacket pocket as he walked to the door and threw it open.

"I might not be able to kill you all, but I'm going to try," he called to them as the men approached, recognizing several of them.

The driver of the van, a stout man with a shaved head who went by the name Ret for *retribution*, held up his hand, and they all stopped moving toward him. "Just want to talk."

Treyton laughed. "Not if CJ sent you."

Ret tilted his head as if considering this. "Any reason CJ would have to send us?"

"None at all. He and I understand each other perfectly, always have. We go way back. Didn't he tell you that?"

"He did mention that you were a McKenna and he didn't like McKennas," Ret said.

"I feel the same way about Staffords. But this is business, right?"

"Right," Ret agreed and shifted his feet.

The change in the four men was subtle, but Treyton didn't miss it. He pumped a shell into the shotgun and fired—just short of where the men were standing.

They jumped back, already going for the weapons they'd brought. Treyton knew that the next few shots would have to stop at least three of them if he stood a chance of this not going south. But killing even some of them would bring its own problems.

He pumped into another shell as those critical seconds swept past. Two of the men were moving toward him fast when he heard the roar of a vehicle coming up the road. The men didn't seem to hear it until the siren and lights turned on and the patrol SUV came to a dust-boiling stop in back of the van.

By then, one of the men had launched himself at Treyton. Rather than pull the trigger, he stepped aside and brought the butt of the shotgun down hard on the man's shoulder. The blow crumpled him on the porch steps. Treyton gave him a swift kick that rolled him back down the steps and into the dirt.

"There a problem here?" the sheriff asked as he climbed out of the patrol car with his own shotgun.

Treyton McKenna had never been so glad to see the law.

BAILEY FELT SOMETIMES as if she was losing her mind. She'd been focused on the man who'd assaulted her for years now, knowing he was out there. As much as she trusted Stuart with her life, but she wasn't about to stop looking for the man of her nightmares on her own. She could feel him watching her everywhere she went. He was coming for her. Had he been biding his time for the past twelve years? Or had seeing Willow brought it all back and triggered something in him? Was he even now closer than she knew?

It was as if she could feel his sour breath on her neck, hear his hoarse whisper in her ears. *I'm right here, Bailey. Only this time I'm going to kill you—like should have happened the first time. Ready?* She could hear his deep, throaty chuckle. *Ready or not, here I come.*

"Bailey, are you listening?"

She surfaced from her thoughts to realize that she was sitting in her SUV parked in front of the family's ranch house. She'd been about to climb out when she'd gotten the call. She'd had no choice but to take it and get it over with. At least here in the car, she would have the needed privacy.

"You aren't going to be able to keep this quiet in a few months," the woman on the other end of the call was saying.

She was well aware her secret would be out soon. Time was running out.

"I had really hoped we could discuss this in person when

you came to Billings. You've cancelled two appointments, but I could stay another day if—"

"No. Don't." She looked in the rearview mirror at her appearance. The scratches on her face were a daily reminder of what was at stake. She knew that R. Durham was only the first to get wind of what she'd been doing. It would be much worse when more people knew. "I apologize for standing you up in Billings, but family issues have kept coming up." She couldn't tell her the truth. Not yet.

"If you're thinking of backing out—"

"No, it's too late for that." She looked away from the mirror to the view of the Powder River Basin stretched to the horizon. She used to love this view, especially this time of year with the cottonwood leaves turning golden along the dark green, quietly flowing river. *Coming back here could be the worst mistake I ever made. The last one as well.*

"Good, I'm glad you realize that it's too late for that. I can understand if you're having second thoughts, but—"

"It's not that." Wasn't it? Not that it mattered. She'd done what she'd done. No turning back now. "It's fine. Everything's fine." She kept saying it as if just voicing the words would make it true, when she knew all along that nothing was going to be fine. In fact, things could get much worse and would if the man coming after her wasn't found and stopped soon.

As a large, male shadow fell over the driver's side of her SUV, she froze for an instant before he bent down, and she saw his face. "I have to go," she said.

"We'll talk next week. This is an exciting time for you. Enjoy it."

Bailey laughed as she disconnected. *Exciting* was putting it mildly.

Her father tapped on her window. "You coming in the house?"

Was she? She could tell by the look on his face that he wanted to talk to her. She could just drive off. Or not. She cut the engine, and he stepped back as she climbed out, dragging her large satchel with her. She saw him look at the bag and then her in question for a moment.

"We need to talk about Stuart," he said.

"Why?" she asked as she started toward the house. She wasn't having this conversation out in the front yard. She could see Pickett over by the corrals working with Holly Jo on one of horseback riding tricks. The girl believed she could be a world-famous trick rider and was determined to make it happen.

Bailey actually admired the thirteen-year-old—not that she'd had anything to do with her since Holden had brought her back to the ranch to live. She was in no place to take the girl under her wing, let alone giggle while they painted each other's nails.

But that didn't mean she didn't notice Holly Jo had grit, something Bailey was sure her father also admired. She remembered when he'd looked at her with awe the way he did Holly Jo. But that was a long time ago, back when there was a reason to have high hopes for her, she thought as she entered the ranch house, her father close behind.

He motioned her into his office-den. "Sit down," he ordered, then softened his tone as he took a chair behind his desk. "Please, Bailey."

She felt like a petulant child as she slumped into a chair across from his desk. She just wanted this over. The news she'd gotten this morning felt as if it had made that already ticking clock tick faster. Now it ticked in time with her pounding heart. She didn't have any time to waste, especially in some futile attempt to explain herself.

"Tell me about you and Stuart," he said as he leaned forward, folding his large, weathered hands in front of him.

"There is no me and Stuart." Not really, not yet. "When and if there is, I'll let you know."

He narrowed his gaze at her. "You spend time with him."

She shrugged. "Sometimes."

"Damn it, Bailey, he told me that he's in love with you."

She'd have rather heard that from Stuart under other circumstances, she thought. Not that she hadn't known how he felt about her. But for so long, she hadn't felt…lovable, so she had questioned how he possibly could love her—especially when he didn't understand her secrets. "He barely knows me."

"He's known you your whole life!"

She had no answer for that. Her father didn't know her either, but he didn't seem to realize it.

"What is going on with you?" he demanded, losing his patience.

"Nothing." She met his gaze, having become good at lying, even to herself.

Holden shook his head, his tone softening again. "I feel like you're angry at me."

"What would I have to be angry at you about?" she asked.

Silence filled the room. He closed his eyes as if in pain, making her wish she could take it back, take it all back, especially her misplaced anger at him.

She got to her feet. For a moment, she searched for words to make it better, but couldn't find any.

"Please be careful," he said, dismissing her. "I worry about you."

"Me too," she said as she went upstairs to get a change of clothes before she left again.

THIRTY-FIVE, TREYTON MCKENNA had longish dark hair and amazing blue eyes, much like his sister Bailey. Stuart figured Willow found the cowboy handsome. She might have taken his arrogance for confidence. More than likely, he wouldn't have shown her his rotten side—at least, not at first.

"Nice to see you, Sheriff," Treyton said as the men with the weapons got back into their van and left.

"Seems my timing worked out well for you. Want to tell me about it?"

Holden's son smiled. "Nothing to tell."

Stuart nodded knowingly. Both the McKenna and the Stafford families' oldest sons were trouble. CJ Stafford was behind bars and hopefully would remain there for a very long time. So far, Treyton McKenna had avoided arrest, but the sheriff figured it was just a matter of time before he ended up incarcerated.

"Got quite the place out here," Stuart said as he glanced around. There were several old buildings that appeared to have been fixed up. "What do you do way out here?" he asked, looking past the buildings to the scrub pine and rough terrain beyond.

"There a reason you showed up when you did, Sheriff?"

He turned back to him. "Willow Branson."

Treyton frowned. "What about her?"

"She's dead." He saw the man's surprise. "You know anything about that?"

"No. What happened to her?" He sounded upset.

"She was murdered."

Treyton blinked and shook his head. "That's awful."

"I was hoping since you knew her that you might have some idea who would have done that to her," Stuart asked. "Maybe someone who hung around the hotel where she worked? Maybe someone in the hotel bar?"

The cowboy was still shaking his head, shock making him seem paler. "I… I don't know."

"You dated her, right?"

He let out a huff. "Not dated exactly. A lot of guys flirted with her."

"Like who?" Stuart asked.

Treyton seemed to have to think about that. "A bunch of old ranchers who had crushes on her. I used to tease her about it."

"Sounds like you were close. You ever tell her to change her hair color?"

He looked surprised. "Her hair color? No, I wouldn't have changed anything about her."

"There wasn't one rancher she was closer to than others?"

Treyton shook his head. "I never paid much attention. She and I had a few laughs at the bar. That's all it was. She wasn't interested in me. I got the impression she was dating someone she was serious about."

Dating someone? "You have some idea who?"

"Sorry. Like I said… I still can't believe…" He shook his head again, sounding truly sorry to hear that she was dead. Maybe Treyton McKenna had a heart after all.

"You going to be okay if those men come back?" Stuart asked. "Because I'm betting they will."

Treyton seemed to get over his earlier shock as he grinned and said, "Don't worry about me, Sheriff. I can take care of myself."

"If you say so." Stuart touched the brim of his Stetson and walked to his patrol SUV. Climbing inside, he wondered again what Treyton did out here all alone. Whatever it was, he'd bet his favorite boots it wasn't legal.

CHAPTER TWELVE

CJ STAFFORD FELT as if he could explode. His heart jackhammered in his chest, each beat like a blow to his chest. That damned Treyton McKenna. He'd kill him when he got out of here, he told himself as he pushed his way through the group waiting to use the prison phone.

After having to bribe and threaten and almost fistfight his way to get the phone, he called Ret. "What happened?" he demanded from between gritted teeth.

"The sheriff showed up when we were about to kick the crap out of Treyton."

He gripped the phone hard. "The sheriff *followed* you?"

"No, why would he? Treyton seemed as surprised to see him as we were. Wasn't even about us, Treyton said when I called him later. Something about some girl."

"Bailey?" She'd always been trouble.

"Naw, not Treyton's sister. That Willow chick who got herself murdered. They found her naked in the river. Didn't you hear about that?"

CJ couldn't care less. "Whatever. All I care about is what I told you to do to Treyton."

"We talked when he called. He's doing what you told him to. He said he would pay your lawyer and send you some money so you could buy yourself a chill pill."

CJ swore. If he could get his hands on that McKenna son of a—

"Seriously, CJ. You need to relax and stay out of trouble. Isn't your trial coming up?"

"Thanks for reminding me." If it went the way his lawyer said it would, he'd be going to prison for the rest of his miserable life.

"Hire yourself a better lawyer with the chill pill money. I know you. If anyone can beat this, it's you."

His time was up. He was going to be cut off anyway, so he merely swore and threw the phone at the prisoner waiting impatiently behind him. All he could think about was that if his mother had gotten him a decent lawyer, he wouldn't be sitting in a prison cell waiting for trial. He would be out running his business, where he should be.

Charlotte Stafford hadn't been taking his calls for months. He hadn't even tried his sisters. Neither Tilly nor Oakley would have taken his collect calls anyway. On a clearer-headed day, he might have admitted he couldn't blame them. He'd almost killed Tilly in his pickup while running from the law. Oakley…well, almost killing her on purpose was why he was headed for trial.

With his mother and sisters not taking his calls, he knew better than to try his two younger brothers, Brand and Ryder. He'd spent years tormenting them both. Which meant he had to depend on the kindness of—not strangers, but criminals he couldn't trust.

It wasn't like he hadn't expected his siblings to turn on him. They'd hated him for years for being their mother's favorite. But he'd never expected his mother to turn on him since he was the one most like her. He'd been the one she'd loved the most because of it, which told him that she wouldn't let him go to prison for the rest of his life.

One of these days, she'd come back to Powder Crossing and the ranch. Because if she didn't help him, he feared what he would do when he finally got out one way or the other.

THE SHERIFF CHECKED in at his office. It had been a long day. Tomorrow, he'd drive out to Jay Erickson's ranch and talk to him. He'd have to wait to catch up with Richard "Dickie" Cline, the last name on Bailey's list until he returned. He hated how little he'd learned today. He felt as if he was spinning his wheels, time running out. Bailey wasn't safe until he found the man who'd killed Willow and assaulted her. He desperately needed a break in the investigation. He couldn't stop until he got it.

As he sat down behind his desk, he went through his messages and thought about what he'd learned. He'd talked to staff at the hotel, the owner and some of the bartenders, especially Luke Graves, who he was told often got Willow to work the bar for him.

Graves had admitted that it was true he got Willow to take his shifts at the hotel bar on occasion. But as far as who she might have visited with at the bar during that time, he had no idea.

"Did she spend time in the bar when she wasn't working a shift for you?" Stuart had asked.

"I never saw her in the bar with anyone, if that's what you're asking," Graves said. "She'd stick her head in after her desk shift was over. I'd make her soda to go on the house, but she never stayed around."

"When she'd stop in for a soda, did you see anyone at the bar leave shortly after that?" the sheriff asked.

Graves hesitated, and Stuart saw that he knew about Willow and AJ. "Was AJ Plummer the only one who left right away?" he asked. When Graves still didn't answer, he added, "I'm trying to find out who was close to Willow. Who might know who killed her."

The bartender swallowed and said, "AJ's the only one I noticed leave right after Willow did."

"They were seeing each other secretly?"

The bartender nodded. "He was separated from his wife, but still married. I suppose that explains the secretiveness."

When asked about Willow's hair color, he said that she did ask him what he thought. He'd liked her blonde and had said as much, so he was surprised when she changed it. As to who told her she should go back to her natural color, he didn't know.

Tomorrow Stuart would talk to Jay Erickson first thing. Then if Richard "Dickie" Cline was back from where his wife said he'd gone, he'd talk to him. Right now, he wanted to bring AJ Plummer in, but he knew Plummer would lawyer up quickly if he tried without more evidence.

The sheriff knew he couldn't ask any of the men to disrobe so he could check for scars—and a small horseshoe brand. It was going to take more than suspicion. He needed proof to make the arrest first. After that, it should be easy to either prove one of the men was guilty—or exonerate all four.

That thought made him feel queasy. Bailey was so sure

it was one of them, but what if she was wrong? Then he would be back to square one.

He shook off the thought. All four fit the description. All four had been invited to the barbecue.

Almost grateful for the interruption, he took a call from the crime lab to let him know that the items collected along the riverbank had arrived. The tech promised to get back to him once the items were tested.

Stuart doubted any DNA would be found in the trash found along the river, but he knew enough about forensics to hold out hope something simple and small could bring down a killer.

He was on his way home when he spotted AJ Plummer's pickup parked in front of the hotel. "Just saved me the drive," he said to himself as he pulled into the lot and went inside.

No surprise, he found AJ at the bar. It was early so he was alone, the bartender nowhere in sight. "Thought you said she was too young for you," Stuart said as he took the stool next to him.

The rancher had the good grace to look shamefaced.

"You failed to mention that the two of you dated for a few months."

"It was only a couple of months," AJ said. "I liked her, okay?"

"You lied about your age with her."

"I never told her my *exact* age. She knew I was too old for her." AJ looked down at his drink on the bar.

"Did she know you were still married?"

"I assume so," AJ snapped, "since everyone knows everyone else's business around here."

"You took off your wedding ring, but now it's back on."

"What are you getting at? Faith and I are trying to work a few things out."

"Now that Willow's no longer in the picture?"

AJ took a drink. "I don't have to put up with this."

"You're right. You could come down to the sheriff's department, and we could make this more formal. You should have mentioned you had a relationship with her."

The rancher sighed. "It wasn't like that."

"Why don't you tell me what it was like," the sheriff said. Again, AJ looked embarrassed. "Let me guess. You knew better than to be seen with her, so the two of you never left the hotel."

"She was of age," AJ said in his defense. "It was consensual."

"Did you tell her to change her hair color?"

AJ's head jerked up. "What?"

"Someone at the bar told her she needed to go back to her natural color."

"It wasn't me. I thought she looked great as a blonde. I liked it better than way."

"Did you ever notice other men flirting with her?"

"Sure." AJ's face flushed with anger. He was still holding his empty glass, his knuckles white. "All the time. They were like bees to honey."

Stuart saw that the rancher had been jealous. So jealous that he stopped Willow from seeing anyone else? "Do you happen to know who got her to change her hair? She didn't mention to you that she was changing it?"

"I told you, I'd broken it off and stayed away from her. We weren't seeing each other the last month or so."

"Why was that?" Stuart asked.

"She was too young for me and…and Faith and I were talking about getting back together."

The sheriff studied him for a moment. It wasn't adding up. What was he missing? "Was Willow seeing someone else?"

"How would I know?" he snapped.

"You don't seem all that broken up over her murder."

AJ met his gaze with a steely one of his own. "You're wrong. It broke my heart. I cared about Willow. I wished like hell that I'd met her when I was closer to her age and not…married."

"Did you know she was coming off of a heartbreak when she moved to Powder Crossing?" He nodded. "She talk about him?" A head shake. "But you knew she was vulnerable."

A muscle jumped in AJ's jaw. "Think of me what you will. Why would I kill her? I was in love with her." With that he threw some money on the bar, slid off his stool and, picking up his Stetson, walked out.

CHAPTER THIRTEEN

It was late by the time Stuart drove home. When he saw Bailey's SUV parked behind his house in the trees, he felt both relief and concern. She'd said she was staying the night in Billings. Had something happened to change her mind?

She'd been in his thoughts all day. Her attacker was still out there. His worry and exhaustion made him feel as if he would never be able to protect her from the man at this rate. His only hope was that whoever the man was, he wouldn't strike yet. Stuart needed the time to find him first.

He reached his front door and started to open it, then stopped as he realized he was angry with her for not telling him why she went to Billings. But more than that, what she was keeping from him.

He wished she had stayed in Billings tonight. He wasn't sure he was up to seeing her without getting into it. Hell, he wasn't up to anything. He'd been looking forward to kicking off his boots, putting his feet up and having a beer or two before passing out on the couch in front of the television. Anything to make him quit thinking about her, worrying about her, wanting her.

The door he'd left locked was unlocked. He pushed it open, surprised by the smell of something cooking. He didn't cook much for himself, making do with leftovers from the café or a fried egg sandwich. When he was this tired, he'd often skip food entirely.

As he stepped into his house, he also heard music. He rounded the corner to find Bailey standing at the stove moving with the soft, almost melancholy music playing on her cell phone. There was something so vulnerable about her, her defenses down, that he didn't speak, couldn't. Bailey had been a force to reckon with for so long. He realized he'd never seen this Bailey.

The sight of her made him go soft inside. He'd wanted her before, the prickly and hard-shelled woman, but this glimpse of her stole the rest of his heart. He no longer pretended he didn't want her more than his next breath.

The song ended, and she turned slowly to look at him. "I cooked," she whispered. "You'd better be hungry—" Unfortunately he'd lost his appetite. "Didn't think I knew how, huh." She seemed to see he was enchanted with this unguarded version of her. "Sit," she ordered, and turned off the music and the food on the stove. That other version of her was gone as if he'd never seen it. He hung up his Stetson and, stepping to the table, dropped into a chair.

Turning back to him, she said, "You look like you had a hell of a day. I made spaghetti. You talk to them?"

"Not Jay Erickson and Richard Cline yet."

"Dickie," she said under her breath.

"I called earlier. His wife says he's out of town—has been for the past three days," he said.

"She could be lying."

He began to kick off his boots. "I would never have thought of that." Silence fell between them as she stood holding a large spoon, looking at him. The rich marinara sauce smelled delicious. But he felt too exhausted to eat.

"Not tonight," she said, turning back to the stove. "Tonight, we talk about something else."

He had started to say that he wasn't up to talking period, but stopped himself. "I thought you were going to Billings?"

"Changed my mind. Took care of it with a phone call." She put down the spoon. "Go in and sit on the couch. I'll bring you a beer."

"I'm sorry," he apologized as he rose stocking-footed from the kitchen chair. "I'm not very hungry."

"Me neither." She stood there as if not knowing what to say or do. "Go. I'll bring the beer."

He gave her a grateful smile and headed for the couch. A few minutes later, she joined him, handing him a cold one. He noticed she hadn't gotten one for herself—just as he noticed there was more going on with her. He thought about their last conversation. Didn't she realize that he knew her, knew when she was holding back something?

She raised her gaze to him, her look almost apologetic as if she knew he couldn't take too much more today. "Something happened. An SUV followed me after I left town again."

Her words felt like an anvil dropped on his chest.

"It was the same one that followed me the last time."

"Ralph Jones's? You're sure."

The last time she thought she'd overreacted when Stuart had told her that he'd run the plates and the vehicle was Ralph's. She'd actually forgotten about it until she saw the SUV behind her again tonight. "Why would Ralph follow me?"

"I don't know, but I'll make a point of asking tomorrow," the sheriff said. "I have to go out that way to talk to Jay Erickson anyway." He could see her doubting herself as she rose and headed into the kitchen.

"I'm going to put the food away," she said over her shoulder.

He worried about her most days, but today had been the worst. Now he knew why. A few moments later he heard her banging around in his kitchen. He wondered if she could be wrong and figured she was struggling with the same thing. Tomorrow he'd pay Ralph a visit. Tonight… He took a long swig of his beer and put his feet up on the coffee table. He knew he should go into the kitchen and apologize for not eating at least a little of the dinner she'd made.

But he wasn't hungry, and worse, he knew he'd ask her why she'd planned to go to Billings again in the first place. The worst part was that he had a feeling she wouldn't tell him. He was trying to keep her safe, find the man who assaulted her, finish this for her. She was making it harder by keeping secrets. There was no way he could keep Bailey safe short of hog-tying her and locking her in his house. Even then, he figured she'd find a way to get herself into trouble.

Except twelve years ago, trouble had come after her. Was still after her.

So why didn't she trust him enough to tell him whatever it was she was up to? Taking another long drink of his beer, he swallowed and closed his eyes.

Hours later he woke, rose and went to see if Bailey was in his guest room. To his surprise, she was.

Some of that weight that had settled on his chest earlier lifted as he closed the door softly and went to his own bed.

When he woke the early next morning, Bailey was gone—as usual. He might have thought he'd dreamed her except for the faint smell of marinara sauce still in his kitchen. As he'd predicted, he'd awakened fully clothed on top of his bed. Alone.

WILLOW'S BROTHER AARON was already sitting in the Cattleman Café in Powder Crossing when Bailey walked in. She liked that he was punctual. As she headed for his table, guilt made her legs heavy with each step. She'd gotten his sister killed.

Often when she forgot why she'd come back home after college, she reminded herself as she did now that she'd come home to catch the man who'd tried to kill her. She'd feared he would do it again – if to her, then to someone else. And now he had killed Willow.

Aaron looked up at her approach, surprise making him blink. She'd forgotten for a moment how much she resembled his sister. She saw in his eyes just how much they had looked alike as he pushed unsteadily to his feet. This was going to be so much more difficult than she had thought.

"Thank you for meeting me, Mr. Branson," she said as she took the chair he pulled out for her. She could feel him staring at her and tried not to let it make her more nervous than she already was.

"Please, call me Aaron," he said as he sat back down.

She nodded. "I'm Bailey McKenna."

"I know. What I don't understand, though, is why you wanted to ask me about Willow. Were you friends?"

Bailey realized she should have expected him to question her motives. "No. I knew who she was." She met his gaze. "I saw the resemblance between us."

He nodded slowly. "It really is striking. You could have been sisters," he said, voice breaking.

"I'm so sorry," she said, and had to swallow the lump that had formed in her throat. "But that's why I hoped you could help me find the person who killed her."

"Are you working with the sheriff's department?"

"Not really." This was going to be much harder than she'd expected. Fortunately, the waitress came to the table to take their orders. Bailey knew she wouldn't be able to eat a bite. "Just coffee. Black. Thank you." The waitress filled her a cup and refilled Aaron's before leaving.

Bailey jumped in headfirst. "This will probably sound ridiculous to you, but I think your sister was killed because she changed her hair color."

"That's weird. The sheriff asked if I knew who talked her into going back to her natural color—something a little darker than your own. But I don't understand why that would—"

"I think I'm next. That's why I need to find him before he finds me."

He stared at her, leaning back in his chair, clearly concerned that she was delusional from his wary expression.

"I know you probably told the sheriff everything, but I'd hoped that since then, you might have thought of something else. Willow might have mentioned the men she came in contact with at the hotel."

Aaron took a sip of his coffee, eyeing her over the cup. As he set it down, he said, "I don't know who told her to go back to her natural hair color. You really think that's why she was killed? The sheriff thinks that too, doesn't he?" His look said he suspected her secret.

Bailey washed down the bile that rose in her throat with some of the hot coffee. It was early enough that the café was empty except for a couple of ranchers sitting at the counter, visiting with the waitress. Still, it was hard to say the words. "He attacked me when I was seventeen," she said, her voice a whisper as she held Willow's brother's gaze.

He started, instantly reacting. "If that's true, then why—"

"I never saw his face."

"But you—"

"I managed to get away from him. That was twelve years ago. After all this time, when nothing else happened, I assumed—"

"That he wouldn't do it again," Aaron said with a curse. His gaze locked with hers. "Because it's you he really wanted."

"That's the assumption. You and the sheriff are the only ones who know this," she said quietly.

He shook his head, clearly having a difficult time with this information. She thought he might storm out. She thought he might take out all his pain by lashing out at her. She'd beat herself up for years. Nothing he could say or do would be worse than what she'd already done to herself.

"I don't know how I can help you," he said as he made a swipe at the tears that had spilled onto his cheeks.

"Willow knew this man well enough that she changed her hair for him," Bailey said. "He made her feel safe. She wouldn't have been afraid when he came for her until it was too late."

He said nothing for a long moment, his long fingers slowly turning his cup around and around as he stared into his coffee. "I asked her if there was anyone special in her life. I knew how badly she'd been hurt before. I was afraid—" He cleared his throat. "There were men who flirted with her. But she said there was one rancher who came into the hotel bar a lot. She never mentioned his name—just that he was harmless when I'd expressed concern she was getting involved again too quickly. He apparently brought her presents, silly little things. I'd forgotten she told me that."

"What kind of silly little things?" Bailey asked, making him glance up in surprise.

He shook his head and looked away. "I should have paid more attention when she called," he said, emotion making his voice hoarse. After a moment, he seemed to remember something. "A tiny windmill he made out of a piece of straw while he was sitting at the bar." He nodded. "Pretty corny, huh. Oh, and fudge. When she told him her favorite, he brought her peanut butter fudge. I'd forgotten. He wrapped the piece of fudge up in silver Christmas paper and pulled it from his pocket like a magician. Sounded so hackneyed I figured he was just some old rancher who saw her more like a daughter."

Aaron cleared his throat again, wiped at fresh tears and said, "But I remember how touched she was by the gestures." Raising his gaze, he asked, "Do you think he's the one who..."

"I don't know, but this might help me find that rancher," she said. "If it isn't him, he might know who else had an interest in your sister."

CHAPTER FOURTEEN

STUART HAD BEEN about to head to the office when he heard a rig pull up in front of his house. He opened the door just as Holden McKenna was about to pound on it. "She's not here."

"But she was, wasn't she?"

"What is this about, Holden?"

The big rancher sighed. "I talked to her. Not that I got anywhere with her. But…" His gaze softened as he looked at the sheriff. "She's going to break your heart."

Stuart laughed. "You drove all this way to tell me that? I could have saved you the trip. I've known that for years."

Holden rubbed the back of his neck for a moment. "I understand what it's like to be in love with someone who is only going to hurt you over and over again. I like you, Stuart. I hate to see you in that same position."

"I appreciate that, I really do, but I know what I'm up against. It doesn't change the way I feel."

"Then I'm truly sorry for you. Let Bailey go before she destroys you." With that, the man turned and walked back to his ranch truck.

Stuart watched him drive away. Holden McKenna's reaction to him and Bailey had left him feeling off balance. Was the rancher worried about him or Bailey? The sheriff had never really thought he'd have a chance with her, let alone… He shook his head. What? A relationship? An honest-to-goodness one with a wedding ring and babies? He tried to imagine having children with Bailey. That he could made him realize he was a lost cause.

He shook off his thoughts, reminding himself that he wasn't even sure he and Bailey were friends at the moment. Right now, though, he had to do his job to the best of his ability. Even the thought made him question that ability.

But he'd do whatever it took. He was anxious to find out if Ralph Jones really had followed Bailey, not once but twice. He also still needed to talk to both Dickie Cline and Jay Erickson, the last two ranchers Bailey hadn't scratched off her list.

On the way to his office, he got a call from the state crime team. They had finished Willow Branson's rental house and her car and would get back to him if they had anything once they ran the DNA and fingerprints that didn't match hers.

He'd already been informed that there had been no sign of forced entry or a struggle inside either the car or the rental property. He'd been waiting before going out to the house himself even though he wanted to see where she'd lived.

But now that the techs were finished, he wanted to see the house. Had Willow's killer been in her rental? Would they get lucky and find his DNA? Had he grabbed Willow somewhere else? Or had he simply driven out to her rental, honked, and she'd come out, thinking they were going on a date?

Holden thought love was blind. Maybe he was right and

it had gotten Willow killed, he mused as he drove. As he came over a small rise, he spotted the house—and the familiar SUV parked outside it. It was the same one Holden McKenna had seen leaving his house the other morning before daylight. What was Bailey doing here?

He drove down the hill to park next to her rig and got out. She must have heard him coming, because a front curtain twitched as he approached the porch. A few seconds later, the door opened.

"I waited until the crime team left," she said, looking as if she'd been caught with her hand in the cookie jar.

He saw emotion in her expression. Pain. "Bailey, what are you doing here?" Clearly seeing Willow's life before it had suddenly ended had already taken an emotional toll on her.

She swallowed. "I need to show you something." She pushed the door open wider.

Even as he stepped in, he was telling himself that if there was anything to find, the crime team would have found it. Just inside the door, he stopped, his gaze following her outstretched arm to a small table next to the couch.

The tiny item on it was so odd that he didn't recognize it at first. As he started to step toward it, she said, "Don't touch it. He made it for her." That stopped him, his gaze flying to her. "I talked to her brother. He remembered that one of the ranchers Willow knew from the hotel bar had given her little presents."

He looked from Bailey to the tiny straw figurine. "What's it supposed to be?"

"A windmill, I think. The man also brought her homemade fudge," she said. "Peanut butter wrapped in silver Christmas paper."

Stuart felt his eyes widen a little. He slowly shook his head. "He could have bought it."

"Or his wife could have made it like she does every Christmas to sell at the toy drive."

He swore. "Her brother told you that?" She nodded. "Why didn't he tell me all this?"

"Probably forgot. Or maybe he didn't think it was important at the time..." She paused. "He really is a creepy, sleazy bastard."

The sheriff knew she wasn't talking about Aaron Branson. "Bailey, I appreciate your help, but you need to back off now, okay? We're getting too close. *You're* getting too close. He might panic and..." He couldn't finish as he met her defiant gaze. It burned in blue flames. "Please."

"What did my father want?" she asked, turning away, breaking eye contact.

"You came by the house after you left this morning?"

"I wanted to tell you what I'd learned from Aaron," she said. "When I saw you were busy, I decided to come out here. You haven't answered my question."

He wasn't finished trying to get her to stay out of this, but knew it would be a waste of breath. "He warned me not to fall for you."

"Too late for that," she said, meeting his gaze.

Stuart nodded. "He told me you were going to break my heart."

"That couldn't have come as a surprise. Is that all?" she asked, looking away.

"He told me to let you go."

She looked back at him. "What did you tell him?"

"That I can't. That I love you, have for a long time."

As if knowing there was more, she seemed to be waiting. "And he gave you his blessing?"

"Something like that." He took a step toward her, but knew better than to try to touch her. Oftentimes she seemed like a broken vase that had been badly glued back together. One wrong touch and she would shatter, the vase destroyed, completely unrepairable. "He said he felt sorry for me if I thought I could ever put a ring on your finger."

"My father doesn't know me," she said, holding his gaze. "But you do."

He wondered about that even as he nodded. "You scare me when I find you out here all by yourself in a place we know he might have been," Stuart said. "He probably watched her from the foothills. He might have grabbed her here that night." He was relieved to see realization in her eyes, along with fear. Fear was the one thing that might save her, he told himself. She certainly wasn't going to listen to reason, not from him.

A heavy silence stretched between them for a few moments before he broke it. "I'll have the crime scene techs pick up the straw figure. I doubt they can get DNA off it, but they might surprise me. For all you know, he accidently wound a piece of his hair into it. You were going to call me after you found it, right?"

"Yes, I was," she said as she stepped past him toward the door. "You have to trust me, Layton," she said as she stepped out into the waning rays of the fall morning, daring him to argue otherwise.

"It's a two-way street, McKenna."

She laughed. "Maybe I'll see you later." With that, she headed for her SUV.

He watched her go, studying the horizon, afraid he'd see

a vehicle pull out and fall in behind her as she left. He noticed a few outbuildings in the distance and called the office. "I need a couple of deputies to search some abandoned buildings near the house Willow Branson rented."

But fortunately, he didn't see anyone following Bailey before she dropped over a rise in the road and disappeared.

THE ANNOUNCEMENT ABOUT Tilly Stafford McKenna's baby shower had appeared in the local shopper, the *Tattler*. Like in a lot of small Montana communities, everyone who got a shopper in their mail or picked up one at local businesses was invited.

This morning, Charlotte Stafford had gotten a copy of the printed announcement via text message from her daughter. It had been days without even a text until this morning, proving what a lousy mother she was. But she figured not answering calls or texts from her offspring was no worse than the other things she'd done.

The truth was, her children were all grown and didn't need her—better for everyone. Not that they hadn't tried to reach her, especially CJ, but she'd ignored the calls, texts and messages. Mostly they wanted to know when she was coming back, and she didn't have an answer for that.

She was looking at the baby shower announcement when her phone rang, startling her. She saw that it was Elaine calling. Before Charlotte had left, she'd told Elaine not to call unless she had to. That left it open to interpretation.

Hesitating for a moment, she picked up. "Hello?" Her voice sounded strange since she seldom used it. She saw no one, hardly left her room. Everything she needed could be ordered at the touch of a button.

"I wasn't sure you'd answer my call," Elaine said.

Charlotte chuckled. "I can tell by your disapproving tone that I'm about to get a lecture. Should I hang up now?"

"No," her friend said, her voice softening. "I'd ask how you are, but you'd lie, so I won't. I'm calling about Tilly. She's pregnant, due in a couple of months, I think. Oakley and Birdie are throwing her a baby shower next week."

"Birdie?"

"Your soon-to-be daughter-in-law. Brand's fiancée. Birdie Malone. Dixon's daughter."

"Yes, Dixon, my dead husband who keeps coming back to haunt me," she said. "Small world, isn't it."

"She reminds me of you, Charlotte."

"Oh mercy, that can't be good."

"They haven't announced a wedding date yet, but I would think you'd want to meet your first daughter-in-law-to-be before then," Elaine said. "You also don't want to miss your daughter's shower—let alone the birth of her baby."

No, she didn't, but all of this news seemed to be about people she no longer knew—even her own blood. She'd burned so many bridges, caused so much trouble. How could anyone miss her?

"Holden's miserable."

The words struck her like a knife to her heart. "I didn't ask."

"He's hurting. Charlotte, you need to come home. You can't keep running. It's time."

STUART DROVE ON out of town on the gravel road toward Richard "Dickie" Cline's ranch. The day was one of those bright, warm fall days when the air smelled like burning leaves and mown hay as he drove. Overhead, white puffy clouds bobbed in a clear, deep blue sky.

The season had changed almost without him noticing it. He knew winter was coming since the temperatures had been dropping at night. This morning he'd noticed frost on his windshield. It was a sign that snow wouldn't be far behind in this part of Montana.

He felt more aware of time passing today as he turned in to the road to the Cline Ranch, sending up a cloud of dust and dried cottonwood leaves. Ahead, he saw the two-story ranch house sitting back from the river and slowed.

Even from a distance, he could make out a horseshoe hanging over the front door. It struck him that he hadn't questioned the brand the man had used on Willow or Bailey. Why a horseshoe?

According to superstition, if the horseshoe was hung over a doorway with the ends up, it caught good luck from anyone who walked under it.

However, if the ends pointed down, the good luck would spill out on those entering. But it was also said to keep evil away.

The horseshoe hanging over the Cline house pointed down, Stuart noted as he climbed out of his patrol SUV and walked toward the door, wondering if it had kept evil out.

Annette Cline opened the door a few moments after the sheriff's knock with a surprised look. "Sheriff?" she said and glanced past him before returning her gaze to him. "To what do I owe the honor?"

A nice-looking woman a good fifteen years younger than her forty-year-old husband, Annette leaned suggestively against the doorframe. She wore a blue short-sleeved dress that matched her eyes, the fabric falling over her curves like running water, accentuating everything.

The look in her eyes had always been a little too predatory. It struck Stuart as he took in her freshly applied makeup that she'd been expecting someone—just not him.

"Is Dickie around?" he asked, noticing how quiet the ranch yard seemed.

"He's out of town," she said, and smiled. "Can I give him a message when he comes back?"

"When do you expect him?"

"A few days. I could have him call you," Annette said, clearly not going to ask him in even as she flirted with him. She was trying to get rid of him.

"I'd appreciate it if you'd do that." He'd started to turn away when she said, "You sure you don't want to leave a message?"

"I'm sure," he said over his shoulder. As he drove away, he passed a large, newer-model pickup coming into the ranch. Wyoming plates. He called the office and had the plates run, but the name that came up, Brock Sherwood, didn't ring any bells.

HOLDEN LOOKED UP to find Elaine standing in his den-office doorway. He'd already had a rough day and wasn't up to more. He'd ridden over to the creek this morning, but there had been no sign of Lottie. He felt like a damned fool, which was probably why he'd said what he had to the sheriff. "If it's bad news—"

"Not necessarily," she said quickly. "I did some checking about this boy Buck Savage." She came on into the room, closing the door behind her since she didn't want anyone hearing and telling Holly Jo that they'd been checking up on her boyfriend. "Talked to the principal and several teachers at the school. Seems like a nice boy, popular."

"But?"

"One of the teachers said she thought Buck had been getting help on his math homework. She said she thinks Holly Jo is doing it for him and trying to pass it off as his."

"Terrific," Holden said with a curse. "What is the teacher going to do about it?"

"Let it go for a while, saying these kinds of relationships never last long."

"Meaning what?" he demanded.

"That if he's only using her to do his homework, he'll probably lose interest in her, and they'll break up."

Holden shoved to his feet. *"The little bastard is using her?"*

"We don't know that for a fact," Elaine said quickly as he came around the end of his desk.

"We know his father. I think it's time I paid a visit to the Savages." He reached for his Stetson as he started for the door.

"Try to be diplomatic, because if it gets back to Holly Jo—"

He slammed the door. "Diplomacy my ass," he said under his breath.

BAILEY FELT A chill as she left Willow's rental. It had been so strange and eerie to see all of the woman's things as if Willow had just stepped out and would be back any moment. There'd been a feeling of expectation in the air along with the faint scent of the woman's perfume. In the bathroom, her makeup had been spread out on the counter, evidence of an important date night.

In her bedroom, a variety of clothes from the closet had been discarded on the bed as if she'd had trouble deciding what to wear. Again, the date had been important to her, given her obvious indecision.

The mess in the bathroom and bedroom told her that Willow hadn't planned to bring her date back to her house that night since she hadn't tried to tidy up. Instead, it almost looked as if she'd been running late.

So where had she been going, and with whom? Had it been him? Had he come to her door that night? Had Willow been expecting him—or someone else? He wouldn't have come into the house. No reason to take a chance of leaving any evidence behind. Since there was no sign of a struggle, she must have gone outside with him. But was he who she'd gotten dressed up for?

Or had it been someone else?

The thought nagged at her as she drove, riding along with her like that ever-present feeling of being watched. Another chill curled around her neck. She quickly rubbed it away, remembering when it had been clothesline cord around her neck. She had to find him and soon, she told herself as she headed into town.

If Willow had a date that night, someone she worked with at the hotel just might have known about it. People might not have been as forthcoming with the sheriff and crime team as they would be with her.

CHAPTER FIFTEEN

ON HIS WAY out to talk to Jay Erickson, the sheriff swung by Ralph Jones's place since the two ranch properties adjoined. Stuart needed to ask Ralph why he'd followed Bailey on the road to Billings—not once, but twice. He also wanted to talk to Ralph's wife, Norma, about her award-winning peanut butter fudge.

When he drove up, he saw Ralph standing in the doorway of a large old shed across from the main house. The rancher was in sunlight, but quickly stepped back as if trying to hide in the shadows behind him.

The sheriff parked, got out and walked toward the shed. He couldn't see the rancher but knew he was still there. "Ralph?" he called as he approached the doorway, suddenly on alert. From inside, he heard what sounded like a wrench hit the wood floor, following by a rustling of movement.

Cautiously, he stepped to the doorway and waited for his eyes to adjust to the semidarkness. A dark figure moved from the back of the shed, stepping in a shaft of light from a crack in the wall. "Back here."

Like the men not crossed off Bailey's list, Ralph Jones was a large, solid man. Twelve years ago, he would have been forty-three, a man in his prime. He'd been invited to the barbecue, but had he gone? Maybe not, and that was why Bailey had crossed him off her list.

Jones held what appeared to be a heavy-looking piece of machinery, the rancher's arms bulging with the weight of it. He watched Jones carry it over to the workbench, put it down, then wipe his hands on the coveralls he wore. "What brings you out here, Sheriff?" he said as if realizing this was an official visit.

Stuart reminded himself that Ralph was the one who had found Willow's body. "I need to ask why you followed Bailey out of town on the road to Billings." Even from a distance, he saw the man start before picking up a hammer. He seemed to weigh it in his hand for a moment before putting it back on a hook on the wall behind the workbench.

With a sigh, he moved, empty-handed, toward Stuart. "I was worried about her." The sheriff raised a brow but said nothing before Jones rushed on. "After finding Willow Branson in the river like that…" His voice broke. "They just look so much like each other. I got to thinking. What if the killer came after her next?"

"So you followed her. Had you planned to follow her all the way to Billings or stop her somewhere along the way?"

"That's just it," the rancher said, sounding flustered. "I didn't have a plan. It was just impulsive. I saw her leaving town, alone, and I… It sounds bad, but it's the truth."

"It doesn't sound impulsive since you followed her twice."

Behind Stuart, a screen door slammed, and a woman's voice called, "Ralph?"

"I'd appreciate it if we could keep this between the two of

us," the rancher said quickly, clearly nervous as the sound of footfalls on the hard-packed earth grew closer. "Norma's worried about me. I haven't been the same since…since I found that girl in the river."

He would imagine it had been a shock, especially when Ralph had thought the body was Bailey's. Stuart realized now why Ralph had mentioned that to him. Because everyone in the Powder River Basin probably knew about the two of them—at least, what they thought was going on when they saw Bailey's rig parked outside Stuart's house at all hours.

"Sheriff?" Norma Jones said directly behind him. Turning, he smiled, tipping his Stetson to her.

"Good to see you, Norma," he said, still surprised that he hadn't realized people knew about him and Bailey. "I wanted to see if you had any of your peanut butter fudge."

A small, demure woman, she put on a scolding expression. "Now, Stuart, you know darned well that I only make that for the county fair and at Christmas." She had for years. Hers always took the blue ribbon, angering a lot of the other wives. Her recipe was a secret and her fudge her pride and joy.

"I missed buying any at the fair this year. I thought you might still have some," the sheriff said. There was no way she'd remember who all bought it from her stand on the last day of the fair. "Was it wrapped in silver foiled paper as usual?"

"You know it was," she said, chuckling. "It's my trademark." She dropped her voice conspiratorially. "Martha Warren's taken to wrapping hers like mine. But don't be fooled. It's not anywhere near as good as mine," she finished proudly.

He laughed. "I don't doubt it." He suddenly had a craving for peanut butter fudge. It had been one of his favorites as a boy. His father used to buy him a piece even though his mother said it would rot his teeth and would hide it from him if he tried to save some of it for later.

"You didn't drive all the way out here for fudge, I hope," she said, eyeing him suspiciously.

"No," he said. "I wanted to talk to Ralph, make sure there weren't any more problems with your neighbor."

"That darned Jay Erickson," she said, shaking her head. "That man's like a mean dog that can't wait to get off his chain and bite someone."

"He hasn't been around lately," the rancher said from deep in the shed. "If he bothers us again, I'll handle it."

"That's what I'm worried about," Stuart said almost in unison with Norma. They smiled at each other. "Call me, Ralph, if there's a problem. Let me handle it."

The rancher nodded from the shadows, knowing that Jay Erickson wasn't the only thing Stuart was talking about. "You got it, Sheriff."

BACK IN TOWN, Bailey parked in front of the Belle Creek Hotel. The yellow-and-white wood structure was a historic landmark with a wide front porch and peaked roof. Inside was an old-fashioned lobby complete with leather chairs and a fireplace. A wide wooden staircase rose to the second floor, this side of the ancient elevator.

The hotel dining room wasn't used except for weddings, holidays and other local events. The lounge though with its long mahogany bar and mirror on the back of the bar highlighting all the different bottle of alcohol was a popular place.

Bailey headed toward the back of the hotel, knowing that the housekeepers were probably still at work. She could hear the murmur of voices over the rhythmic hum of the washing machines in the hotel laundry. An older woman named Sylvia Day was busy pulling towels from a large clothes dryer as her younger companion, Nicky Browning, folded them onto their carts for the next day.

They both turned, looking surprised but not concerned as Bailey stepped into the room, closing the door behind her. "I'm trying to find out who killed Willow," she said. Neither woman questioned why the daughter of a wealthy local rancher would be looking into the murder. "I was hoping you could help me." When they said nothing, she continued, "Do you know if she had a date the night she was killed?"

Sylvia finished dragging out the last of the towels and closed the dryer door. "What makes you think we'd know anything?"

"You're women. You notice things men do," Bailey said simply. "Has anyone questioned you about Willow?" They both shook their heads. Just as she'd thought. They didn't work in the same area, weren't the same pay grade. But Powder Crossing was a small town, and there wasn't a lot to do but speculate on other people and what they were up to. It was why she'd been able to get information so easily about everyone *but* the man she was looking for. People out here in the middle of nowhere made butting into other people's business an Olympic sport. Every house had binoculars and usually at least one nosy occupant.

"She always wore this one perfume when she had a date after work," Nicky said as she kept folding towels. "She had this look," she said with a shrug. "Kinda smug."

"Like it was an important date?" Bailey asked, and got

a nod from Nicky. “Like the look of a woman in love?” Another shrug. “Any idea who he was?” There was a general shaking of heads. “Did some of her dates pick her up at the hotel?”

“Not this one,” Sylvia said, lips pursing. “She kept looking at her watch like she was going to be late meeting him. No idea where. But I got the impression he was older.”

“A rancher?” she asked feeling her pulse throb under her skin.

“Probably,” the old woman said, disapproving. “The men who flirted with her were all too old for her.”

“Like who?” Bailey asked.

Sylvia shook her head. “She never mentioned any names, and I never saw her go out of the hotel with anyone. I got the feeling she’d been hurt before she came here and was taking it slow. If she was seeing someone special, she liked her privacy, something hard to come by in this town.”

How had she kept her “dates” a secret? “She ever mention going to Miles City or Billings on one of these dates?”

The younger housekeeper ducked her head for a moment. Bailey kept her gaze on her. “Nicky?” she asked. “If you know something—”

“I know she went to Billings with him,” the woman said.

“Do you know where they might have stayed? Maybe the Northern?” A lot of ranchers stayed there because it was downtown and close to the airport.

Nicky shook her head. “They couldn’t stay there. That’s apparently where he always stayed with his wife. Heard her telling someone on the phone. Wasn’t happy about that.”

THE SHERIFF SLOWED to turn in to the Erickson place. He’d been to the ranch last year when Jay and neighboring rancher Ralph Jones had gotten into a verbal argument that ended in a fistfight. Jay had gotten his wrist broken, and Jones lost a tooth.

The fight had to do with coalbed methane drilling. The Powder River Basin was the single largest source of coal mined in the US and contained one of the largest deposits of coal in the world. It had always been a matter of time before crews showed up to drill for coalbed methane.

Jay Erickson had a well drilled on his property and had been threatening to have one dug near Ralph's.

Coming up the road to the ranch house, he saw Jay Erickson leaning against his pickup as if he'd been on his way somewhere before he'd spotted the patrol SUV coming up the lane.

"Jay," Stuart said as he climbed out of his rig. "You headed somewhere?" Erickson wasn't dressed for town. He looked as if he'd just stepped out of his blacksmith shop. He was a big man who owned a small ranch by eastern Montana standards. He'd always supplemented his income by working as a blacksmith.

Wearing a wifebeater T-shirt, he was muscled at forty-five. His biceps bulged. He'd always been strong and still was. He'd also always had an anger problem as far back as Stuart could remember. What the sheriff found most interesting was that Jay had made regular-sized branding irons for several people in the area. He definitely could make a small one.

Without answering the sheriff's question, Erickson said, "That bastard call you again?"

"Which bastard would that be?" Stuart asked.

"Jones."

Ralph Jones, his neighbor, Stuart assumed. "You two get into it again?"

The rancher-blacksmith shook his head and looked back down the road as if expecting someone else to drive up.

"I need to know where you were the past few nights—and mornings," the sheriff said.

"Why?"

"Someone was murdered."

"And you think I did it?" He laughed and looked away. "Jones put you up to this, didn't he?"

"Why would you ask that?"

"Because he threatened to call the law on me."

Stuart sighed. "I hate to even ask."

Erickson shook his head. "Why else are you out here?"

"I told you. I'm investigating a murder."

"Well, I didn't kill no one." He started to get into his pickup.

"Don't you want to know who died?"

The rancher grunted and turned back to him.

"Willow Branson," Stuart said.

"Who?" Something flashed in Erickson's eyes before he looked away.

"The young woman who worked at the hotel in town. She sometimes filled in at the hotel bar." Stuart knew that Erickson more than likely drank at the Wild Horse Bar rather than the hotel. Maybe he didn't "know" Willow, but he would have seen her around. He definitely knew who she was.

Also, Jay was at Holden McKenna's barbecue twelve years ago shortly before he'd married his long-time girlfriend, Angie Durham, and inherited the Erickson ranch.

At a dripping sound, Stuart realized the noise appeared

to be coming from pickup bed. He stepped closer. The truck bed had been recently washed out and was still wet.

With a shudder, he realized that the rancher might be not only the killer, but the man who'd assaulted Bailey. He felt heat rush to his chest and cramp his stomach. When he spoke, his voice sounded stilted, each breath a struggle.

"There a reason you washed out your pickup bed?" When Erickson hesitated, the sheriff said, "I'm going to need you to come into town and make a statement under oath about where you were the night Willow was abducted and the morning she was dumped in the river."

Erickson swore and took a threatening step toward him. There was that instant when Stuart welcomed it. His hand went to the gun strapped at his hip. "Don't make me do something you're going to regret."

As the front door of the house swung open with a bang, Erickson stopped coming at him and raised both palms. A woman as wide as she was tall yelled, "Somethin' wrong, Sheriff?"

"Just need a moment with your husband, Angie." His pulse hammered so loudly in his ears, he could barely hear. He stared at Jay Erickson, trying to picture him twelve years younger, dressed up at the McKenna barbecue, then later in that old cabin, stripped down. He'd have the scars to prove it—including where Bailey had gotten him with the small branding iron.

Angie came out to the edge of the porch. "Don't say nothin' to him, Jay. You got a warrant?"

"It isn't that kind of visit," Stuart said.

Her gaze went to her husband and back to the sheriff. "It sure looks like that kind of visit," she said, crossing her arms on her ample chest.

Stuart looked at the rancher. He seemed more afraid of her than even the armed lawman.

"What did he want to know?" Angie demanded. When her husband didn't answer, she picked up an old iron rake leaning against the porch and descended the steps.

Stuart tried to keep both Jay and Angie in his sights as she lumbered toward them. He could see how this could go south real fast. "I asked Jay where he was the night Willow was taken and the morning her body turned up in the river."

"Where do you think he was?" she snapped. "Home with me."

"You'll swear to that under oath?" Stuart asked.

Her eyes narrowed. "You betcha. But what's it to you?"

"She was murdered."

Her brows shot up as she stepped closer. "You think my *husband* had somethin' to do with it?"

The sheriff hoped like hell that this didn't escalate. He dropped his hand to the butt of his gun, afraid drawing it and trying to take Jay in right now would only make things worse. Clearly neither Jay nor his wife had any respect for the star he was wearing or the gun on his hip.

He studied the two of them, reminding himself that this was another reason why he'd typed up his resignation with the best intentions. He'd learned quickly why domestic disputes were so ugly and dangerous for law enforcement.

"I think you better get off our property," Erickson blustered.

"Jay, I need you to come in to my office. You're welcome to bring your lawyer."

"And if he don't?" Angie demanded, brandishing the rake.

"Right now, he's only wanted for questioning. I'd hate to

have to come back out here and escort him in handcuffs." He looked at Jay. "Don't make me come after you."

With that, Stuart tipped his hat and walked past Jay's pickup toward his patrol car. All the time, his ears were tuned in to movement behind him as if there were two rabid dogs foaming at the mouth who could be nipping at his heels at any moment.

He told himself that if Jay Erickson was guilty of the murder, then he'd tried to wash away any evidence.

But the pickup was an older model, and Stuart was betting that if Willow Branson had been in the bed of that truck, the crime team techs would find evidence of it—even if the bed was dry by the time Jay Erickson reached town.

Had he found the killer? The man who had assaulted Bailey? If so, it should be easy to prove given the marks Bailey said she left on him. As he climbed behind the wheel, his hands were shaking. Was it possible this would be over so quickly?

He started the patrol SUV, thinking about what Bailey had said about the man who attacked her. Someone would have had to help him cover it up. Pulling away, he glanced back to see the Ericksons, grim-faced, standing together, watching him go.

CHAPTER SIXTEEN

HOLLY JO GROANED when she saw Pickett's truck and him standing next to it as the bus rolled up to let her off. This was all his fault for going to HH. She'd pleaded with him to let her ride with Buck, but HH had been adamant. She could go to the dance with him but had to be home by ten, and she would continue to ride the bus until further notice.

"What are you doing here?" she said as she crossed the road to where he was parked. Behind her, the school bus engine revved and pulled away in a cloud of dust. "I don't need a ride. I'd rather walk."

"Fine with me," Pickett said. "The walk will do you good, but first I have something for you."

She weakened. "What is it?" She saw him hesitate. She'd always liked Pickett. He felt like a big brother—not that she'd ever had one. Cooper was kind of like that, but Pickett was funnier, and he knew a lot of horseback riding tricks.

He seemed to make up his mind and handed her a plastic bag he pulled from his pickup. "I talked Holden into it."

She recognized the logo on the bag. "A cell phone?" she

cried as she pulled the box out, looking from it to him. "You're not just teasing me, are you?"

"I wouldn't do that," Pickett said.

"I don't understand. HH said—"

"It's just for emergencies."

She smiled at that.

"You know why he didn't want you to have one," Pickett said. "He was afraid you'd be on it all the time. So, use it wisely or lose it. I just want you to have it on you if you ever need to call someone for help."

She couldn't believe this. "For help?" She was so sick of being the kidnapped girl. Especially adults treating her weird.

"You get stuck somewhere, you know. Call me. I put my number in there."

Holly Jo eyed him warily. "Just because I got kidnapped once—"

"It isn't about that. This is about Buck."

"Buck?" She shook her head. "Why can't you just let me be a normal teenager?"

"That just it, you are. I know you Holly Jo. You're smart and strong, but his is your first boyfriend. I was a teenaged boy, okay? I want you to be able to call if you ever need me. Middle of the night? Any time and I'll come get you. You understand?"

"Not really, but okay."

"You will if you need someone older you can trust to get you out of a bad situation. Just promise you'll call if you're ever in trouble."

Holly Jo swallowed the lump in her throat, thinking of another time she was in trouble. She'd assured her therapist she'd been seeing that she was doing fine. She was—most of the time now. "I promise."

"Now," he said, smiling at her. "You still want to walk home, or would you rather have a ride?"

BACK AT HIS OFFICE, Stuart was more than a little surprised when Jay Erickson and his wife showed up with Alfred "Tick" Whitaker, a geologist originally from Texas.

"I have a law degree and even passed the bar in Texas," Tick said at the sheriff's raised brow. "I'm here only in an advisory capacity."

Stuart figured they could get this over with quickly if Tick could handle Angie. "I need to see Jay alone."

"Ain't happening," Angie cried. "Tell him, Tick."

"This can be over in a matter of minutes if I can see Jay alone," the sheriff said. "Either way, Angie isn't staying."

She started to go off on a rant about police injustice, but Tick strong-armed her out of the office. He was no small man, which was good because Angie was built like a small tank. Once outside the office, he bent down to say a few choice words to her, then pushed her into a chair before returning.

"Lock the door," Stuart said.

Tick hesitated, but only a moment. As the sheriff began to put down the blinds in his office, the geologist and part-time lawyer said warily, "What exactly is going to happen here?"

"Jay, I'm sure you want this over as quickly as I do," Stuart said. "If you would remove your shirt."

Erickson laughed nervously. "You can't be serious."

"I'm looking for the man who killed Willow. I need to see your legs. It will only take a minute. Either show me or I'll read you your rights and hold you for questioning. Up to you."

He shook his head as he took off his shirt.

Stuart looked at the man's upper body. He had burn marks all over him—except on his left shoulder—and while there was a scar on his side, it was impossible to tell if it had been a knife wound. He took photos with his camera, but what he hadn't taken into consideration was that whatever injuries the killer had gotten when he'd attacked Bailey, the wounds had twelve years to heal.

"You can put your shirt back on," Stuart said. "But I need you to drop your pants."

"Come on!" Erickson protested.

"I'm looking for the man who killed Willow. I need to see your legs. It will only take a minute. Either show me or I'll read you your rights and hold you for questioning. Up to you."

"I've never heard of such a thing," the rancher said, and looked to Tick.

Tick merely shrugged and said, "I'd show the man your legs. Unless you have something to hide."

Erickson considered that for a long moment. "I can't believe this."

"Did you drive your truck into town?" Stuart asked. "If you don't comply, I'm also going to have to take it into evidence until the crime team out of Billings can look at it. Or, once I see your legs, I let you get in it, and you and Angie go home."

Swearing, the rancher unbuckled his belt, popped open the buttons on his jeans and dropped them to the floor.

"You're going to have to take off one boot and slip out of

that jean leg," Stuart said. The swearing grew louder, but Erickson did as he was asked.

"This is highly irregular," Tick pointed out, and the sheriff agreed as he set his phone to Record.

He photographed the front of Erickson's hairy legs, then the back, noticing a few scars, one that could have been a knife wound low on the left thigh. "Please put your free leg up on that chair."

The rancher started to object, but Tick said, "Just do it."

The moment the man did, Stuart saw the scar. It was jagged and deep, high inside the thigh. "What caused that?"

"Bull horn. I used to be a bull rider until one got a little too close to the jewels."

Moving in, the sheriff photographed the scar. "Okay, thanks," he said, shaken by the violent-looking scar and his disappointment. He'd thought this was going to be over quickly, but Erickson wasn't the man. At least, he couldn't prove that he was. "You can get dressed." Outside his office, he could hear Angie causing a commotion and was glad the door was locked.

"So, this person who killed Willow Branson," Erickson was saying. "You hear he had some kind of scar you're looking for?"

Stuart feared that everyone in the county had heard about the horseshoe-shaped brand by now. "Something like that."

The rancher nodded knowingly. "You could have just asked me if I had it."

"I could have," the sheriff said as he sat down again behind his desk. "But who's to say you would have told me the truth?"

Erickson smirked at that. "Well, anything to help, Sheriff."

"Appreciate that." He didn't sound any more sincere than the rancher had.

"A little unorthodox, but we got it done," Tick said as he unlocked the door. "Let's go see to Angie."

Stuart slouched in his chair as the two filed out. He could hear Angie screaming at the top of her lungs that she was going to sue for false arrest.

"Jay wasn't arrested," Tick was saying. "It was just a misunderstanding."

The sheriff closed his eyes. He'd been so sure it was Erickson, so sure that once he got him in here, saw the injuries he'd been expecting, he'd have the man before he could come for Bailey again.

Instead, he was no closer to finding him.

"Sheriff, we've got trouble out front," came over his radio. "There's an altercation on the lawn."

He rose to his feet and rushed out of his office. "What the hell?" he said as he went past the dispatcher.

"Want me to call for backup?" she called out to him.

He could hear Angie screaming obscenities. "No, I'll take care of it." But as he pushed outside, he saw Angie going for someone's throat. He caught a flash of dark, curly hair. Bailey?

Stuart rushed forward and pulled Angie off as she clawed and kicked and screamed. Fortunately, Deputy Dodson drove up, jumped out and came running. "Restrain her until I can find out what's going on," he ordered as he handed the woman over.

Dodson, being Dodson, threw the still-fighting Angie Erickson to the ground and cuffed her behind her back. Jay started yelling, and Stuart had to step between him and Dodson.

"Everyone settle down or I'm going to arrest all of you," the sheriff ordered.

Jay looked like he was up for a fight, but Tick restrained him. Angie was still screaming, clearly furious. Stuart looked to Bailey. She shook her head. Of course she wouldn't want to press charges. He sighed and said, "I'll speak to you in my office."

As she walked past and into the sheriff's department, Angie yelled, "I'm going to kill you! You hear me?"

Stuart turned to Erickson. "I'm not sure what's going on here, but if you can get your wife to calm down, I just need to know what this was about. If you can't—"

"She didn't do anything," Erickson said. "Why don't you ask Bailey McKenna?"

"I plan to," the sheriff said, and turned to Deputy Dodson. "Angie, if you settle down I'll have my deputy uncuff you. Or we can arrest you for assault."

She swore, then mumbled obscenities under her breath as Dodson took off the cuffs. Jay helped her to her feet, and Tick stepped in front of her to keep her from going after Stuart and getting arrested.

"Now, what was that about?" the sheriff asked.

"Your…girlfriend butting into other people's business, that's what," Angie snapped. "I don't know who she thinks she is, but carrying tales about me and my family will get her killed."

"Let's not make death threats in front of the sheriff," Tick said. "Jay, why don't you take your wife home."

"I'm going to sue," Angie cried as Jay and Tick led her to his pickup.

Seeing that Dodson had everything under control, Stuart went back inside to his office, where he found Bailey waiting for him. She was disheveled, a new scratch on her cheek, a grass stain on one knee of her jeans, and her shirt sleeve torn and hanging down.

"Does everyone want to kill you?" he asked from the doorway.

"Not yet, but soon," she said as she wiped her nose with the back of her hand and smeared the fresh blood on her jeans.

Stuart stared at her, realizing that he couldn't love her more than he did right at this moment. "I'm afraid to ask."

She nodded. "Maybe we could talk about it back at your place? I made some pretty good spaghetti sauce last night, and I'm starved. After that?" She held his gaze. "I'll tell you. I'm just afraid that when I do, you'll resign and leave town."

Great, he thought. "It's that bad?"

Bailey nodded, then shrugged, her eyes shining with tears. He saw her swallow and turn away.

"Are you sure you don't want to press charges. The woman assaulted you." She shok her head. "Okay, then. See you at home, then," he said to her retreating back, wondering if she'd show up.

HOLDEN WARNED HIMSELF to keep his temper, even as he felt his heart racing and sweat making his shirt stick to the seat of his pickup. He'd had a run-in with the large Savage family in the past, a dispute over a horse. Frank Savage and his brothers worked on the Durham place, had a passel of kids, and often ended up fist fighting out behind the bar in town on Friday and Saturday nights.

As Holden pulled up in the ranch hand's yard, a half dozen little kids scattered. The screen door on the large, sprawling former main house swung open, and the oldest Savage stepped out. Frank squinted as the dust settled around the McKenna Ranch pickup and Holden stepped out.

"I need to talk to you about your son," he said as he stalked toward the house.

"Which son would that be?" Frank said lazily, still standing in his doorway.

"Buck. Seems he's been using my daughter, Holly Jo."

"That right?" Frank let the screen door slam behind him as he walked to the top of the porch steps. "I heard you were adopting her but didn't think it had gone through yet."

Holden waved that away. "He's using Holly Jo to do his homework, pretending to be her boyfriend, and I'm not going to stand for it," Holden said, glaring up at the man.

The ranch hand frowned, then turned and yelled back into the house. "Buck! Get your scrawny behind out here."

The lanky teenager who came out of the house was just what Holden had expected. He could see right away what Holly Jo saw in the surly expression on the boy's face, the too-long blond hair the sixteen-year-old flipped back nonchalantly, the confident way he leaned against the porch pillar to glare down at him.

"Have you been getting someone else to do your homework?" Frank asked.

"Why would I do that?" Buck asked.

"Either because you're lazy or you're not all that bright," Holden said, and Frank shot him a warning look before turning that look on the boy.

Suddenly not looking so confident, Buck said, "She's been helping me with my math."

"You need help with your math, your mama will help you," Frank said, and looked at Holden. "That all?"

"One more thing," he said. "Holly Jo won't be riding

with your son from now on. She'll be taking the bus." Buck shrugged like it was no big deal and headed back inside. Holden shook his head and started to walk away.

"Now that we got my kid straightened out, how about you do the same with your daughter," Frank said from the porch.

Holden turned to look back at him. "What are you talking about?"

"Bailey. Maybe you should have a talk with her about what she'd been up to before she gets hurt."

He felt his pulse punch up at the threat and started to take a step back toward the house when Frank went inside, slamming the door behind him.

BAILEY DROVE AWAY from the sheriff's department, planning to go straight to Stuart's house. But she remembered that they were out of beer. She wasn't looking forward to the discussion they were about to have. She knew she was going to need at least one beer, maybe more, to get through it.

She hadn't been kidding about her concern. Once she told him, she didn't fear so much that he would resign and move away from town and leave her high and dry. She feared he would never look at her again with such pure love in his eyes. The thought of losing that love would maim her in a way not even her attacker had.

After hurrying into the local general store and coming out with a twelve-pack, she climbed behind the wheel and started to drive to the sheriff's house. But when she looked into the rearview mirror, she saw a familiar gray SUV parked down the street, the engine idling.

With a curse, she jumped out and stalked down the street toward the vehicle. Why was Ralph Jones still following her? She couldn't see his face with the afternoon sun glinting off the windshield, but she wasn't surprised when he hurriedly tried to back up and get away.

She picked up a rock from the edge of the road as she reached the driver's side door, ready to break out the window. But as she grabbed the door handle with one hand and lifted the rock with the other, she saw that it wasn't Ralph Jones.

It was Norma, his wife, and her expression gave her away.

Apparently realizing that she couldn't escape, Norma put the SUV into Park and tried to put the window up before Bailey could stop her.

Bailey tapped on the window and waited as Norma put it back down. "It was you. Why have you been following me?" she demanded, feeling a little off balance as she saw the woman's obvious fury.

"I know about you and my husband, you homewrecker," Norma spat as she glared at her.

Bailey took a step back. "What?"

"Don't bother to lie. I saw how shook up he was when he thought you were the one who was lying in that creek. He couldn't eat, couldn't sleep. I'd never seen him like that. He'd been acting strangely for months. The way he got all slicked up to take a horse to Wyoming. Nicking some of my fudge to take to you since he'd never liked it." Her voice broke. "You'd have thought the old fool would know better than to fall for a…a…woman like you, and at his age!" Tears filled her eyes. She wiped at them. "After all these years of marriage."

"Norma, I have not been seeing your husband. It wasn't me." Had he taken the fudge to Willow? Had it simply been platonic? She reached in, touched the woman's arm, thinking she could convince her how wrong she'd been, but Norma jerked it back.

"Stay away from my husband, or so help me..." The ranchwoman shifted into gear. "Best step back. Wouldn't want to run over you." With that she roared off, leaving Bailey standing in the road, wondering what had just happened.

Walking back to her SUV, she saw that her driver's side door was open. Had she left it like that when she'd hurried over to confront Ralph Jones, only to find Norma behind the wheel?

Maybe, she thought as she approached the SUV more slowly, all the while looking around warily. Sometimes, for seconds and even minutes, she'd forget that the man who killed Willow was out there. Sometimes, she could even lie and tell herself that Willow's death hadn't been a message to her, and the man wasn't coming for her next.

As time had passed since the murder, she'd even started to sometimes think he'd only wanted the younger version of her.

But then she reached her SUV and looked in, her heart dropping as she saw what he'd left her.

CHAPTER SEVENTEEN

OAKLEY STOOD IN the small bathroom of the ranch cabin where she and Pickett lived while their house was being built. The light was dim, but it was too early to look anyway. She stood there trying not to make deals with God that she knew she couldn't keep.

"You just need to relax and let it happen," Pickett always said. "Have faith that when the time is right, we will make a baby."

Her chest squeezed at the thought of holding their infant in her arms. She wanted this more than she had ever wanted anything—except Pickett. She'd so hoped that by the time their house was finished, she'd be looking like her sister—lumbering around with a big belly, wanting only to talk about babies.

She could feel the plastic stick dangling from the fingers of her right hand but was afraid to look. She wondered if their mother had had difficulty getting pregnant. Apparently not, given the number of children she'd had fairly quickly.

It was too late to call her—even if Charlotte was taking

their calls. Her sister hadn't had any trouble getting knocked up. Oakley hoped having unkind thoughts of her pregnant sister wasn't going to jinx this pregnancy test.

Time was up. It was now or never. She lifted the stick up to the light and mentally crossed her fingers as her eyes burned with tears.

WHEN STUART RETURNED HOME, he saw at once that Bailey's SUV wasn't parked in front of his house. She'd said she was headed there. A lie because she hadn't wanted to tell him what that altercation with Angie had been about?

He swore, aware that he might not see her for days or even weeks now—if she made a point of avoiding him. What was going on with her? More than just having a killer after her, apparently. He shook his head as he parked, got out and headed for his house. He'd thought he'd made some progress with Bailey, that she trusted him. Now he didn't know what to think. Clearly there was a whole lot he didn't understand, but apparently Angie Erickson did.

He'd just stepped inside when he heard the sound of a vehicle engine. He turned to see Bailey drive up and park. As she got out, she reached back into the back seat to pull out a twelve-pack of beer. Relief made his heart beat faster. She'd just stopped to get beer.

Their gazes met. She seemed to hesitate, but only for a moment, before she walked toward him. He told himself that the two of them would get through this together even as he doubted it in the next second. As she grew closer, he saw something heartbreaking in her face and almost reached for her.

"Stuart—" There was a catch in her voice before she rushed to him. He grabbed the beer an instant before she threw her arms around him. She clung to him, her body warm, soft in all the right places, before she kissed him. He couldn't help but respond even as he knew in his heart that something must have happened on her way here, something that had her running scared.

Or this was a ruse to put off telling him the truth.

He didn't care. She felt so right in his arms. He buried his hand in her wild, dark curls, losing himself in the kiss, in the scent of her, in the taste of her, the feel of her. He wanted this, wanted Bailey, body and soul, even if she broke his heart.

After a few minutes, she drew back, catching her lower lip in her teeth. She looked so young, so vulnerable. He could see the fear in those river eyes. "What is it, Bailey?"

A tentative smile played at her lips before she shook her head. "You know me. Trouble. Only this time..." Tears filled her eyes. She looked away.

"Let me help you."

"You don't know how much you already have," she said before she kissed him hard, then stepped out of his arms. "I found out who's been following me," she said, her back to him. "It wasn't Ralph. It was his wife, Norma. She thinks I've been having an affair with her husband."

He grasped her arm and pulled her around to look at him, knowing that couldn't be all that had happened since he'd last seen her.

"When I got back from talking to Norma, my driver's side door was open," Bailey said, and swallowed. "*He* left me something in the passenger seat."

"Tell me you didn't touch it," he said, instantly in sheriff mode. He looked out at her SUV. "Is it still there?"

She nodded. "It's unlocked."

Stuart grabbed gloves out of his patrol SUV and approached her vehicle. Even with the light fading, he could see a bundle on the passenger seat. He carefully opened the side door to find what appeared to be something wrapped in a towel stained with dried blood. Willow's?

His stomach roiled as he carefully unwrapped the fabric, sick at the thought of what he'd find inside the towel. To his relief, it was only a small horseshoe, not even four inches, the kind used on ponies.

But the message was clear. The man was coming for Bailey. He was through waiting. Bailey had been right. He wasn't finished with her.

After calling the state crime lab, he bagged the evidence to be picked up at his office tomorrow. He locked it in his patrol SUV and went inside the house to find Bailey heating up last night's dinner and cooking pasta in his largest pot.

"You looked inside it," he said.

"I didn't touch it. I used a pen to open the towel a little. It's her blood, isn't it?"

"We won't know until the crime lab runs DNA on it, but probably." He stepped closer to her, remembering her in his arms, remembering the kiss. He'd thought the smell of marinara sauce would make him nauseous, but he heard his stomach growl. In a way, it felt good. He and Bailey were still alive, still hungry, still determined not to give up.

He pulled her close from behind. She leaned into him as she continued to stir the sauce. He wanted to believe that everything had now changed between them, that from now on she would trust him, that this had brought them closer.

But he didn't delude himself—even after a couple of passionate kisses. With Bailey, he suspected he didn't know even the half of it.

BAILEY HAD BEEN so determined to tell Stuart everything—before she'd spotted the gray SUV, confronted Norma and found what *he'd* left her in her car.

She had every reason to stall as they sat at his small table in the kitchen, eating the spaghetti she'd made, like they'd done this dozen of times before. It was warm and cozy and felt so normal that she wanted to forget everything but this moment since after she told him, they might never do this again.

"This is really good," he said, sounding so surprised that she had to laugh. "I didn't know you could cook."

She grinned and shrugged. "There's a lot you don't know about me." She'd meant it as a joke, but realized after the words came out of her that it wasn't funny, because it was true. She stood up and got them each another beer before sitting down again.

As she opened hers, she said, "I'm glad you enjoyed it. It's my mother's recipe. Elaine's mom kept it for me after my mother died. I've never made it before, but I've always wanted to try it."

"That's the first time I've heard you talk about your mother," he said as he put down his fork and looked at her.

She could tell that he was waiting. His look said that he knew she would tell him when she was ready, as if he'd learned that prodding her would only make her dig her heels in. She realized she was wrong about one thing. He knew her—even if he didn't know all her secrets.

"Did you know that I always dreamed of being a writer?" she blurted out.

"I knew you loved to read, so I'm not surprised. Didn't you major in English at college?"

She nodded. "English with a minor in criminology."

He cocked one eyebrow. "Criminology? I guess I could see that, given what had happened before you left for college. So, you haven't given up on being a writer?"

Bailey rose, avoiding his gaze as she began to pick up the dirty dishes. Before Willow was killed, she could have come up with a lot of reasons for keeping everything to herself. But she couldn't anymore—especially from Stuart.

"I started gathering information after I got back from college," she said, her back to him.

"Information?" he asked, already sounding suspicious.

"I've written a book," she said as she rinsed the dishes and put them into the dishwasher. "It's almost finished."

"What kind of book?"

"At first it was just an excuse to get closer to the ranchers here in the Powder River Basin," she said, avoiding the question. "I was sure one of them knew the truth." She kept her back turned to him.

She heard his sharp intake of breath before he said, "You were looking for the man who'd attacked you by talking to the women in their lives."

Bailey didn't care what other people thought, even her family. But Stuart was different. She didn't want to see his reaction, which was why she had tried for so long to keep it a secret. She especially didn't want to see his disappointment in her.

But as her editor had pointed out, she couldn't keep it a secret much longer. The book would be published soon.

"You'd be surprised how many people wanted to tell me their stories," she rushed on, unable to look at him. "Or even better, stories about their neighbors. I wrote it all down, thinking there was a thread that would lead me to *him*. But instead, I realized that I had a book." She took a breath and let it out before she said, "It's a tell-all book about the people of the Powder River Basin."

The silence that followed felt thick as mud. When she couldn't stand it any longer, she turned to look at him. To her surprise, she saw no judgment in his gaze. When he finally spoke, it wasn't a criticism.

"The night outside the bar, when someone tried to mug you…"

"A man tried to take my bag. It wasn't *him*. Whoever it was, I'm not sure if he wanted my money or my laptop, or he could have suspected I was writing a book and was afraid about what was in it. Afraid he or his family was talked about."

Stuart shook his head as his gaze met hers. "The injuries to your face."

"A deputy from another county with relatives in this one."

"No wonder I suspected you were in trouble," he said with a shake of his head. "You do realize that it's going to be hard to differentiate between the killer and some random person who wants to stop this book of yours from ever seeing print. Have you already sold it?"

She nodded. "I just need to write the final chapter—the finding and killing of the man who attacked me."

The sheriff groaned. "Who all is in the book?"

"Pretty much everyone."

"Your family? Your father?" She nodded. "You blame him, but why everyone else in the basin? You can't blame them too for what happened to you."

"I don't expect you to understand, but I think Willow would."

He sighed. "It was one bad man."

"Who blends in so seamlessly with the residents of the Powder River Basin that I can't find him," she said, feeling her ire rise. "Someone knows him, really knows him, because he came home with a small horseshoe branded on his left shoulder and knife wounds that someone had to bandage. Why haven't they come forward?"

"Maybe he's a bachelor who lives alone, and he bandaged himself. I assume you checked the hospital and those in the surrounding area."

She nodded. "Someone stitched him up. I wouldn't be surprised if he has a wife who lies in bed next to him at night. Or a sister or daughter who senses something wrong with him. Or a neighbor who saw him covered in blood twelve years ago. Or a rancher or his wife who passed him on the county road near the river where Willow lay drowning. Maybe even someone who saw him come out of the woods where her body was found."

"Not everyone recognizes evil when they see it," Stuart said.

"Or they see it, but they don't want to get involved. Or they refuse to see—let alone do anything about it." Bailey shook her head. "Don't get me wrong. I'm no better than any of them. I let Willow get killed knowing the monster was out there because I was too traumatized to come forward all those years ago, asking myself what was the point since I couldn't identify him."

He seemed thoughtful for a moment. "You said everyone is in this book?"

"Anyone with a secret, so pretty much everyone. I didn't set out to unearth the stories, but once I did, the writer in me had to tell their secrets and unlock the mysteries and local legends." She saw his expression change as he realized who else was in the book.

"My mother," he said on a shaky breath. It wasn't a question.

CHAPTER EIGHTEEN

"STUART—"

The sheriff shoved back his chair and rose abruptly to his feet. "I don't want to know." A lie. He'd spent his life wanting answers as to what happened to her. But he also wanted to know if the nightmares he had about her were real or just a child's fear of monsters manifested out of nothing.

The last thing he was going to do was ask Bailey about his mother. That was a deep, dark well he couldn't go near, not now, maybe not ever. *This* certainly wasn't the time. He had enough on his mind that he feared he couldn't handle the truth.

Nor did he need anything distracting him. He had a killer to find. A killer who had only today reminded Bailey that he was still close, still coming for her. That was enough to deal with. He hadn't been in the greatest head space when this had all started. The only reason he was still sheriff was Bailey.

"I want you to know," she said, sounding worried, "I didn't set out to do this, I swear. I just wanted to find him, but the more wives and girlfriends and daughters I talked to, the more I realized that he couldn't have gotten away with what he did to me without their help."

"We should get some rest," he said, glancing at the time. Where had the night gone? He could feel the weight of everything she'd told him. It dulled the memory of their kisses, their embrace. "Promise me you'll stay in the guest room and won't leave on your own before it gets light."

BAILEY NODDED, FEELING BEREFT. *This is why I didn't want to tell you.* She thought about earlier, throwing herself at him, safe in his warmth and the solid shelter of those arms, his chest pressed to hers, their heartbeats in tandem. It had felt so right. Just like their dinner in the kitchen tonight. She remembered thinking how she never wanted it to end.

"I promise I'll stay." She watched him turn his back on her, go into his bedroom and close the door, surprised by the ache of longing knotting in her chest. Tears burned her eyes. All those months she'd come here, keeping Stuart at arm's length, she'd known in her heart he was here for her unconditionally. She'd felt she could always depend on him.

But right now, she wasn't so sure about that. He had planned to resign as sheriff. He'd only changed his mind because of her. She wondered if he was regretting that decision at this moment. He'd been through so much, almost dying. Maybe he wasn't up to this. She knew that she often felt she wasn't.

What if she'd dragged him into this only to get him killed? The thought was like a blow to her chest, stealing her breath and making her heart race. He was risking his life for *her*, and she'd never asked him why he had wanted to resign, why maybe he needed to step away.

She certainly longed to put the past behind her. For so many years, she'd believed that she could—once she found the man and stopped him, once she told the world what he'd done, what she'd done, because she planned to kill him.

But would it ever truly be over?

She'd promised Stuart she would stay the night, but going to the spare bedroom was harder than it had ever been, knowing that he was only in the next room. She desperately wanted to go to him, to curl against him, to hold on to him as if their lives depended on it.

Instead, she lay down on the spare bed, listening to the night sounds. *He* was out there. *He'd* left her a reminder that he wasn't far away, that *he* was watching her and could get to her at any time.

You're safe here. The thought rang truer than any she'd had.

STUART EXPECTED BAILEY to be gone the next morning. He didn't expect to see her making French toast and bacon for breakfast. He raised an eyebrow. He hadn't had bread or eggs or bacon in the house.

"I called my brother Brand. He just happened to be on his way into town," Bailey said. "He was happy to help since apparently he's been worried about me."

With good reason, the sheriff thought. "How fortunate for me," he said, and sat down in the chair she indicated while she poured him a cup of coffee. "He wasn't curious about you being here, cooking us both breakfast?"

"Apparently he'd already ready heard about your declaration of love," she joked as she handed him the full cup of coffee and sat down.

"Holden," he said with a shake of his head as he studied

her. She'd been shaken last night, first after finding out that Norma Jones had been following her and then seeing what the man had left for her in her car.

They ate in companionable silence for a few minutes. "I don't normally eat breakfast," Bailey said.

"Me either. But waking up to this—" he took her in "—was a special surprise."

She grinned. "I promised I wouldn't leave last night. But Stuart, you wanted to resign, and I never asked you why you—"

"I'm not going to stop looking for the man," he said, and met her gaze. "And neither are you, and I couldn't stop you even if I tried."

She held her fork in the air. "I guess that about covers it."

He nodded, averting his eyes as he cut off a piece of French toast on his plate. "What do you make of the package he left you?"

Clearly, she'd expected him to want to talk about her tell-all book or his mother or why he'd wanted to resign. Those were the last things he wanted to talk about.

He watched her consider him for a moment before she said, "He wanted me to know that he can get to me—and will when he's ready."

"You don't think he's ready yet." That surprised him, because he was thinking the same thing. The man had taken a chance leaving the bundle for her right there on the main drag of Powder Crossing. "Did you see anyone around when you went back to your vehicle?"

She shook her head. "Town wasn't busy at that hour. Even if it had been, I doubt anyone would have noticed."

"Except for one person—Norma, who'd been facing in the right direction to see it."

Bailey stared at him. "I'll drive out to her place and talk to her."

"Might be better if I questioned her, under the circumstances."

She shook her head. "I can handle it." She took a sip of her coffee as his phone rang.

The moment he answered, Deputy Dodson said loudly and excitedly, "I think I found where he did it. Where he assaulted Willow. There are pieces of cut rope, some torn clothing, the remains of a small fire in one corner and what looks like dried blood."

Stuart stepped into the other room as the deputy gave him directions to an old outbuilding some distance from the house Willow had been renting. "Okay, stay in your vehicle. Don't go back inside. Stay there until the crime team gets there." He disconnected and turned to see Bailey standing in the doorway.

"You found where he assaulted her," she said. "Can you find out if there was a gas can there? He told me he was going to kill me and then burn down the cabin. He'd brought a small can of gasoline. He was going to destroy any evidence and make his escape back into the barbecue crowd as if he'd never been gone. That old cabin would have burned quickly. When my body was found..."

"He would have covered his tracks. But he underestimated you."

"I got lucky," she said with a shake of her head. "I know the area you told the crime team to go to. That outbuilding is back off the road, isolated, perfect for what he had in mind. So why did he take Willow to the river? Why move her at all? Why take the chance? If she hadn't drowned..."

He saw what she was getting at. "He changed his routine."

"Or something or someone forced him to. If the gas can is there, then he might have been interrupted and, for whatever reason, he was afraid to go back there to clean it up."

Stuart quickly called his deputy, asked about a small gas can, then hung up. "It was there," he told Bailey. "Which means we might have gotten lucky," he said, hoping it was true.

WHEN PICKETT SPOTTED the remains of a pregnancy test in the trash that morning, he felt instant heartbreak. If the pregnancy test had told Oakley what they both wanted to hear, she could have told him before she left earlier, saying something about the last-minute preparations for the baby shower.

Why did Oakley put herself through this constantly? Put him through it? If only she could just give it time and relax. He had no doubt that it would happen. He wanted children as much as she did, maybe more. He'd been an only child. He couldn't wait for the patter of little feet racing through the home they were building. He had to believe that they would conceive.

Not that he'd proven to be very good in the parenting department. He'd certainly bombed out with at least one thirteen-year-old he knew. Holly Jo wasn't quite as mad at him after he gave her the phone, but when he reached the arena, he found her horse still out to pasture and no sign of her.

"She must have forgotten," Elaine had told him when he stopped up at the house and found out she wasn't home. "Or it skipped her mind since she's gone with her friends to decorate the gym for the dance tonight."

It hadn't been all that long ago that trick riding was the only thing Holly Jo was interested in. Now it was Buck

Savage and a dance. He tried not to take it personally, but he couldn't help it. He and Holly Jo had been buddies. He'd loved working with her. She was a natural. He loved seeing her talent, enjoying her sense of humor, feeling like he had what it would take to be a dad.

"She's mad at me because I told Holden about the boyfriend."

"He's glad you did. If it makes you feel better, she's avoiding him too," the housekeeper said.

It didn't.

"Actually, she's probably going to be much angrier with him than you. He went over to the Savages' and told them what Buck had been up to."

Pickett groaned. "I wish he hadn't."

"You aren't the only one," she said with a sigh. "It will blow over. At her age, things can change in an instant."

That was what he was afraid of. "What about the dance? She sounded like she was really looking forward to it."

Elaine nodded. "Holden said he would drive her to the school, then pick her up afterward. She declined in tears, and he relented and said Buck could pick her up and bring her home. But that if she missed curfew… I'm sure you know the rest."

Pickett couldn't help feeling somewhat responsible. Maybe he should have kept it just between him and Holly Jo. He was just a ranch hand on this spread, and she wasn't his responsibility. But she was only thirteen. This boy was older. If she got into trouble, he didn't think she'd call Holden or even Elaine. Pickett wanted her to know she could call him, because he remembered being a boy about that age.

BAILEY DROVE OUT to the Jones Ranch, hoping to talk to Norma alone. She was glad to see that the dark-colored SUV was parked in front of the house, but it appeared Ralph's pickup was gone.

Getting out, she walked to the front door, not sure what kind of reception she was going to get. Norma was often as sweet as the fudge she made, too sweet for Bailey. But she'd definitely seen another side of Norma yesterday evening.

The woman who answered the door was wearing an apron over her house dress. Norma prided herself on being old school from her neatly trimmed nails to her perfectly coiffed helmet of brown hair. If she was surprised to see Bailey, she didn't show it.

"You're timing is perfect," Norma said brightly. "I'm about to take rhubarb muffins from the oven, and I always have a pot of coffee on for unexpected guests." She stepped back to let Bailey enter.

"Actually…" Bailey hesitated. She didn't want muffins. All she wanted was to ask Norma if she'd seen the man who'd put the bundle in her SUV yesterday evening. But she found herself stepping into the house as the timer went off on the oven and Norma disappeared into the kitchen. She followed the scent of rhubarb muffins, coffee, and whatever perfume Norma was wearing.

As she did, Bailey couldn't help but feel a sliver of concern. Had she convinced the woman that there had never been an affair between her and Ralph? Or was she going to come around the corner into the kitchen to find Norma armed with a butcher's knife?

At the kitchen doorway, Bailey stopped short at the sight of Norma filling two cups of coffee. She'd already put a muffin on a plate along with a fork. She carried the cups of coffee over to a table. The table, Bailey noted, had a lace tablecloth on it, along with a vase filled with the last of the flowers from her garden, no doubt. It was no secret that Norma prided herself on making a cozy home for her hardworking husband. She taught a class on it at her church, stressing the part about honoring and obeying the man of the house.

"Sit," Norma said as she motioned to a chair and took one across from Bailey. "Isn't this nice."

"I suppose you're wondering why I came to see you," she said.

"You must try the muffin while it's still warm. Would you like butter on it?" She started to get up before Bailey told her no, it was fine as it was.

"It's about yesterday evening in town," Bailey said after humoring the woman by taking a bite.

"How is it?" Norma asked, leaning toward her. "That's rhubarb from my garden."

"Delicious." She swallowed the bite, determined to get to the point. "I want to know if you might have seen someone put a package into my SUV."

Norma frowned. "A package?"

"Actually, something bundled in a stained white towel."

She wrinkled her nose. "Why would someone leave you a stained towel?"

"You were facing in the right direction. Do you remember seeing anyone near my SUV? They left the door open after they tossed it in."

"Was that your SUV? Yes, I guess it was. I'd forgotten what color it was. Is it supposed to be a green?"

"Norma, it's important that I find the person who got into my car."

"I would think so. A stained towel." Her nose wrinkled again. "I did see someone. I didn't know what she was doing. I just assumed she was putting something into her own car."

"Her?"

"Annette. She seemed to be in a real hurry. Looked right at me after she tossed it in. I thought it was so rude to leave the door open as she hurried away."

"Annette *Cline*? Dickie's wife?"

"Why would a grown man call himself Dickie?" Norma said, and motioned for Bailey to finish her muffin.

Bailey had no idea. She ate the last of the muffin and washed it down with coffee. "Do you need to talk about our conversation from yesterday?"

Norma blinked. "You said you weren't interested in my husband. That conversation?"

"Yes. It's true. I'm with Stuart Layton and have been for some time. I have no interest in your husband, nor does he have any in me."

The older woman nodded and smiled. "So glad we have that cleared up," she said, getting to her feet and scooping up Bailey's plate and empty coffee cup. The muffin had been dry, not that she would have told Norma that to save her life.

Dismissed, Bailey rose. "Thank you for your help and the muffin."

Norma waved it off. "I'm just glad you stopped by. If you don't mind seeing yourself out, I have a lot to do today. A woman's work is never done."

"So true." She left and almost made it off the Jones Ranch before her stomach began to roil. She was throwing up beside the road by the time she reached the edge of Powder Crossing and remembered something that had seemed out of place in Norma's ultra-clean kitchen. A small plastic bottle of eye drops next to the coffeepot. That evil woman, Bailey thought as her stomach cramped again.

DEPUTY DODSON HAD called to say the crime team had arrived when the dispatcher told Stuart there was an urgent call from a woman, but she wouldn't give her name.

The moment he answered the phone, Stuart could hear a woman crying hysterically. "Take a breath," he ordered even as his pulse began to pound. Bailey had said she was going out to see Norma Jones. "Tell me your name and what's wrong." He could hear her struggling to gain control of her sobbing. At first he couldn't understand what she was saying and felt his frustration rising.

Then he heard what she was trying to tell him. "He's dead," Annette Cline sobbed. "He's dead."

"Annette, tell me what's happened? Is it Dickie?"

She sucked in a breath on a sob. "It's…it's my friend Brock."

Brock Sherwood, the Wyoming man Stuart had seen driving to her house when Dickie was gone.

"He's *dead*."

"Where are you?" the sheriff asked, and listened as she told him the name of a motel in Miles City. She went on to say that she'd gone to get them something for breakfast before they had to leave, and when she came back…

"I opened the door and…" She began sobbing again. "It's so awful."

"You're sure he's dead?" She was.

"He'd been worried, thought someone had been following him and was afraid, but I didn't really think…" She broke up again.

"Don't touch anything. Just stay there. I'm sending help. Where is Dickie?"

Between sobs, she told him that Dickie had called yesterday to say he was on his way home, but since she hadn't gone to the house yet, she hadn't seen him. Dickie's return explained the motel in Miles City.

Stuart disconnected and called the police in Miles City. He'd just hung up when the dispatcher said Dickie Cline was on the line.

"I got a text from Annette to call you when I got home," Cline said.

"Are you going to be at the ranch for a while?" the sheriff asked.

"I guess so. What's this about?"

"I'll tell you when I see you."

CHAPTER NINETEEN

HOLLY JO TRIED to contain her excitement. Her very first dance, and she was going with Buck Savage, the dreamiest boy in school. She couldn't help smiling to herself as she waited for Tana and her friends to pick her up to go decorate the gym. She hoped Buck came. The last time she talked to him, he'd said he would come by before the dance to give her a ride.

Fortunately, she'd talked HH into letting her go with him. She couldn't imagine how embarrassing it would be to have her soon-to-be adoptive father take her and pick her up. The thought mortified her.

Seeing dust rising down the county road, Holly Jo felt that rush of excitement again. Soon she would be with her friends. But when the car pulled up, it wasn't Tana. It was Buck.

She frowned, then broke in a huge smile.

The passenger side window came down. "Get in!"

Holly Jo bristled at his tone. She'd been so happy to see him, but now hesitated. Why was he acting like this. She glanced back down the road. No Tana. Buck must have told her that he would be picking her up. She looked back up the ranch road. No sign of HH or Pickett or anyone else. Still, she hesitated. "What's wrong?"

"Who said anything was wrong? Come on," Buck said, softening his tone. "You coming or not?"

The cutest boy in school wanted to give her a ride to class. Why was she hesitating? She knew Buck. Had spent time with him at school. Tana thought he was great. She'd been hoping Buck would ask her to the dance, her first dance with a boyfriend. It was just a ride to school, she told herself and climbed in.

He sped off before she even had a chance to put on her seat belt.

"Your old man came over to our house and gave me and my dad a ration of shit," Buck said.

She blinked. Her old man? HH? He'd gone over to the Savages'? She tried to breathe. "What?"

He finally looked over at her, and she realized he was furious. "Are you deaf?"

"No. I just don't understand," she stammered.

"You're turning out to be more trouble than you're worth."

She couldn't believe he just said that.

He was driving too fast, and yet he looked away long enough to glare at her. "I thought you were smart. Why would you tell your father about us?"

"I didn't," she cried as she looked from him to the narrow gravel road. Towering thick cottonwoods lined both sides beyond the narrow barrow pit. Her heart pounded. She started to ask him to slow down when he hit the brakes, making her glad that she'd managed to get her seat belt on.

The car rocked and began to fishtail before he hit the gas and went down a path through the trees that led to the river. He brought it to a stop just feet from the bank.

She realized that she'd been hanging on, her fingers gripping the door handle white-knuckled.

He killed the engine and slumped in the seat, running his hand through his hair before looking over at her. "Did you tell him I was using you? That you were doing my math homework for me?"

"No," she said quickly, even though she *was* doing his math homework for him.

"Well, someone did."

Pickett, she thought, and felt like crying. "I wouldn't do anything to hurt you," she whispered.

They sat in silence. An occasional magpie squawked from a nearby tree. "I thought you didn't mind helping me with my math so I could play football."

"I don't," she told him quickly. "I know how much footfall means to you. Isn't there a game next weekend?"

He didn't answer as he looked over at her. His gaze softened.

Her heart beat faster when he looked at her like that.

"I thought you and I had something."

Holly Jo nodded, unable to speak about the lump that had formed in her throat.

"You're my girl, right?"

"Right." The word came out thick with emotion.

"That's what I thought. "You know I'd do anything for you, and I know you'd do the same for me. Unless you don't want to be my girl and go to the dance with me."

Pulse pounding she smiled and nodded. Buck started the car and headed for the school.

BY THE TIME the sheriff reached Richard "Dickie" Cline's ranch, he'd already been briefed by the Miles City Police Chief on Brock Sherwood's cause of death. His throat had been cut. He'd bled to death.

Stuart assumed whoever had killed him had waited until Annette left the motel room.

"A pickup truck was seen leaving the scene shortly before Mrs. Cline returned to find the body," the chief was saying. "I just ran the plates. The truck is registered to Richard Cline."

"I'm on my way to talk to him now. He's apparently been gone for a few days. I wanted to speak with him about our murder over here. I can bring him in if you want to come over to Powder Crossing to talk to him."

"I'd be interested to hear what he has to say," the chief said.

"I'll get back to you," the sheriff said, and disconnected.

Dickie had motive and opportunity and was seen leaving the scene of the murder. He was also the last one on Bailey's list that they hadn't already scratched off. Stuart was anxious to talk to him.

As he drove into the yard, he parked next to the rancher's pickup and got out. He put a hand on the hood. Dickie hadn't been home long—the engine was still ticking as it cooled.

Turning toward the house, he saw the rancher looking out the window. A moment later, the door opened, and Dickie stepped outside. He was a large man, muscular, but not what Stuart would call handsome. He had a thick head of dark hair that was wet from a recent shower. He ran his fingers through it, the scent of shampoo and body wash strong.

Stuart looked past him. "Annette around?" he asked casually, aware that she wasn't.

The rancher looked over his shoulder back into the house. "Wasn't home when I got here. Must have gone into town for something." He looked at the sheriff. "Her text said you wanted to talk to me." He frowned as if he couldn't imagine why.

The sheriff had a few ideas. "Mind if we go in and sit down? I have some questions I need to ask you."

Dickie shrugged, but pushed open the door behind him, letting Stuart lead the way into the house. He could hear the washing machine chugging away down the hall. Seemed the rancher had time to shower and do a load of clothing.

"Why don't you have a seat," the sheriff said, and walked down the hall to open the washing machine. Looked like jeans and a shirt or two.

"What the hell?" the rancher said behind him as Stuart pulled out the shirts and dropped them into the sink next to the washer and dryer. Any blood might already have been washed away, but he thought the crime lab would still be able to find some embedded in the jeans, because it appeared the wash had just started.

He turned to Dickie. "I'm going to have to ask you where you were this morning."

The rancher looked at his shirt and jeans in the sink, then at the sheriff. "Not until I talk to my lawyer."

"You're going to have to talk to him at my office," Stuart said, reaching for his handcuffs. "Richard Cline, you have the right to remain silent..."

OAKLEY TOLD HERSELF that all she had to do was get through the baby shower. She felt as if she would burst with the knowledge. *I am pregnant! Pregnant!* She wanted to shout it from the rooftop, and yet she'd told no one, not even Pickett. She'd been afraid that she would jinx it.

"Are you all right?" Birdie asked her as she shoved another shower card over to her to log into the gift book Tilly had provided. "You're getting behind, and if you mess up... Well, you probably know your sister better than I do, but she scares me."

Oakley laughed. She liked Birdie and thought she was going to fit into their strange family just fine. "I'm so glad you're helping me with this." The young woman was perfect for her brother Brand. He needed someone who challenged him, and boy would Birdie challenge him.

"I got your back," she whispered as Tilly opened yet another present, something so cute and adorable it made Oakley hold on even tighter to her secret.

"Did you two get this one?" Tilly asked pointedly, her gaze going from Birdie to Oakley and lingering. Her sister knew her too well. She dropped her gaze, but not before she saw a spark in Tilly's eyes. She knew and was probably worried that Oakley would announce it at *her* baby shower.

There was a time when they'd been so competitive, so immature and resentful of each other, that Oakley might have done just that. But not today. She quickly updated the presents log as everyone began to migrate into the dining room for cake and coffee.

She pushed herself to her feet, the first time she'd gotten a chance to stand for at least an hour. For a moment, she felt a little dizzy. Birdie had gone into the dining room to help serve. Tilly was busy making sure everything was perfect when she looked up and caught Oakley's eye.

The room seemed to spin as she felt the warm wetness between her legs. No! No! She looked down and saw a trickle of blood run down her bare leg past the hem of her skirt.

Her sister was to her in an instant, taking her arm and leading her quickly into the bathroom. Oakley hadn't even realized that she was crying until she saw her reflection in the mirror over the skin.

"I'm so sorry," Tilly was saying as she handed her sister a warm washrag and helped her over to the toilet.

Oakley pulled off her soaked panties. Tilly took them from her and began to rinse them in the sink. "It's your shower," Oakley protested. "You should be—"

"I'm right where I want to be," Tilly said. "Here." She handed her a tampon. "I'll get you something to wear and be right back."

She sat on the toilet, numb even as tears streamed down her face. No baby. All she'd had was a matter of a few precious hours believing she was going to have a baby. Hadn't she known it was too good to be true?

IN THE INTERROGATION room at the sheriff's department, Stuart sat next to the Miles City police chief across from Richard Cline and his attorney, a man best known as Shorty Gilmore.

"I swear I didn't kill the man," Cline cried even as Shorty advised against his talking. "Yes, I followed her there. I waited until she left to go across the street, and then I saw that she hadn't closed the motel room door all the way, so I went into the room." He shook off his lawyer's hand. "They already know I was there. I want to get this cleared up."

"You had the knife with you?" the chief of police asked.

"No," the rancher snapped. "I didn't have a knife. I was going to beat him up—not kill him. I saw he was still in bed. I went over there and jerked back the covers. That's when I got blood on my clothes. It was everywhere." His lawyer groaned. "I panicked and got out of there."

"You were just going to beat him up?" the cop asked.

"He was sleeping with my wife! I was going to beat the hell out of him."

"Which could have also gotten you arrested," Shorty whispered.

"Where have you been the past few days or so?" Stuart asked, and he saw the rancher hesitate.

"I had business down in Wyoming."

"What kind of business?"

Cline looked away. "I knew Annette was seeing someone. I wanted to find out who this man was and how serious it was, okay?"

"You do understand," his lawyer whispered, "that makes your actions sound premeditated."

"What did you find out?" the chief of police asked, ignoring the lawyer.

"The son of a bitch was a womanizer and flat broke. He was after my wife and my ranch," Cline said, making his lawyer groan again.

"You weren't giving up either, huh," the cop said. "Kind of gives you a motive for murder, I'd say."

"I told you. I didn't kill him."

"Then who did?" the chief demanded. "Your wife wasn't gone long enough that two men could have gone into that room."

"I'd been waiting across the street. I saw Annette leave and started over there but had to wait on some traffic. As I crossed the street, I saw a man walking away from the motel. He could have come out of her room." He looked from the chief to Stuart. "He must have."

"What did he look like?" the sheriff asked.

"Big, stocky..." He shrugged. "I only saw him from behind."

"Did you see what vehicle he got into?"

Cline shook his head. "I had other things on my mind."

"Let's say the man had just come out of the motel room where you were headed," the chief said. "Who else had motive to kill your wife's lover?"

The rancher hung his head. "I don't know. Maybe someone Brock Sherwood owed money to. When I asked around about him down in Wyoming, I found out that he owes everyone and was about to have his pickup repossessed."

"Little chance of anyone collecting the money they're owed if the man is dead," the cop pointed out as he rose. "We're going to be talking to your wife, but in the meantime, you'll be a guest of our Miles City jail. You don't have any trouble with that, do you, sheriff?"

"Just one thing," Stuart said. "Mr. Cline, would you mind removing your shirt?"

CHAPTER TWENTY

STUART WAS EVEN more discouraged as he watched the chief of police lead Dickie Cline away. There had been sign of a burn on his shoulder. Nor was there any sign of an old wound on his left leg. He'd been the last man on Bailey's list, and Stuart had struck out.

It had seemed simple since she had wounded the man. Even after twelve years, there should have at least been a scar. He couldn't understand why he hadn't found Bailey's attacker and Willow's murderer.

Most ranchers had scars because of a lifestyle that exposed them to dangerous situations. A horse putting them into barbed wire or dumping them onto the rocky ground. Using equipment that maimed. Or growing up trying to ride the wildest horses and bulls.

Stuart had found injuries, but none that corresponded to those Bailey had left on the man. Certainly not a brand in the shape of a small horseshoe. It had seemed so easy. Too easy. What he hadn't realized until he'd done a little research was that in order for the brand to be permanent, the hot branding iron had to be pushed down hard for three to five seconds so it burned through the first two layers of skin and grazed the third.

He doubted Bailey had been able to hold the iron on her attacker that long. Depending on what the attacker had done after being burned with the iron, he could have known what to use on it to make the scarring less noticeable too. Otherwise, after twelve years, there might not even be a scar.

Like the others he'd checked, Cline didn't have a brand on his shoulder. Like the others, he had scars, but none Stuart could definitely say were from a knife wound, since clearly the wounds hadn't killed the man.

On top of that, the crime lab had been unable to obtain any fingerprints from Bailey's door handle or the horseshoe wrapped in the bloody towel. Nor was it a surprise that the blood on the towel matched Willow Branson's.

Stuart realized that the only man he hadn't checked for a shoulder tattoo was Earl Hall. The condition the man had been in when he'd stopped by his house had led him to believe that the man couldn't have killed Willow. But maybe that was what Hall had wanted him to believe.

He told himself he'd go back out there tomorrow. Tonight, he just wanted to go home. All his insecurities about not being able to handle this job taunted him. He was no closer to finding the killer who, if the bloody towel and horseshoe were any indication, was coming for Bailey soon.

Stuart hated what he'd see in Bailey's face when he told her the news.

BAILEY HAD SEEN right away that the sheriff had had a rough day. She knew the feeling. She'd been sick for a few hours, but was feeling better. She could tell that Stuart had hoped

Dickie Cline was the man—especially after he'd been seen coming out of his dead wife's lover's motel room.

"It wasn't him," he said as he took the beer Bailey offered him and joined her on the couch.

"But the crime team found evidence left in the outbuilding, right?"

He nodded. "They think there's a chance they might get lucky and find some fingerprints or DNA at the site. Hopefully enough to tie the man to Willow Branson and her murder. We just won't know for a while. How are you doing?" he asked, studying her. She knew she was still a little pale after heaving her guts out.

"Better. I went out and talked to Norma. She insisted I have coffee and one of her muffins straight from the oven so she could drug me."

"What?" he demanded, looking upset.

"Eye drops in my coffee. Made me sicker than a dog, but the good news is that she did see someone put a bundle into my SUV the night before. She swears it was Annette Cline."

Stuart shook his head. "Do you believe her?"

"I do, and yet she also said she believed me that I didn't want anything to do with her husband. I suspect that was a lie. Otherwise, why drug me?"

He swore. "I always suspected there was something amiss under all that sweetness, you know?"

"I do. I should have been smarter about eating or drinking anything at her house. She was once questioned for trying to poison her first husband," Bailey said. "It's all in my book." She saw his expression change and wished she hadn't mentioned the book.

"I didn't realize that she'd been married before," was all Stuart said about it though. "Annette Cline? Norma's sure?"

Bailey shrugged. "Don't forget, she drugged me. She could have been lying. Annette was having an affair. Norma, in all her righteousness, might have wanted to get her into trouble because Annette was doing something she shouldn't, sleeping with a man who wasn't her husband. Who knows what Norma would have done if she really believed I was messing around with her husband?"

"I pity anyone who was after Ralph," the sheriff said. "He took Willow's death hard. He might have been the one plying her with Norma's peanut butter fudge."

"Which would give Norma motive for murder. You can't think she killed Willow, though."

He shook his head. "The first thing I'm going to do tomorrow is talk to Annette. Then I'll go see Ralph and Norma." He yawned. "Once the crime team gets through at the outbuilding, hopefully we'll have him."

Bailey nodded, but she feared it wouldn't be in time.

He reached for her hand. "We're going to find him. We're getting closer all the time." She nodded. "Don't give up hope."

That made her smile. "Don't worry. I'll be fighting right to the end."

Those words seemed to send a chill through him. "Not alone," he said, squeezing her hand. "Not alone."

STUART HAD BEEN looking forward to talking to Annette Cline, especially after what Bailey had told him. The police chief had released her yesterday, telling her not to leave the area. She'd claimed that she was only going home, that she had nowhere else to go.

That's why he was surprised to get her call so late that

afternoon saying she needed to talk to him. "I need to talk to you too," he'd told her.

Now as he drove out to the Cline ranch, the sun dropping behind the mountains, he felt tired and anxious. If Norma was telling the truth, Annette had put the bloodstained towel bundle into Bailey's SUV. Where could she have gotten it? Had someone put her up to it? The man Stuart was desperately searching for?

The woman who opened the door at the ranch looked nothing like the one only days earlier. Annette wore no makeup. Her hair was pulled back in a ponytail that appeared still wet from her shower. She wore a T-shirt and a pair of worn jeans. Her feet were bare.

She opened the door wide and motioned him in without a word. "Coffee?"

He declined, thinking of Norma's coffee. "Why did you want to see me?" he asked the moment they were sitting at the kitchen table. Annette had both hands wrapped around a mug of coffee as if she was cold on this fall afternoon.

"It's about my friend, Brock." She looked up, tears filling her eyes. "The one who was killed in Miles City." He nodded. "He's been driving up from Wyoming to see me. I guess you already know that. Well, this one morning…" She stopped to take a sip of her coffee as he felt his pulse jump at the thought that he already knew what morning she was referring to.

"He saw the killer," the sheriff said.

"He wasn't sure at first," Annette said quickly. "The man was coming out of the river, fully clothed, soaking wet. He seemed surprised to see Brock drive past. They'd looked at each other for those few seconds. Brock didn't think too much about it until he heard about Willow's murder." She sniffed and touched a paper napkin to her eyes. "I can't believe he's dead."

"Why didn't he tell someone what he'd seen?" Stuart asked, not about to let her get distracted right now.

"He was scared. The man had seen *him*."

"Did he describe the man to you? Or the vehicle? There should have been one parked close to the river's edge." The killer had carried Willow's body out into the river. He would have parked as close to the bank as possible.

"Big, strong-looking. Scary, that's all. Brock said he didn't get a good look, just a glance in passing. He said the man's truck was gray, but that's all he knew." Annette took another sip of her coffee.

There must have been fifty gray pickups in the Powder River Basin alone. "So Brock saw him again." She looked up in surprise. "How else did he get the bloody towel bundle to give to you?"

She looked shaken. "How did you—"

"You were seen putting the bundle inside Bailey's SUV."

"It isn't what you think." He wasn't sure what he thought. "Brock found it in his truck. It had a note on it saying he was to see that Bailey McKenna got it or he would get another visit—one involving his own blood."

"He knew who left it for him?"

"He knew when he looked into the bag and saw the towel and the small horseshoe."

So it was public knowledge about the brand, Stuart thought. Also, Brock Sherwood's prints and DNA would be all over the towel and its contents. He swore under his breath. "How did he talk you into delivering the bundle to Bailey's SUV?"

"Brock was scared. Dickie had called to say he was coming home. We decided to go to Miles City and get a motel for the night," Annette said. "He still had the horseshoe wrapped up in the towel. I told him to get rid of it, but he said he was afraid that if he didn't get it to Bailey, the man would kill him too. We were driving through Powder Crossing, and I saw Bailey talking to Norma. I had Brock pull around the corner, and I jumped out and took care of it. I didn't think anyone saw me, and if they did, they wouldn't think anything of me putting something in her car."

She looked up at him. "I assumed that would be the end of it, but Brock was still scared. He said he was going to come talk to you, but…"

But he hadn't lived long enough.

Annette's eyes filled with tears as she reached for her coffee. "I can't believe Dickie killed him."

Yet she seemed to. "Maybe he didn't," the sheriff said. "Maybe it was the man who he saw coming out of the river the morning Willow Branson was murdered. The man who knew who Brock was and left him a present to give to Bailey."

Her eyes widened in new alarm. "Does that mean he'll be coming after me next? I didn't see him, but what if he thinks Brock knew more than he did and told me?"

"You might consider staying with a friend or relative for a while," Stuart suggested, although he thought it was a long shot that the man would come after her. Then again, if the man had killed Brock, he might indeed be afraid Annette knew more than she did.

On the way back into town, he called the Miles City police chief and told him what he'd learned. "Dickie Cline might be telling the truth."

Unfortunately, Stuart had little to offer as to who had killed Willow Branson and possibly Brock Sherwood as well.

HOLLY JO COULD feel the housekeeper studying her in the large full-length mirror. She wondered what Elaine was looking for. She hated that everyone worried about her so much now. It made her feel uncomfortable.

"You look so pretty," Elaine said. "I'm glad you decided to wear that dress. The one you borrowed from Tana was a little too grown-up, and I like your hair down. It's so beautiful."

She studied herself in the mirror, wishing that her mother could be here. Her mother would have made her wear the more grown-up dress and insist on putting her hair up for her first dance. But her mother wasn't here. Nor did she know anything about Holly Jo or her life now.

The thought made her sad.

"I know you wish your mother was here," Elaine said as if reading her mind. "You can always come to me if you—"

"I'm fine," she said, moving away from the mirror.

"I should get downstairs."

Elaine checked the time. "Yes, I would imagine Buck will be here soon. You told him what time you had to be home?" She nodded. "Maybe you could plan on getting home just a little early."

"I know." She couldn't help being annoyed. How many times did she have to be told that if she was late, she wouldn't be able to ride with Buck again? If HH had his way, she'd never be able to leave the house.

She thought about earlier, when Buck had talked her into leaving before the decorating was done at the gym. Tana had asked if Buck had kissed her yet. Not yet, but she'd been waiting. It would be her first kiss. She'd been so excited thinking it would be a rite of passage.

Buck had stopped on the way back from the ranch. She'd been excited anticipating this moment. He'd grabbed her, pulled her to him and kissed her. She'd been expecting something like in the movies.

When he'd put his tongue in her mouth, she'd jerked back, grossed out by how wet the whole kiss had been and unable to hide her disappointment.

"I need to get home," she'd said as she'd turned to secretly wipe her mouth so he couldn't see.

Buck had swore and started the car. "Some times I don't know why I brother with you."

For a moment, she'd been afraid he would change his mind about the dance, but he said nothing even as he'd dropped her off at her bus stop, staying he had to get home.

"You're sure you're all right?" Elaine asked, still studying her.

"Just excited about the dance." There was so much she didn't understand. Her life right now felt confusing, scary and yet exciting. She wished she could ask Elaine about boys and kisses, but she couldn't. She'd ask Tana maybe. She felt as if she had so much to learn.

At the sound of a horn, Holly Jo hurried down the stairs, only to have HH stop her.

"He'll come in to get you," Holden said. "Or you won't go with him at all." He stepped to the door and motioned for Buck to come to the house.

Holly Jo could almost imagine Buck rolling his eyes and driving off. But a few moments later, he appeared at the door.

"That's the way a gentleman takes a lady on a date," HH

said as Buck walked her to his car and opened the door for her. But the moment her soon-to-be adoptive father turned his back, Buck gave him the finger and laughed. "What an old fart," he said as he started the car and took off in a hail of gravel.

He put his free hand on her leg, pushing her dress up to get to her thigh as he grinned at her. "We are going to have fun tonight."

She slid her dress back down as he reached into the glovebox and pulled out a flask and took a gulp before handing it to her. She hated even the smell of booze and quickly put the cap back on.

Buck didn't seem to notice as he turned up the radio, then reached for her again. He'd made it clear earlier that she owed him after getting him in trouble with his dad. "You owe me big time tonight," he'd said with a leer, then laughed.

CHAPTER TWENTY-ONE

"IT'S ALL MY FAULT," Bailey said as Stuart brought her another beer from the kitchen. "If I had gone to your father right away, the man's wounds would have been fresh. Maybe he would have been caught."

"You know that's not necessarily true," he said, taking his place on the couch. He'd hated having to tell her that they'd struck out. That he'd stuck out. He didn't want her ever blaming herself. "You didn't see his face. You couldn't identify him. My father would have had to check every man who came to the barbecue, but with no evidence to demand. It's not like he'd have a DNA evidence kit handy."

"Still," she said.

"You didn't expect him to ever do this again. As time went by, even though you were still actively looking for him, he stayed hidden."

"So why kill Willow?" she demanded. "Why come out of hiding *now*? It has to be more than her change of hair coloring. He'd gotten away with what he'd done. Twelve years had gone by. He was safe. Why take a chance?"

Stuart didn't know. "Maybe Willow triggered something because she looked so much like you at that age—and with your hair color. Maybe he couldn't help himself. He'd gotten away with it once. He probably thought he could do it again."

"He'd almost gotten caught and was definitely wounded enough that someone had to help him get away twelve years ago," Bailey pointed out. "Maybe it scared him, but as time went on..." She shook her head. "None of it makes any sense."

"I really doubt we will ever know what went on in the man's head," Stuart said, thinking about the woman who had almost killed him. "He's obviously sick. Maybe he'd fallen for Willow—just as he'd fallen for you. Only this time, he was hoping he wouldn't have to kill her. If he uses the branding iron to mark what he feels is his property, then why destroy that property?"

They fell into a tension-filled silence for a few minutes.

"We are no closer to finding him than I have been in the past twelve years," Bailey said. "We know he's still here since I got his message." She sat up little, her eyes suddenly bright and shining. "What if we call him on it?"

"I'm not gambling with your life."

As if not hearing him, she continued, "What if my father throws another barbecue and invites the same people?"

Stuart was on his feet. "Not a chance in hell. You're talking about using yourself as bait."

"I'm already bait," she said. "This puts the ball in his court."

"You're confusing me with all these metaphors."

She stood to face him, clearly excited. "Once he hears the news, he'll get that I'm calling him out. He won't do anything until the day of the barbecue. We'll have control over when he is going to make his move."

"You're not giving him a lot of credit. What makes you think he'd fall for that?"

"Because of his arrogance, believing he can outsmart both of us. He has so far. Why wouldn't he think he can do it again? He assumes we don't have a clue who he is."

"We don't," the sheriff pointed out. "I can't let you do this."

"You can't stop me." She stepped closer to put a finger over his lips before he could respond to that. "Do you know how much I've wanted to come to your bed at night?" He was taken aback for a moment by the change of topic. "I haven't been with any man in all this time. I thought I'd never feel desire." She met his gaze as her finger traced his lower lip before she moved her hand to cup his cheek. "I want you, Stuart Layton, but I can't until I know this man is gone for good."

He heard what she was saying. Not just caught, but dead. "Women have tempted me with sex before, Bailey, but not so blatantly."

"I'm not talking just sex, Stuart, but I think you know that."

The sheriff shook his head at even the idea of the two of them having the future he'd dreamed of. He'd be a fool to think it possible. Worse, he knew she was right. He couldn't stop her. All he could do was try to keep her alive, whether they had a future together or not.

"If we don't do this, then he could strike at any time. We offer the bait, he'll come. This time we'll know he's coming and be ready."

"As ready as we can possibly be at a big barbecue with over fifty ranchers and their wives there."

She leaned into him. "But it will be worth it when it's over."

He wished he could believe that with all his heart. But she was right. She didn't need his approval. Clearly, she'd already made up her mind. "Damn, woman, you drive hard bargain."

She laughed and kissed him, hugging him as she looked into his eyes. "We can do this."

He wished he had her confidence. They still had no idea who he was or if he'd fall for this. Even if he did, he couldn't use the same ruse he had last time. They might not see him coming until it was too late.

The sheriff thought about the resignation letter still in his desk drawer down at the department. He'd had the nightmare again last night, reminding him that there was a very good chance he wasn't up to this.

He looked into Bailey's face and felt his heart float up as if filled with helium. He'd do anything for this woman, even die to save her.

It gave him an idea. He just hoped she'd go along with it. But first he had to drive down to the general store before it closed. "I have to run an errand, and then you and I are going out to dinner."

"GO OUT TO dinner tonight?" Bailey said, already shaking her head. All this talk about the man and now the barbecue had drained her. She knew it was the only way to draw him out and get this over with one way or the other.

Not that she could say that to Stuart. He wanted to believe the best. Bailey didn't think she'd ever been an optimist. After what had happened to her, she pretty much expected bad things to happen. Not that she could tell Stuart that either.

"We're going out, you and me, on a date," he said.

"A date?" she repeated. She couldn't remember the last time she'd been asked out, let alone gone out to dinner with a man. "Stuart—"

"At dinner, I'm going to tell you my plan."

She started to groan because she knew he didn't like the idea of the barbecue and her using herself as bait. Who would? But she wasn't changing her mind, and he should know that about her by now.

"Trust me. My plan works with your barbecue plan." Bailey highly doubted that.

He wasn't gone long. Somehow he'd managed to get to a store before it closed, because when he walked in, he was carrying a plastic bag. "I bought you something to wear tonight."

When he pulled out a yellow-and-white-checked sundress, she blinked in surprise, her gaze going from the dress to him. "Are you sure about this?"

"We've been hiding out here in my house long enough."

She wanted to argue. Mostly, she wanted to curl up on the couch, drink beer and watch something mindless on the television, but she could see how much he needed this. He'd even bought her a dress to wear.

"Let me change," she said, taking the dress from him. Seeing this side of Stuart warmed her in a way that also scared her. She hadn't let herself think about the future, believing she didn't have one once the man came for her.

Nor did she want to let herself dream now. It would have been too easy to see herself with Stuart for the long haul. Yet she felt a thrill of excitement at the idea of going on a date with him—even only as far as the local Cattleman Café.

THE SHERIFF COULDN'T help being nervous as he and Bailey took the only empty booth at the café. "Busy night, huh, Penny?" Stuart said to the waitress after she told them the specials and asked for their drink orders.

It was dinnertime on a Saturday night and one of the reasons he'd insisted on dinner here tonight. He'd wanted them to be seen together. As they'd walked to their booth, he'd felt all eyes on them. He could imagine what the other patrons were thinking—if not saying. What an odd couple they made. He doubted anyone was thinking he and Bailey were perfect for each other, not that it mattered.

They both ordered the chicken-fried steak special. "Could we also have two empty glasses?" Stuart asked. The owner of the café allowed the less unruly patrons to bring in their own beverages on a Friday or Saturday night.

When he pulled out a bottle of red wine, Bailey's eyebrow shot up. "Stuart?" she whispered, leaning toward him.

"Just go with whatever I do, okay?"

She laughed and looked at him warily as he opened the wine, one with a twist cap, and poured a little into each of the glasses Penny had brought them. He raised his glass in a toast. Bailey raised her glass too, her gaze locked with his.

"To the future," he said, and saw her wince. "May it be everything I know it can be." They clinked glasses, and he watched her take a sip of the wine, her eyes shiny, as he took a sip of his own, then put down his glass and got to his feet.

She looked at him in alarm. He could feel eyes on them as he dropped to one knee, making Bailey gasp, her eyes as wide as the café's famous pancakes.

"Stuart?" she said again as he pulled a small, worn velvet box from his pocket.

"Bailey McKenna, you make my life so much more interesting. You make it worth living. Also, your father said he'd throw us a party, a barbecue to celebrate our engagement. I've always wanted to go to one of his barbecues." That got a few chuckles from the crowd that seemed to be holding their collective breaths. "Marry me."

For a moment, Stuart feared she'd get up and run out. Or just as bad, say no. Her gaze locked with his. "You're serious?" No one seemed to be breathing, including himself, as he nodded and smiled. He figured at least a few of the crowd were taking bets on whether or not she would turn him down.

Tears filled her eyes. "Stuart Layton…yes, I'll marry you."

The full café erupted in applause and well wishes. He saw more than a few people taking photos with their phones. Everyone in the Powder River Basin would be talking about this by tomorrow morning.

"It was my grandmother's," he said as put the ring on Bailey's finger. He wasn't sure she'd heard because of all the noise around them. The café had taken on a party feel. He'd known it would fit, and it did.

Stuart rose, heart in his throat. He'd dreamed of this—the real thing, not a pretend engagement for a barbecue to draw out a killer. He wondered if Bailey would ever forgive him for springing it on her. But he'd needed her reaction to look as real as possible.

As he sat back down, he smiled at the people smiling at him and wondered how he'd ever be able to eat his meal when it came. He'd pulled this off, but at what cost? How could he ever ask Bailey to marry him for real now?

With a jolt, he was reminded why he was doing this. He would never have the chance to ask her for real if his plan didn't work. It all hinged on keeping her alive. He looked across the table at the woman he loved. Bailey was staring down at the ring on her finger. When she looked up, her blue eyes shone with tears, but not of joy. Clearly, she didn't like being surprised. She didn't seem all that happy about being engaged either. He worried that she'd convinced herself she had no future. He hoped to hell he could change that.

He poured her some wine and himself more as well. "I'd let you do the toast, but I think it's better if I do. To us, Bailey. Come hell or high water, we're in this together." He raised his glass. She did the same, clinking hers a little too hard.

They were engaged.

At least until after the barbecue her father was about to throw for them.

CHAPTER TWENTY-TWO

PICKETT WAS WORKING at the house when he got the call from his sister-in-law. "Tilly, if you're looking for Cooper, he's right here," he said with a chuckle. His friend looked up from where he and some of the other crew from the McKenna and Stafford Ranches were helping hang sheetrock. He was determined to get this house finished before winter.

"I was calling you, Pickett," Tilly said, and quickly told him what had happened at the baby shower. "Oakley's headed home. She's devastated."

He looked down at the floor and groaned in pain for his wife, for himself. "Thanks for letting me know. I'll go find her." *Oh, Oakley*, he thought, his heart aching. And to have it happen at her sister's baby shower. Pocketing the phone, he turned to Cooper. "I need to go."

His brother-in-law came over to him, looking concerned. Pickett whispered, "Another miscarriage." Cooper put an arm around his shoulders for a few moments. They'd always been like brothers since Pickett had come to work on the McKenna Ranch when he was a teen.

"Go. We'll keep working," Cooper said. "You need to get your woman into a decent home. Could change everything."

Pickett nodded. "Thanks."

He found Oakley in the stable, saddling up a horse as if nothing had happened. His wife had always been happiest out riding. "Want some company?" he asked from behind her.

She didn't turn but did stop what she was doing for a moment. "I thought you were working on the house?"

"Was. Cooper is keeping the crew going until I get back." He desperately wanted to turn her around, pull her into his arms, make everything right.

"Well, you should get back. We need walls in our house. I'm fine. I'm going for a ride."

Pickett wasn't fine. "I need a hug." They'd heard somewhere that to have a happy marriage, they needed to hug for twenty seconds every day no matter how busy they were.

"Please don't," she whispered, emotion making her voice break.

"Twenty seconds, Oakley," he said. "I really could use one. I hit my thumb with a hammer. It hurts like the devil."

She dropped her head for a moment before she turned. He saw the anguish in her eyes as he quickly pulled her into a hug. He didn't want her to see how badly he hurt for her, for them. At first her body was stiff, but slowly she began to soften against him. She buried her face into his neck, leaving wet tears as she clung to him.

He never wanted to let her go even as he felt his own heartbeat slow. They stayed like that, well over twenty seconds, before he was the one to pull away. "Best get back to that sheetrock and let you go on your ride." Their gazes met for a moment.

Oakley sniffed and wiped at her cheeks, avoiding his gaze. "Watch that thumb," she said, and turned to swing effortlessly up into the saddle.

Picket would have gladly stood there and watched her ride off into horizon, but Cooper was right. He needed to complete their home. One of these days they would have children to fill it—even if they had to adopt.

Turning, he walked back to his pickup. He heard the jingle of the horse's tack as Oakley spurred her horse. Once he was behind the wheel, he finally looked to see her riding across the pasture, silhouetted against the golden leaves of the cottonwoods, a woman in her element.

He told himself that she was going to be all right. They were going to be all right. They had to be.

HOLLY JO HAD been excited but also anxious about her very first dance, especially after the way Buck had been acting. She'd made excuses for him insisting she leave the gym before they were finished decorating. She hoped they would have fun tonight and that he might kiss her again and this time it would be better. She was determined to have a good time. She'd be dancing with the cutest boy in school.

But when they arrived at the school, Buck had taken the time to refill his flask from a bottle he had behind the seat before they went into the school gym.

The moment they entered, he spotted his friends and left her standing in the doorway. She'd been looking forward to their first dance. Nothing was going like she'd thought it should. Buck was still angry about HH getting him in trouble with his dad. He'd hardly said a word on the way to the dance. She could see him now passing his flask around to his friends and laughing, not even looking in her direction.

She was fighting tears when Tana joined her. "You look so pretty," her friend said the moment she reached her. "Everyone's over here. Wait until you see Claire's dress. I think it was her mother's when she went to school here."

The night became a blur with her gossiping and dancing to a few songs with her friends. She tried to have a good time despite Buck avoiding her the whole night. By the time the DJ played the last song, she was ready to go home. Her feet hurt in the dress heels she'd worn, and she was pretty sure that Buck planned to break up with her after tonight.

More than anything when she felt like this, she wanted her horse. Often when she was sad, she would go out to the stable, loop her arm around Honey's neck and talk to the mare. She wished she could do that right now as she watched Buck stagger across the dance floor toward her. When he reached her, he threw his arm around her and kissed her. He tasted like alcohol and made a show of sticking his tongue in her mouth. She shoved him away as his friends all howled in laughter.

"Let's get out of here. I know where there's a party," he said, slurring his words as he reached for her.

She stepped back out of his reach

"I have to go home. If I'm late—"

He stumbled back from her, his expression one of anger as if she'd been the one to ignore him all night. "Then go." He breathed alcohol fumes on her as he lurched toward her and whispered loudly, "I can do better." He laughed. . "See ya." Turning, he walked off, his friends joining him as they headed for the door, all of them laughing. She felt her face burn.

"I can give you a ride home," one of her friends offered.

"No, it's fine. I have a ride," she said despite the sobs

that threatened to burst from her. She didn't even want to be around her friends as humiliated as she felt. She waited until they'd left and the two young teachers who'd chaperoned were packing up to leave before she stepped outside. She didn't want one of them waiting with her. She wanted to be alone.

Pulling out the phone Pickett had given her, she made the call. He answered on the first ring. At just the sound of his voice, she burst into tears.

BAILEY DIDN'T REMEMBER eating dinner. The night was a blur of well-wishers and gawkers, who seemed to be watching them as if they weren't a likely pair. But the worst part was the disappointment she felt, because it made her angry with herself. She was the one who'd called the shots when it had come to their so-called relationship. She'd been the one to push him away—and was still doing that.

So why did she hate that it hadn't been real? She tried not to look at the beautiful ring Stuart had put on her finger. How could he dare make a promise of a future—even pretend—knowing what was at stake? Not that it wasn't a good plan, but she wished she'd been in on it so it hadn't hurt so much.

When he'd gotten down on one knee, her heart had broken. She'd never been much for tradition. It was hard for her to even admit why she was disappointed. So far nothing about her and Stuart had been traditional by any means. This was their first date, for crying out loud. She had wanted to stay home and watch TV at his house.

And it wasn't like she'd grown up dreaming about her wedding day. She'd been more interested in horses than boys. At seventeen, she'd never been in love. Then *he* had happened.

Now she was engaged to the only man she'd ever loved, and it wasn't real. The only thing real in her life was that there was a killer out there coming for her. Had she dreamed of her future, this was not the way she would have wanted it to go.

It only made it worse when Stuart looked at her, his eyes full of love and concern for her. She'd stared back, angry with him even as she had to admit the reason she was so disappointed. She loved this man. Because of that, she wanted the romance, the real engagement, the dream of a future together.

Damn him for making her ache for it when she didn't believe it possible—as much as her heart yearned for a happy-ever-after with Stuart.

CHAPTER TWENTY-THREE

HOLDEN SADDLED UP and rode out as the sun rose over the mountains. There was a chill to the fall air this morning. The leaves on the cottonwoods had turned to golds, dark reds and browns. They rustled overhead as he rode along the river.

He couldn't help the melancholy he felt at this change in season. Winter would be on its heels. He'd heard on the news this morning that it had already snowed in the high country. The weather changed quickly in Montana. In a single day, the greatest temperature change in history happened not all that far away. It had gone from fifty-four degrees below zero to forty-nine above—a shift of one hundred three degrees Fahrenheit.

It wasn't just the thought of winter that had him down today. Summer was Charlotte's favorite time of year. He'd been so sure his Lottie would return. Now he feared she would never come back. He'd held out hope with each hot, cloudless-blue-skied day, thinking how much she loved their spot on the creek with the deep green of the cottonwood leaves a canopy overhead. They'd spent hours there when they were young, lying on the warm, flat rocks, staring up at the cottony clouds drifting past. They hadn't known then how their lives would turn out, and he was thankful for that.

He picked up the scent of the creek even before he saw it through the trees. His horse shuffled along through the fallen leaves, the air colder, the deeper he went into the trees. He followed the creek to their spot. Ahead, he could see that there was no one along the opposite shore.

Why had he thought there was a chance Lottie might be here waiting for him? How many days could he ride over here, filled with hope, only to have it bashed? She wasn't coming back. He had to accept it. As he reined his horse in to leave, though, he knew he would continue hoping. It was all that kept him going.

Just as he'd started to turn away from the spot where he and Lottie used to make love as teens, he saw something that made him pull up short. At first he thought he was seeing things, that his imagination was playing tricks on him, that the flash of red was no more than wishful thinking.

Turning his horse, he rode deeper into the trees. He spotted what appeared to be a piece of red fabric tied to a tree limb. It fluttered in the breeze by the edge of the creek bed near a large boulder.

Dismounting, he worked his way across the creek from stone to stone until he reached the spot where it was tied. He saw that it was her scarf, one he remembered her wearing. He took the end of it in his fingers and brought it to his face. It smelled of her perfume. Red was definitely Lottie's color.

His heart began to pound as he looked around, spotting her tracks and her horse's in the earth along the bank of the creek. Lottie had been here. She'd left her scarf. To let him know she was back?

Holden felt his pulse pound. He dared not to believe it for fear the disappointment if he was wrong would knock him to his knees. But if Lottie was back… He thought about the way he'd left things. He had to see her. After moving quickly to his horse, he mounted and rode back toward his ranch, determined to get changed and drive over to the Stafford Ranch. He had no idea how long she'd been back, but he couldn't wait another minute to see her. She had to know how he felt about her. She'd come home.

For the first time in years, he felt as if she might have found her way home to him. But when he reached his house, Bailey and the sheriff were waiting for him.

THE SHERIFF WATCHED Holden look from him to Bailey warily. When the rancher had seen them waiting for him, he hadn't looked happy about it. When they'd told him they had to speak to him right away, he'd been clearly irritated.

"I don't understand," Holden said once they were all seated in his office. "What is so important that you can't even let me change clothes after my ride?"

Stuart reached over and took Bailey's hand. He knew how hard this was for her. Earlier, he'd seen her turning the engagement ring around and around on her finger as they'd driven to the ranch. While they hadn't talked about it, he could tell that she was still mad at him for not warning her. After their dinner last night, they drank more at the hotel bar and came home to pass out—in separate rooms.

"This can't wait," Stuart said now and explained what they needed.

Holden let out a curse. "You're…engaged? Since when?"

"Last night," Bailey said. "Stuart surprised me at dinner at the café. I would have thought you'd have heard."

"And now you want me to throw you a barbecue engagement party immediately?"

"And only invite people from the old invitation list I wrote up for you," Bailey said.

"What the hell is this really about?" her father demanded. "Are you pregnant? Is that why you're in such a rush?"

"I'm not pregnant."

Stuart noticed the way she avoided his gaze. They hadn't even slept together. He'd almost given up on the idea all together. "It's better if you don't know why it's so important."

"Like hell," Holden bellowed, and looked at his daughter. "I held that barbecue you're talking about right before you went off to college. When you came back..." The sheriff caught the sudden change in the man as if he'd glimpsed something in his daughter's eyes that was like a closing fist around his heart. His voice broke when he spoke. "Did something happen at that barbecue?"

Tears filled her eyes. Holden looked from her to Stuart again. "Tell me."

It wasn't the sheriff's story to tell. Bailey had only finally broken down and trusted him enough to tell *him*. Stuart wasn't about to betray her trust. "It's up to Bailey."

"I was assaulted at the barbecue," she blurted out.

"What?" Holden was shaking his head. "How is that even possible?"

"You remember telling me that someone mentioned one of our horses was out? I went down to take care of it, and he was waiting for me."

"He?" her father asked.

"I never saw his face. He grabbed me from behind, injected me with something that put me out for a little while. When I woke up…" She stopped to swallow. "I was naked. He raped me and then tried to…brand me."

Holden swore and shot to his feet. For a moment, he swayed as if he was going to pass out. He pushed his palms down hard on his desk, dropped his head and seemed to be fighting hard to catch his breath.

"Are you all right?" the sheriff asked, alarmed.

"Of course I'm not all right," he snapped as he raised his head and looked at his daughter. "Why didn't you come to me, tell me…"

She shook her head. "He planned to kill me, but I managed to fight him off. I injured him. He was bleeding badly when he left the cabin." She stopped, took a breath and said, "And now he's done it again. He murdered Willow and did the same thing to her. I've been looking for him for twelve years. I know he's still here. He's one of the ranchers you invited to the party."

Holden slumped into his chair. For a moment, he broke down, dropping his face into his hands. After a few moments, he said, "Now I understand why you've been so upset with me. I sent you out to the stables, right to him."

"You didn't know," she said. "I shouldn't have blamed you."

He lifted his head and looked at Stuart. "You're on board with this…barbecue?"

"We know he's coming for her," he said carefully. "Bailey feels he'll wait until the barbecue to strike again. This time we'll know he's going to try to abduct her, and it will be on home ground. But no, I'm not exactly on board. It terrifies me that we might not be able to keep her safe. We can't bring in a bunch of undercover cops. This man knows everyone. He'd back off, and who knows when he'd come for her?"

"He has to suspect that he's walking into a trap either way," Holden said.

"He's done this twice and gotten away with it," Bailey said. "He'll think he can do it again."

"Only this time," her father said, "he could kill you."

No one said anything for a few moments as his words hung in the air. "Is this really what you want?" he asked his daughter. Bailey nodded. Holden sighed. "Then I'll send out the invitations to the barbecue. When do you want it?"

"As soon as possible," the sheriff said. "Bailey's convinced he'll wait to try to redo what went wrong the first time he attacked her. I'm not so sure that he'll wait. So the sooner the better."

Holden nodded.

"You can't tell the ranch hands or anyone else," Stuart said. "If you mention this to the wrong person—"

"I understand," her father said, and looked to Stuart. "You do realize that you are taking one hell of a chance with my daughter."

"I do, but it's what Bailey wants. We've been trying to find him. We haven't been able to. She's been looking for twelve years. We both believe he plans to come for her again. If she's right about him, he'll wait until the barbecue. At least we'll know when and where."

"You're sure he's still here, that he's local?" Holden asked.

"He's still here," she said. "He'll come." Stuart could see how hard this was for her. "I know it's been twelve years, but please try to remember who told you that one of the horses had gotten out."

The rancher shook his head. "There were so many people..."

"It would have been a man you trusted," the sheriff said. "Someone who wouldn't have taken it upon himself to put the horse back in the pasture."

He saw Holden's expression change and felt a jolt as he realized how true his words were. No rancher would warn his host that he had a horse out. He'd try to put the horse back himself.

"It wasn't a rancher," Holden said. "It was a woman. One of the wives?" He frowned as if trying to remember. "I'm sorry. I can almost see her..."

Stuart exchanged a look with Bailey. This was new information. He considered what she'd said about the man getting help after he was injured from someone he trusted. What if he'd gotten help before the attack as well?

Then he'll probably use his accomplice again, the sheriff thought.

WHEN CJ STAFFORD heard he had a visitor, he'd been more than a little surprised. He hadn't had any visitors since his arrest, other than the one time his mother's attorney had stopped by to tell him she wasn't going to help him.

He couldn't imagine Treyton McKenna coming here. As far as most people in the Powder River Basin knew, he and Treyton were mortal enemies—just like their parents.

Nor was there any reason CJ's sisters or his two younger brothers would come visit him. He'd tormented them their whole lives. At least he'd never almost killed Brand and Ryder, so maybe...

But when he walked into the visiting area, he stopped short. Sitting on the other side of the Plexiglas window in the small booth was his mother. He couldn't imagine what she was doing here. On top of that, Charlotte Stafford looked different, he thought as he walked slowly toward her and sat down. He couldn't put his finger on what it was, though. She'd aged, but she was still beautiful, still regal in the way she held herself. Yet there was something different in her eyes.

She pulled her phone off the hook and put it to her ear. He did the same on his side of the clear partition, his mind racing. Surely she hadn't come here just to tell him she never wanted to see him again, she wasn't going to help him, and she'd left the ranch to his siblings. She'd already made all that clear the last time he saw her, before the cops arrived to take him away in handcuffs.

"Chisum Jase," she said quietly, catching him off guard even more by calling him by his full name.

"Mother," he said, his heart pounding. He still had no idea what she was doing here, but the way his luck went, this wasn't going to end well. He felt his free hand fist against his thigh, his nails biting into his palm. "I never expected to see you. I heard you left the ranch."

"I did. But now I'm back. I had to see you."

He waited, expecting to take a verbal beating that would be worse than some of the physical ones he'd already endured behind bars. "I can't imagine why."

"You're my son, the one most like me, as you've pointed out many times."

"Your greatest disappointment, as I recall."

She nodded. "I need to ask you something." He held his breath. "Is there any chance you think you could change?"

The question caught him flat-footed. His first instinct was to lie. Lying had always come easy to him. "I don't know."

"Would you be willing to try?"

He laughed and looked away from her green eyes so like his own, before he licked his dry lips and met her gaze again. A bubble of hope rose in his chest, making it ache. "What are you asking me?"

"I've thought about change a lot in the time I've been away from the ranch. I have changed, but I have a long way to go." Her eyes focused on him. "If I can change, I wondered if you could."

His throat had gone dry. "I don't know what you want me to say."

"Yes, you do, or you would have lied right away. Why don't you think about it. You have time. I'll come back when you have an honest answer." She hung up her phone before he could say another word.

He watched her rise. What was she offering him? At what cost? He reminded himself what he was looking at if he stayed here. His trial was coming up soon. Even his cheap lawyer had been able to put it off for a while, but he was headed for prison.

He was still sitting there holding the phone when the guard came to take him back to his cell. He'd known seeing her would upset him. He hated her and loved her. He knew he'd done wrong, but when she'd turned on him… He still tasted that bitterness after all these months.

"That your mother, huh?" the guard asked with a chuckle as they reached his cell.

"I have no idea who that woman was," he said, stepping in and letting the door slam behind him.

HOLDEN SAW THAT Bailey had sent over the original list of ranchers he'd invited to the barbecue. It would take a few days to get the invitations out and a few more to get the RSVPs back. Some ranchers wouldn't respond. Bailey and Stuart seemed to think that the announcement of their engagement would get the man who'd attacked his daughter to attend.

Elaine had been shocked when he told her about the barbecue. "Isn't it risky this time of year with the weather changing?" she'd asked. When she'd seen that the event was only two weeks away, she demanded, "What's the rush?"

"The weather," he'd snapped back, and felt her knowing gaze on him.

"I need some time to get everything ready."

"Bailey has already lined up a caterer," he'd said without looking at her. "Hire all the help you need to get the house and property ready. Just make sure they are all finished by the day of the barbecue and gone." At her silence, he turned to see if she was still in the room. She was. She looked at him as if he'd lost his mind.

"What is going on, Holden?"

"A barbecue. I thought I made that clear."

His even more clipped tone didn't stop her in the least. "I've known you all my life. You think I don't know when something is going on?"

"Elaine, please. Just do this for me, and no more questions."

"I can see how upset you are," she said. "This isn't just about an engagement party, is it?" He gave her a don't-ask-any-more-questions look. "Fine, I'll do my part, but I'm going to be watching you, Holden."

"I'd prefer you watched Bailey," he said, then started to turn away. This woman knew him too well. She would weasel it out of him if he wasn't careful. He'd already said too much. "By the way, have you heard if Charlotte is back at her ranch?"

"I believe she is, but you could drive over and see for yourself," Elaine said. For years she'd encouraged him to mend fences with Charlotte and end the long-standing feud between their families. He'd been shocked to learn that Elaine and Charlotte had some kind of old friendship.

"I have too much to do getting ready for this barbecue, but after that...maybe I will," he said, and left the house. Bailey's confession, her so-called engagement to the sheriff, and now this barbecue had him where he couldn't eat or sleep. It also had him out walking the property at all hours. There were no old cabins left standing. No place for this monster to take her, he told himself.

He couldn't believe he was being asked to invite the man back here. He told himself there had to be another way, even as he remembered that his daughter had been looking for the man for twelve years. Twelve years!

Holden knew he would do what Bailey asked. He owed her. He'd let his daughter down last time. He wouldn't this time. He checked out where vehicles would be parked. The sheriff had suggested valet parking so no one could leave without someone knowing it.

He would put Pickett in charge of parking since he trusted him with his life. He didn't know what more he could do. But even as he thought it, he questioned how he could play host at this barbecue, pretending his daughter wasn't using herself as bait for a killer. Any one of the ranchers he'd known most of his life could be the one who'd assaulted and tried to kill Bailey.

The thought turned his blood to ice and made him question if he'd ever known his neighbors in this river basin.

But his biggest fear was that he wouldn't be able to stop the bastard from succeeding this time.

CHAPTER TWENTY-FOUR

PICKETT HAD ALWAYS thought of himself as a nonviolent person. But last night, it took everything in him not to go find Buck and beat some sense into him. The only thing that had stopped him was Holly Jo's reassurance that Buck hadn't hurt anything more than her feelings

Still, he wanted to kick the kid's butt. He knew he couldn't, that it would only make things worse for Holly Jo. Instead, he'd stayed cool. He'd gone to the school, and there was she was, waiting outside. One of the chaperones must have seen her waiting and had also waited nearby in her car as if she'd known that Holly Jo was embarrassed and wanted to be alone. He'd found her sitting on the front step of the school.

It had broken his heart, but he'd done his best to hide it from her.

He'd waved to the chaperone and they'd driven home in silence. Holly Jo curled against the door most of the way home until he'd gotten her to open up to him. Pickett had really believed that after Holden had paid the Savages a visit, Buck wouldn't dare act up. He'd been wrong.

"I'm sensing that you don't want to talk about it," he said.

"You think?"

"I know you want us all to put the kidnapping behind us so you can. We're trying." He'd glanced over at her. "But it's hard. We all worry about you."

"Because you think I'm going to get kidnapped again?"

"No, because we care about you and hate what you went through. We just want to keep you safe."

He'd dropped Holly Jo off at the house and gone home to his cabin down by the stables. He'd found Oakley sleeping soundly and crawled into bed next to her.

This morning, while she was still asleep, he'd slipped out to walk up to the main ranch house. He found Elaine in the kitchen, baking apple turnovers. The smell of cinnamon and apples drew him right to her.

"They're not quite ready," she said when she saw him. "I just put them in the oven." She glanced at the clock, then at him, as if realizing he hadn't come for breakfast. "What's wrong?"

He pulled up a chair and tried to keep his voice calm as he told her about the phone call from Holly Jo and how he'd picked her up and gotten her home.

"That little bastard didn't bring her home?" Elaine said angrily as she joined him. "I'd like to get my hands on his scrawny neck." She stopped speaking, her eyes welling. "Is she all right?"

He nodded. "Still, someone needs to talk to her about—"

"If you say birds and bees—"

"She needs to know that no all boys are jerks. I think she'd done with Buck, I certainly hope so. She told me she just wants to be a normal teenager. But someone needs to warn her about boys."

"Poor baby. Of course someone should talk to her." The housekeeper shook her head and sighed. "Certainly not Holden. I'll do it." The timer went off on the oven. "You should stay for breakfast."

Pickett rose, shaking his head. "But I would love to take a couple of those back to my cabin. Oakley could use one." Elaine didn't ask why, and he was grateful for that and pretty sure she probably already knew that they were trying for a baby without much success.

"Let me wrap up some for you to take. Then I'll go up and see how Holly Jo is this morning. I don't know what Holden was thinking. He isn't equipped to raise another daughter. He'd be the first to tell you that he wasn't all that equipped to raise the first one."

Taking the wrapped hot turnovers she handed him, Pickett smiled. "Thanks. I'm glad Holly Jo has you. Holden too."

She scoffed at that, but smiled as she took off her apron and headed for the back stairs.

EARL HALL LOOKED surprised to see the sheriff again so soon. His appearance had changed drastically since the last time Stuart had been there. He was recently shaved, hair trimmed, and he was fully dressed, including boots on his feet. No black crocodile. Not buckaroos either.

From what Stuart could see of the house behind Hall, the place was neat and clean. "If you have a moment, I'd like a few words with you. Mind if I come in?"

Hall glanced over his shoulder, then hesitated for a few moments before he said, "Sure, Sheriff," and pushed the door open for him to enter.

Plastic covered the living room couch, and a plastic runner ran up the hallway over the carpet. He heard the rattle of pots and pans coming from the kitchen and headed in that direction.

"The wife's making breakfast," Earl said behind him, sounding as if he'd prefer to talk to Stuart alone, which made the sheriff even more curious.

He wasn't sure who he'd thought he'd find in the kitchen. The last time he'd been here, he'd gotten the feeling that Iris might not ever be coming back. But he'd also suspected that *someone* had been here and peeked out the window.

A small, thin woman with a plain face and a turned-down mouth was standing at the stove.

"Iris," Stuart said, and took off his hat. "I'd like to talk to you and Earl if you have a few minutes."

She looked past him to where Earl was standing, still in the kitchen doorway as if afraid to enter the kitchen.

"Mind if we sit at the kitchen table?" the sheriff asked. "I don't want to keep you from your breakfast." He didn't wait for an answer, just moved to the table and pulled out one of the chairs to sit. Neither Iris nor Earl joined him, though.

He crossed his legs to balance his Stetson on his knee, the tension in the room making him a little nervous—also a little suspicious. "I'm sure you've heard about that woman who was murdered and dumped in the river."

A look passed between Iris and her husband before she said, "Horrible thing to happen."

"How was Fargo, Iris?" he asked, startling her. She appeared confused. "Last time I was here, Earl said you were in Fargo visiting a sister? Or one of the girls? Sorry, I can't remember."

"Sister," she said, her mouth tightening into a straight line. This time she didn't look at Earl.

"Earl, I can make this quick. I'm going to need you to remove your shirt."

Iris grabbed hold of the kitchen counter and looked down at the floor without a word, but from her expression, he thought he knew what he was going to find.

"Earl?" The man hadn't moved, didn't even seem to be breathing. "If you prefer not to do this here, I can take you in to the sheriff's department."

Slowly, as if sleepwalking, Earl began to unbutton his shirt, his frightened gaze on his wife, who was still looking at the floor. He pulled out one arm, then the other.

"Step over here into the light, if you don't mind, and turn around," Stuart said.

Earl shuffled over. The look of dread on his face had the sheriff's heart thundering in his ears. Something was definitely wrong here. If it was what he thought it was…

The rancher walked into the light, baring a back to Stuart that looked painful and sore. There were patches of red, some oozing and some flaking around the large, swollen tattoo as if someone had tried to scrape it off Earl's back. The tattoo was of a naked woman. The woman looked nothing like Iris.

He shot a look at Earl's wife, who still had her head down. The sheriff rose and motioned for Earl to follow him outside. "When did you get the tattoo?" he asked once they were outside, when what he really wanted to ask was why.

Earl looked as chagrinned as his wife as he buttoned up his shirt. "Last week. I was drunk."

That was a pretty safe bet, Stuart thought. "What day?"

Turned out it was the day Willow Branson was murdered.

"Where'd you have it done?"

"Billings. I guess I told the tattoo artist to surprise me."

The sheriff nodded, feeling for the man. He'd bet Earl Hall hadn't been drunk but a few times in his life. "I'm guessing you weren't alone."

Earl looked up and swallowed before he shook his head and then looked back toward the house. "It was just someone I met at the implement dealer's yearly picnic. She dared me."

"Iris didn't go to Fargo, did she?" The rancher wagged his head. "Okay, Earl. I'm still looking for Willow Branson's murderer."

"Don't know anything about that." He frowned. "How'd you hear about my tattoo?"

"I didn't," Stuart said. Settling his Stetson onto his head, he started for his patrol SUV. "But it sure looks like it hurts."

"You have no idea," Earl said.

HOLLY JO DIDN'T want to go to school Monday morning. She was embarrassed, even though Elaine had assured her that she had nothing to be embarrassed about.

"Buck behaved badly," Elaine said. "The kid's a jerk. I'm proud of you for standing up for yourself and calling Pickett for a ride home. You can also call me or Holden, you know."

She nodded.

"Buck should be embarrassed, but don't expect him to be," the housekeeper told her. "He behaved horribly."

Holly Jo hesitated. "My first kiss was awful."

Elaine laughed. "So was mine. You were just kissed by the wrong boy – just like was. When you kiss the right one, one who respects you and wants it to be a good experience for you too, I think you'll like it."

"I hope you're right."

"Now to basics. You know about periods? Good. I bought you some options and put them in your bathroom. Holler if you need help. If you have any questions about anything, please come to me. I'll try my best not to make it embarrassing."

She'd smiled. "I will."

And while Elaine had made her feel better, she still worried about facing her friends—and Buck and his friends.

"Head up," Elaine had said Monday morning when Holly Jo came down ready for school. "You are the master of your own fate and one amazing trick rider. Remember that. You deserve a boy who appreciates you."

She'd nodded and even smiled as she sat down to have breakfast. She'd spoken with Tana over the weekend. "Buck was such a jerk," her friend said. "If I were you, I'd never talk to him again."

When the bus came, Holly Jo had climbed aboard, surprised to see Tana, who usually caught a ride with a friend's older sister.

"My mother thinks it would be better for me if I rode the bus," Tana said, mugging a face as Holly Jo sat with her. "I missed curfew the other night." She shrugged. "But if you're going to be riding the bus too, it's not so bad."

They talked about homework, teachers and upcoming school events, staying clear of mentioning Buck and the dance. For that, Holly Jo was thankful.

But when the bus pulled up to the school, her butterflies came back. She found herself looking for Buck and worrying about what would happen when she saw him. She'd reached her locker and was digging out what she needed for first period when she heard his voice.

A moment later, he came up next to her and threw his arm around her. "Hey," he said. "Forgot to give you this Friday." He shoved his unfinished math homework at her. "I need it by lunch."

Holly Jo had thought he'd say something about what had happened at the dance. She stared at him for a few heartbeats as if seeing him for the first time. He'd seemed so cute, so sweet, so pathetic when it came to math.

She shoved the papers away. "I won't be helping you with your math assignments anymore." She grabbed her books and slammed her locker.

"If this is about the dance—"

Head up, Holly Jo walked away. She heard him mumbling something about how irrational girls were and swearing as he went to his own locker. She didn't look back. At lunch he sat with his friends at another table.

"Buck Savage is such a jerk," Tana said, and the girls at her table all agreed. Holly Jo changed the subject, and soon they were laughing about something silly one of their teachers had said.

She wanted the fiasco of her first boyfriend to be behind her, but all that day in school, her heart ached. Not for the Buck she now knew, but for what could have been. Elaine had said it would get better. Right now, it didn't feel that way.

BAILEY GOT THE call from her father that the invitations for the barbecue had gone out. He sounded gruff, his voice edged with emotion.

"I'm so sorry I let you down."

"Dad, you didn't—"

He made a strangled sound, and she wondered how long

it had been since she'd called him Dad. "Oh Bailey, if only I could go back and—"

"You're helping me now. That's what I need. Once this is over…" She was afraid to make promises she might not be able to keep. The future was a black hole, as if it didn't exist. The thought terrified her—just as crossing paths with *him* again did. She knew that if he got the chance, he planned to hurt her again before he killed her. "Let's just get past this barbecue."

She got off the phone, knowing her father wanted and needed more from her, but she didn't have it to give right now. Not to her father and not to Stuart, she thought, looking down at the ring he'd put on her finger.

Seeing it surprised her and reminded her it wasn't a real engagement. It made her wish that she was happily planning her wedding right now. That alone shocked her. Wedding? If she'd given getting married any consideration, she would have thought that she'd want to elope or maybe not even get married.

Instead, she wanted more than anything to marry Stuart. She ached for a future with him. That's why it had broken her heart when he'd put that ring on her finger. She'd loved him and hated him because it was only pretend. He couldn't promise her that future any more than she could promise her father they'd have the time to mend the pain between them. She couldn't plan anything past the barbecue. That's if *he* didn't show up sooner. Surprise!

She had no idea how much time she had left or what she should be doing with it. For twelve years, she'd taken the offensive and gone looking for him. She'd peered under every rock, and look where that had gotten her. She'd written what she'd found, and now it would be coming out for everyone to read. She pushed the thought away. Nothing she could do about that. She might not even be alive when the book came out.

All she could think about was the barbecue and coming face-to-face with the man who'd ruined much of her life. Her life had been on hold for so long. The years of searching with only two thoughts in mind. *Find him. Kill him.*

But she'd never thought past that. Because she'd thought that she would fail, that he would kill her, that there wasn't anything past this? She looked down at the ring on her finger. Stuart. Her fiancé. Yet the only place they acted like they were in love was in public.

At his house, they were as they had been before. Distant. Her fault. She could see in his eyes how badly he wanted to take her to his bed. He had no idea how badly she wanted the same thing. But she couldn't. She felt damaged and had for twelve years. It wasn't just the scar on her breast. It was much deeper than that.

She told herself that once the man was dead, she would be ready to trust another man enough to make love with him. That man was Stuart Layton, she knew in her heart. But she couldn't turn to him—not until this was over. If they made love, she would want a future with him so badly that she feared she couldn't go through with the barbecue, let alone what she had to do when the man came for her.

All she could do was wait, something that went entirely against her nature. But there was no longer anywhere to look. She'd gotten her list down to four men—Earl Hall, Jay Erickson, AJ Plummer and Dickie Cline. None of them had a scar from the branding iron she'd hit the man with.

Yet all that had proven, Stuart told her, was that she hadn't burned him enough to leave a lasting mark—unlike what he'd done to her. Even without the scar from the brand he'd burned into her flesh, he'd left his mark on her. Some days, she feared she'd never be able to overcome that.

So she waited, wondering if she would recognize him when he came for her. She had a feeling that this time he wanted her to know who he was—and why he was going to kill her.

CJ WONDERED WHEN his mother would be back to the jail. Or if she would at all. Maybe her visit the other day had been a trick. Mental torture. Offer him a way out and then take it back. Like something he might do.

Wasn't there some expression about a leopard not being about to change his spots? He thought that was probably him. Doomed to make the same mistakes out of anger or greed or just plain meanness.

Changing would mean giving up his so-called business, the one Treyton McKenna better be running for him if he knew what was good for him. It would mean going back to the ranch with his mother still running it.

He shook his head. He'd never been good at taking orders. But at one time, he was in line to take over the ranch. His sisters wouldn't be a problem, and he'd always been able to buffalo his younger brothers.

But Brand and Ryder had been running things with their mother gone. They might not be as malleable as they'd been before. No, he couldn't see himself fighting for the ranch again. Look what had happened last time. Fortunately, he hadn't killed either sister, but his actions now had him behind bars, facing years in prison.

When the guard came by to tell him that he had a visitor, he got up off his bunk, determined to do whatever he had to to get out of here. Lying, cheating, stealing, and even stooping to attempted murder hadn't been a problem in the past.

Being someone he wasn't? He didn't know if he could pull that off, but he had to try.

Except when he walked up to the booth and sat down, it wasn't his mother who was sitting on the other side of the partition.

CHARLOTTE STAFFORD WAS back in the Powder River Basin. Rumors ran wild as people speculated on where she'd gone. She'd been at some fancy spa that had taken ten years off her face. She'd been locked up somewhere, taken by one of her enemies as payback. She'd had a secret lover who'd flown her off to an island in the Caribbean.

Holden didn't believe any of them. After the way the two of them had left things, he figured she'd gone away needing time. He'd hoped that when she was ready, she would come back.

He suspected he knew why she was back now. Her oldest son CJ's trial was coming up soon, and he'd always been her favorite. Her oldest daughter, Tilly, was pregnant with her first grandchild, and even though Holden's son Cooper was the father of the baby, Charlotte wouldn't want to miss the birth. He didn't kid himself that she'd ever come back because of him.

There was also a rumor that she'd come back to sell the ranch. Few people believed that. "She'll die out there, be buried in a pasture, before she'll give up that place. She'd never sell," he'd heard a rancher saying at the general store.

"I don't know," another had said. "Heard there's been some out-of-state billionaire interested in buying up ranches in Montana. For the right price, hell, I'd sell."

"Anyway, aren't Brand and Ryder running the ranch now?" the clerk had said as Holden stood in the back, listening. Other patrons jumped in since out-of-state billionaires were the boogeyman to locals. "I heard that they're buying up the whole damned state."

Holden could only shake his head. He couldn't imagine Lottie selling the ranch she'd fought to keep for so many years. But then again, he couldn't imagine her leaving the way she had either.

Right now, all he cared about was seeing her. He didn't care where she'd been or why. He was just glad that she was back. It was odd, since they'd been alienated for years, even more so before she'd left, but he'd missed her. He'd liked knowing she was just next door on their adjoining ranches, a horseback ride away.

But until this barbecue was over, until his daughter was safe, he was in no mental shape to face Lottie. There was so much he wanted to say to her, so much he wanted to make up for. There was also a good chance she wouldn't want to see him. He had to be ready for that outcome, and right now, he didn't think he could handle it.

Nor could he tell her about what was going on. If he saw her, he knew he'd break down and tell her everything. Lottie was his heart. He'd give anything to be able to share this burden. He couldn't even tell Elaine.

"Aren't you going riding today?" Elaine said, startling him from where she stood in his office doorway.

"I have to do some things for this barbecue."

She narrowed her eyes at him. "As long as you're feeling all right. You wouldn't lie about *that*, would you?"

He heard perfectly what she was saying. She knew he

was lying about the barbecue, what he had to do to get ready for it and a lot more. "I'm feeling fine." Even that was a lie.

She stood in the doorway as if waiting for him to level with her. Then, with a huff, she left.

He put his head in his hands, admitting only to himself how terrified he was that everything would go wrong at the barbecue, and he would lose his daughter for good.

CJ WATCHED HIS sister Oakley pull down the phone on the other side of the glass partition and put it to her ear. All he could think was that this couldn't be good. As far as he could remember, he hadn't seen her since he tried to kill her the second time.

He took down his phone and put it to his ear, ready for her to go off on him. They'd been at each other's throats since they were kids. True, he instigated it, but Oakley always held her own. He'd actually admired her on occasion. But then again, she was the reason he was locked up now.

"Mother asked me to come see you," she said, making it clear this hadn't been her idea.

Another test? "It's good to see you. I heard you got married."

She gave him the stink-eye, not buying it. Oakley had always been able to see right through his lies. Of course, that was why their mother had sent her.

"What do you want me to say? I'm sorry for what I tried to do to you? *I am.*"

"Sorry I'm alive or sorry you got caught?"

"Sorry I've been such a shitty brother," he said, and realized a part of him actually meant it. He'd bullied his siblings because he could. Also, because they were often in his way to get what he wanted.

"Mother wants to believe that you've reached rock bottom and might now see the error of your ways," she said, glaring at him. "I think she's deluding herself. You're incapable of changing even if you seriously wanted to. Oh, you'd say anything to get out of this. But I know you, CJ. You're rotten to the core. If you get out of here, you'll go back to your old ways in a heartbeat. No one will be safe from you."

He told himself to keep his cool. Oakley had always known how to get under his skin. Maybe that was exactly what she was trying to do. "If this is reverse psychology—"

"It's the truth."

"Then why did you bother to come here?"

"Because I had to look into your eyes to make sure."

"And now you're sure?" He held her gaze for a few moments before dragging it away. "You're right. I'd do anything to get out of here, let alone not go to prison for years. Who wouldn't? But maybe I'm not all bad. Maybe there's hope for me. Don't you believe in second chances?"

Her look said she didn't believe a word of it.

"How's life with Pickett? I heard he's building a house for the two of you."

"You aren't really interested in my life."

"Heard Tilly's pregnant. Do we know if it's a boy or girl yet?"

"Stop, CJ."

"You think I don't know that things have changed?" he demanded. "Tilly's married to a McKenna, and you're practically married to one too. Both of you will be living on the McKenna Ranch. Brand and Ryder have taken over the family ranch. Brand's now with the daughter of Dixon Malone, mother's murdered second husband? I hear about all of it. Isn't it possible that I wish I'd done things differently so I'm a part of it? It's like you've all written me off, all going on with your lives, completely forgetting that I existed."

Oakley smiled. "There's the CJ I know. Poor you. If you'd gotten your way, I would be dead right now. You would have kept the feud going between the families. It's been a relief not having you around." Her voice broke. "A lot has changed because you weren't part of it. You will never be part of it. You're the family's bad seed. You will never change."

With that she rose, slammed down the phone and, without even a look back, walked out.

He sat for a moment, surprised at the emotion he felt. Fury being utmost. He wanted to make her pay for what she'd said, because it had hurt a lot more than he'd thought it would. But an even stronger emotion had him wanting to prove her wrong. Prove everyone wrong about him as the guard came to take him back to his cell.

But the only way he could do that was to make his mother believe he could change. That's if she came back to see him after she talked to Oakley. He swore. He was never getting out of here.

CHAPTER TWENTY-FIVE

THE SHERIFF TOLD himself that he'd done everything he could to make sure Bailey would be safe today as he dressed for the barbecue. He felt as if the two of them had been holding their collective breaths for days, afraid the man wouldn't wait, that he would strike when they least expected it.

Finally, it was Saturday. His nerves felt raw. He regretted even going along with this even as he knew Bailey wasn't about to back out. That meant he'd be there doing everything he could to keep her alive. The problem was that anything could happen. They'd gone through various scenarios until she'd finally told him to stop.

"Don't you think that I've already thought of what I would do if I were *him*?" Bailey had demanded as she'd paced his small living room. "How to get me away from the crowd. Couldn't use the same ruse. Would need possibly a diversion. Maybe start a fire. Or set off firecrackers in the crowd to panic everyone that it was gunfire." She'd looked over at him. "What?"

"You. I know it's strange, but I love the way your mind works—even though it scares the bejesus out of me," he said.

She'd smiled and had looked as if she was going to say, *When this is over...* But she turned away, biting down on her lower lip. "We're ready. We've done all we can."

Stuart nodded. He had deputies standing by, close but not too close to the McKenna Ranch. He couldn't chance that the man might spot one of them and not show up.

He and Bailey would be going out to the ranch together. He wasn't about to let her go alone for fear she'd never make it there. His plan was to try to be by her side as much as possible. After all, she was his fiancée, and this party was to celebrate their engagement. It would be odd if he didn't stick close to her.

But he knew that he couldn't watch her the whole time. He'd actually gotten the feeling that she didn't want him to. She wanted the killer to make his move today so this could end—one way or the other.

The thought terrified him. He would do whatever it took to make sure that when this day was over, Bailey was alive and coming home with him.

Yet he knew the odds were against them. Just like the first barbecue, there would be a lot of people. It would be impossible to watch them all.

But he told himself that this time, the killer would have to be more creative to get to Bailey. She knew he was coming. He had to suspect that this was a trap. But if she was right about the man, he would see it as a challenge. He and his accomplice, Stuart reminded himself. The man wouldn't come to the barbecue alone.

BAILEY TRIED TO breathe as Stuart drove the patrol SUV into the McKenna Ranch. The place looked like it had twelve years ago. Lights were strung around a huge deck that had been constructed for the event. A mixture of classic country played from a sound system. Several makeshift bars had been set up.

As Stuart parked, she could already hear the clink of ice in glasses, the murmur of voices as the caterers finished up work to leave as per plan and the ranch hand bartenders got ready for the rush to begin. Other ranch hands had set up tables and were taking care of barbecuing the meat.

The fall day was perfect, all blue sky and puffy white clouds drifting on the warm breeze. The air even smelled the same, the scents of dried fall leaves and grasses mixing with those of the beef and pork roasting on the spits.

Bailey felt herself freeze, her heart pounding. The thought of stepping out into the coming chaos stole her breath. *He* might already be here waiting for her. She took a breath and then another.

"You can change your mind," Stuart said next to her.

She smiled over at him and reached for his hand, squeezing it and feeling his strength as well as his love. "You have no idea what you've done for me. I'd never be able to thank you enough."

"Bailey—"

"Don't worry, I'm not saying goodbye. I just needed to tell you that I couldn't get through this without knowing that I'm not just fighting to stay alive. I'm fighting for a happy ending I never dreamed possible. I love you, Stuart, with all my heart."

He squeezed her hand back, his eyes shiny. "I never thought I'd hear you say those words."

"I should have sooner, but—"

"You weren't ready."

She shook her head, glad he understood. "I'm ready for whatever comes next." She checked the knife strapped to her thigh beneath her sundress. Her phone was in the small cocktail bag she carried. She doubted she'd have time to use it, but Stuart could track the phone if he lost sight of her.

"You look beautiful," he said, and leaned over to kiss her. It was the most passionate kiss they'd shared. For a moment, they stayed locked in each other's arms.

At a tap on the side window, they both started.

HOLDEN HAD THOUGHT the engagement was part of the ruse—just like the barbecue to celebrate it. But seeing the two of them locked together, he realized that Bailey and Stuart were actually in love.

He'd hesitated for a moment before tapping on the patrol SUV window. They pulled apart, both not happy to see him. But he needed to talk to them before things got crazy. More rigs were pulling in. Stuart had parked in a spot where he would be able to get out quickly if necessary. Pickett was directing valet parking and taking keys so no one left without him knowing it. As if Holden could forget what this event was really about.

"Some of the family has gathered in the house," Holden said. "They want to congratulate the two of you on your engagement before everyone else gets here." Of course, family would come to the barbecue because of Bailey's engagement, and their family had grown in the past twelve years.

He wondered if Stuart had taken that into consideration before he and Bailey had come up with this plan.

"Are you doing all right?" Stuart asked.

The rancher swore. "Why wouldn't I be?" He looked past the sheriff to his daughter and felt emotion choke off any words he might have uttered. Turning, he headed for the house, telling himself he could do this. He hadn't lived almost sixty years and survived everything he'd been through not to be able to play his role. He shook hands with one of the ranchers, kissed the man's wife's cheek, and excused himself as he entered the house.

"The engaged couple has arrived," he announced. "They're on their way in. I had to break them up." There were chuckles around the room.

"Bailey and Stuart, who knew," Tilly said, her hand on her large baby bump. She looked as if she might have the baby before the day was out.

"They make a great couple," her husband said. Cooper had been Stuart's best friend since they were boys. If he'd been surprised by the engagement, he didn't show it.

Holden wondered what they would all say when they found out the real reason for the barbecue. He figured not much—unless this day had a tragic ending.

He pushed that thought away as Stuart and Bailey entered the house and the family swept around them. Holden watched as even Holly Jo joined them. The only McKenna family members missing were Treyton, who had been scarce for months, and Duffy, who was still working down in Wyoming.

But some of the Stafford family was here, including Oakley and Pickett and her younger brothers Ryder and Brand with his fiancée, Birdie. The women all had to see the ring. The men had to slap the sheriff on the back.

At one point, Stuart caught his eye. "I better get busy," Holden said. "Sounds like our guests are arriving." His job was to play host and not get duped by one of the wives into putting Bailey in danger.

For the life of him, he couldn't remember who'd told him about there being a horse out at the barbecue twelve years ago. It was driving him a little batty trying to recall.

But better to worry about that, he told himself as he stopped to hug his daughter on the way outside, than what might happen today. He held Bailey too long and too tight, but she let him.

BAILEY WISHED AGAIN that this was all real. She was so touched by the family's sincere best wishes. She'd never thought the McKennas and Staffords could ever come together the way they had. She'd grown up in the middle of the feud between her father and Charlotte Stafford. All of the children and the ranch hands had gotten dragged into it over the years. To see peace between at least the offspring made her heart swell.

She hated how emotional she felt when Elaine came out to draw her into the kitchen with the promise of a surprise. Bailey felt Stuart tense next to her.

"She'll be fine," Elaine said. "I won't keep her long."

The moment they reached the kitchen, the housekeeper, who'd been more like a mother to her, demanded to know what was going on.

"I don't know what—"

"Don't even bother lying to me," Elaine snapped. "I've had enough of it from your father."

Bailey looked toward the closed door. "In a nutshell? At the barbecue twelve years ago, I was assaulted and almost killed by one of the ranchers invited here today." Elaine's hand went to her mouth, her eyes filling with tears. "Recently he killed Willow. He plans to kill me. This barbecue is to lure him out."

"Oh, my God," Elaine breathed. "No wonder your father didn't tell me. What can I do?"

"Watch for a diversion. That's when he'll make his move. Just don't get hurt."

The older woman nodded and impulsively pulled Bailey into a hug. It had been years since they'd touched. Bailey hadn't realized how much she'd missed human contact.

Elaine drew back, wiping her eyes with the end of her apron. "Thank you for telling me. I thought your father had lost his mind." They both chuckled at that, but the sound of laughter died quickly from their lips. "Be careful."

Bailey nodded. "You too. I'm worried things might get out of control and innocent people will get hurt." She started to leave when Elaine said, "Your engagement?" She turned back and shook her head.

"I was afraid it wasn't real," the housekeeper said.

"But Stuart and I do love each other."

Elaine smiled. "Good."

"You don't happen to remember who told my father that one of the horses had gotten out twelve years ago, do you?"

Elaine frowned. "Good heavens, no. It wasn't me. Is that…" Her voice broke, and she shook her head as if not letting herself go there. "I wondered why you changed so much." She cleared her voice. "It's good to have you back. I've missed you."

Bailey nodded, their gazes locking for a moment, before she left the kitchen. Yes, she was back—at least for the moment.

STUART QUICKLY MOVED to Bailey as she came out of the kitchen. From her expression, he could tell what had happened with her and Elaine. The women had been close, almost like mother and daughter. Until twelve years ago.

He pulled his fiancée into his arms, giving her a smile of encouragement. It was going to be a long day. He wanted to pull the plug on this and get her the hell out of here. If they left Montana, left the country… He brushed a kiss on her neck and felt her shiver before he whispered, "Say the word and we skip town and don't look back."

She laughed softly as if he'd said something sweet and endearing before pulling back to look at him. "I'm in this for the long haul, and you know it."

"I suppose we'd better mingle, then," he said, glancing toward the crowd that had gathered outside under the twinkling lights.

Stuart took her hand, and they stepped out of the house and into the crowd of ranchers and their wives. It quickly became a blur of voices and faces, handshakes and good-old-boy slaps on the back. He didn't want to let go of Bailey, but they were pulled apart as ranchers wanted to talk to him and their wives wanted to hear about the wedding. *Have you found a dress yet...how long have you been seeing each other...you two have certainly kept it a secret... let me see that ring again…it's so beautiful.*

The sheriff kept track of her by the sound of her voice that he knew so well until the roar of the crowd grew too loud. He looked for her, trying not to panic when he didn't see her at once. One of the wives appeared to be talking her ear off, drawing her to the edge of the crowd.

He recognized the woman. Angie Erickson, Jay's wife. He excused himself from a discussion about the rise of vandalism and pushed his way toward the two of them. Even from a distance, he could tell that they weren't talking about weddings or dresses or marriage.

"There a problem here?" Stuart asked as he joined them.

Angie, her face screwed up in obvious anger, had been in the middle of warning Bailey about something. She checked her expression and took a step back, her gaze going to Bailey before settling on him.

"You have any idea what kind of woman you're marrying?" Angie asked, and looked at Bailey again. "If she publishes that so-called book of hers…" Her gaze swept back to him. "Well, it might be a short engagement, let alone marriage."

"I hope you're not threatening my fiancée," Stuart said. "There is a law against it. Unless you want to see the inside of my jail…"

Angie's mouth snapped shut. With a glare at Bailey, she huffed off.

"You all right?" he asked, noticing that Bailey looked pale.

"I'm fine. I've dealt with the Durham family before," Bailey said. "I thought at first that Angie was trying to get me alone for something else. We haven't completely ruled Jay out, right?"

"Right."

She looked past him, back toward the bar. "I could use something to drink." They'd agreed earlier that neither of them would eat or drink anything that could have been tampered with. It seemed paranoid, but then again, was it paranoia when the killer was real?

"I'll get you a bottled water, but don't set it down, okay?"

Bailey nodded. "I know he's here," she said, looking into the crowd. "I can feel him." She closed her eyes for a moment. "I just want him to make his move."

CHAPTER TWENTY-SIX

STUART FOUND HIMSELF looking at the ranchers' boots as he and Bailey headed for the bar. If she was right, the man was arrogant enough to think he could get away with it again and might not even change the way he'd been dressed before.

But would the man really wear the same boots and would Stuart be able to tell if they were black crocodile buckaroo boots, tall, with the cut heel. All he could do was look for expensive black ones, in case the man was as cocky as Bailey thought. Most of the ranchers had worn their dress boots, so looking for expensive ones in this crowd was like looking for the proverbial needle in a haystack.

The crowd undulated along with the low rumble of voices. The sheriff saw AJ Plummer with a drink in his hand, talking to Holden. Next to him was his wife, Faith. She looked uncomfortable. Probably because everyone knew that she and AJ had been separated. Were they back together? She had a drink and seemed to be searching the crowd for someone.

A burst of laughter close by startled Stuart. He turned

swiftly to see Jay Erickson's wife, Angie, entertaining a small group of men with a bawdy story. From the way she was speaking, she'd already had a few drinks before she got to the barbecue. Jay stood nearby, looking bored.

Stuart got a bottled water from the bar for Bailey, but when he looked back, she was gone. For a moment, he panicked, afraid someone in the crowd had grabbed her. With relief, he spotted her. Annette Cline had hold of Bailey's arm and was leaning toward her as she spoke intently.

He began to make his way toward the two, curious what Annette was telling her and why she seemed to be drawing Bailey away toward the trees.

"I BROUGHT YOU some bridal magazines I kept from when Dickie and I got married," Annette was saying. "I thought of you right away when I heard about your engagement to the sheriff. I have them in the truck if you want to escape this madhouse for a minute. We can go get them." She chuckled. "I almost didn't come, figured everyone would be talking about me. I was surprised when Dickie insisted. These things give me a headache."

Bailey smiled as she thought of a line from a line from some old movie. *"The one who comes to you with a deal is the traitor."* But bridal magazines? "Where's your truck parked?" she asked, curious.

"Since we were some of the last to arrive—my fault, it takes me forever to get ready, Dickie says—we're parked almost to the county road. But we can cut through the trees. It's such a beautiful day, I wouldn't mind following the river."

"You know, Annette, I really appreciate—"

"Here's your water," Stuart said, joining them. "Talking wedding plans?"

"Don't you know it," Bailey said. "Annette brought me some bridal magazines from when she and Dickie got married. We were just discussing going to her pickup to get them."

"That'll have to wait," the sheriff said. "Your father's about to make an announcement. He wants us front and center."

"Well, maybe later," Annette said. "It was just a thought. I better find Dickie. He's lost without me."

"Maybe I should have gone with her," Bailey whispered as Stuart led her toward the house. "She wanted to go through the trees along the river."

He swore. "I'm surprised after what happened with her boyfriend that she and Dickie even showed up today. I'd heard he'd been released on bail. I'd like to think both of them are harmless, but I've been in this business too long to believe that."

"If this was about him, then she'll try again, maybe more forcefully next time," Bailey said.

"Pleasant thought," Stuart said, shaking his head. "How did I ever let you talk me into this?" He realized Bailey had stopped walking and was looking back at the crowd.

"It's probably nothing, but Annette said she was going looking for her husband. Instead, she went straight to AJ Plummer."

The sheriff glanced back. Annette and AJ seemed to be having a serious talk before he walked away from her and joined his estranged wife, Faith, at the bar.

HOLDEN FINALLY GOT everyone's attention as Bailey and Stuart joined him. He had tried to write up something last night but couldn't make himself. This wasn't a real engagement party. What did you say when the happy couple believed the killer was out there in that crowd, drinking McKenna Ranch booze, and would soon to be eating his food? The thought made him sick to his stomach.

But he'd known once he'd heard what the man had done to his daughter that he would do whatever it took to catch the bastard. He just wasn't sure this was the best way. It was definitely the most dangerous, though.

He cleared his throat as everyone began to settle down. "Thank you all for coming here today to celebrate with us." He told stories about Bailey growing up, her love for horses and the ranch, how glad he was that she'd come back, and how he hoped she would always stay here. "I know she and Stuart will be happy. I've seen how much they care about each other. Everyone needs the love of their life to complete them. Bailey," he said, his voice breaking, "I'm glad you've found yours. Here's wishing you many, many years together."

The crowd clapped and cheered, and the day dragged on. Holden knew his words probably wouldn't have any effect on a killer, but he could hope, couldn't he? He'd wanted to say out loud, *Please don't take my little girl from me, you monster!* even as his heart cried out those words.

He saw Bailey on the edge of the crowd with Stuart and prayed the sheriff could keep her safe, because her father had failed her twelve years ago and feared he'd fail her again today.

STUART FOUND HIMSELF watching four of the men at the barbecue—the four that Bailey had narrowed down on her list. He hadn't been able to prove that one of them had assaulted Bailey and killed Willow. But he also hadn't been able to disprove it.

Earl Hall still looked uncomfortable, his wife Iris dutifully staying right by his side. Jay Erickson stood in a group of men drinking silently as his wife, Angie, had become more vocal and argumentative the drunker she became.

Annette had danced with AJ Plummer and anyone else she could get onto the dance floor, while her husband Dickie stood morosely on the sidelines. Stuart figured that marriage had been doomed from the beginning when Dickie had married a woman so much younger than him.

He thought about Annette attempting to get Bailey to walk with her out to their pickup to get the bride magazines. Maybe she was just trying to be friendly. Maybe her husband had killed her lover, had assaulted and tried to kill Bailey, and had killed Willow. Would a man out on bail come to a barbecue planning to kill again? Anything was possible, and that's what worried Stuart the most.

When AJ asked Bailey to dance, the sheriff couldn't help but tense. He watched Bailey's face for an indication something was wrong and saw none as they moved on the small dance floor. When the song was over, Bailey walked in Stuart's direction.

Annette had started to ask AJ to dance when his estranged wife, Faith, came up to them. She only said a few words quickly and then walked away. AJ said something to Annette and then went after his wife, catching up to her as the chow bell rang.

The ranch hands served the barbecued beef and pork along with baked beans and coleslaw. As Bailey joined Stuart, he asked, "Hungry?" She shook her head. He could tell she was worried that they'd both been wrong. The man wasn't going to make his move.

They got in line eventually, but barely ate anything on their plates. Next to them at a large table, ranchers were arguing about coalbed methane drilling. Bailey rose to take her and Stuart's empty disposable plates to the trash. They hadn't said two words to each other during the meal, no doubt both thinking the same thing. The man hadn't taken the bait. This setup hadn't worked. Which meant he would still be out there, waiting until he was ready to kill her. He'd seen through the trap.

Stuart had thought about what they would do now. He would resign. They'd leave town and go as far away from the Powder River Basin as possible. But even as he thought it, he knew they would always be looking over their shoulders—that's if he could even get Bailey to go with him. Sometimes he forgot that the engagement wasn't real. If she didn't get closure, he wasn't sure even their love could survive.

"BATHROOM," BAILEY MOUTHED to Stuart, who was still sitting at one of the long tables where she'd left him. As she headed for the row of portable outhouses brought in for the party, she felt a strange mix of emotions. This barbecue had been a mistake, a waste of time and money, a too obvious ruse to draw the man out. She had thought that the man's arrogance would make him take the bait. She'd been wrong.

She walked the line of toilets, looking for an empty one. Experience had taught her that the last one would be the least used. As she did, she saw that people were already leaving as the evening dimmed to darkness. Deep black shadows hunkered in the trees toward the river.

She hardly noticed the night slipping over her. She'd been so sure that *he* would strike today. Stuart hadn't let her out of his sight. Was that why the man hadn't made his move? She'd promised Stuart she would trust him. That she wouldn't lie or keep anything from him. Not in words, but still a promise she didn't want to break. She needed him, something that was hard to admit. She'd lost her trust in men after the attack. Stuart was more than a just a man she could trust. She loved him, but how could they move on? She couldn't. Not until this was over.

Which made this all so much harder since she couldn't lose him. She knew he would die trying to keep her safe, and because of that, she had to find the man before he came for her. She had to end this herself, but it might mean doing the last thing Stuart wanted her to do.

She finished and pushed open the outhouse door, determined to put some space between her and the sheriff. She desperately wanted this to end today, one way or the other. She couldn't keep living like this.

Her mind on drawing out the killer, she stepped out of the portable toilet and collided with Norma Jones, who must have been about to try the door and had been standing too close. The older woman grabbed her arm as if for support, bony fingers and nails biting into Bailey's flesh.

"We just keep running into each other, don't we," Norma said, hanging on as she seemed to have trouble regaining her balance. Had she been drinking? "You have been the bane of my existence for such a long time. I watched you grow up, saw how the men all buzzed around you like bees to honey."

"Norma, if this is about Ralph again—" She tried to pull

free, but the woman's talons were embedded painfully in her flesh, making her wince in pain.

"Don't pretend you don't know how Ralph feels about you," she snapped.

Bailey was glad no one was around to her the woman's wild accusations.

Norma dug in deeper as Bailey tried to pry her fingers off her arm. The woman's grip was so strong that Bailey stumbled as Norma tried to pull her into the nearby trees, away from prying eyes and ears of anyone who might come along.

Bailey finally yanked the woman's fingers off her arm, having enough of this. As she did, she noticed the deep cuts she'd left. She rubbed at them. "How many times do I need to tell you?"

"That you didn't tempt my husband? That it's not your fault you're all he's thought about for years?" Norma's voice broke with emotion. "You put a curse on him. Don't act like you didn't know." Bailey was beginning to wonder if the woman was in her right mind.

The cool breeze here in the trees felt good since Bailey realized that she was sweating and a little lightheaded. "Norma, there is nothing I can say since you aren't going to believe me. I need to get back to—"

"Your fake engagement?" Norma asked, the tone of her voice seeming to change as she studied her long fingernails. Speaking of fake, those nails looked so odd on the woman, who, as far as Bailey knew, had never worn them before. She tried to remember if Norma had been wearing them at the house when she'd drugged her.

She raised her gaze to the older woman's face. Had she gotten fake nails just for the party? That seemed so out of character for this conservative, matronly ranchwoman.

Bailey took a step, stumbled, and had to grab a tree for support. Her mouth had suddenly gone dry. She tried to lick her lips, but she could no longer feel them. "What did you do?" The words came out slurred, barely audible. Realization struck her hard as she became aware of how much her arm burned with a strange fire where Norma had drilled her fingernails into her flesh. Worse, she couldn't move. Her legs didn't even feel as if they would hold her up much longer.

Norma was smiling. "Let me help you, dear," she said as she took hold of Bailey's arm. She pulled her further into the trees and whispered, "It will be over soon. Ralph will get you out of his system for good. Ralph's a good man who lost his way. It wasn't his fault. He couldn't help himself. If he'd killed you the first time…" She tutted. "We won't let that happen again, will we."

She tried to shake the woman off her, but her limbs no longer worked as Norma drew her deeper into the growing blackness of the trees. "I'd hoped killing the other one would release your hold on him. But even when I got Willow to change her hair color, it didn't work. I argued against it at first, but Ralph's right. The reason Willow didn't work was because it takes you to break the curse. Once you're dead, he'll be free of this sinful need inside him, and we can finally live in peace like we were meant to."

She didn't even hear *him* come out of the woods. Suddenly *he* was there, taking hold of her, lifting her off her feet as he had before and taking her into the woods. The sounds of the barbecue grew more distant. She could hear the river, the sigh of the breeze in the drying leaves of the cottonwoods, the sound of Ralph's heavy breathing. She recognized it and felt her heart pound even harder than it already was.

Ralph Jones was going to kill her, and his wife, Norma, was going to help him.

STUART HAD LOST track of time, he realized. Bailey hadn't returned from the portable outhouses. He'd assumed when she didn't come right back that she'd had to wait for one. He could see that a line had formed at this end.

He'd been about to go check when he heard a disturbance break out. Angie. Jay was trying to help her up from where she'd fallen on the dance floor. At the same time, Stuart saw Pickett hurrying over to another dining table where Holden was sitting. Stuart watched him lean down to whisper something to the rancher. At once, Holden was on his feet.

"What's happening?" the sheriff asked, getting up to rush over.

"Tilly. She's in labor," Pickett said. "Cooper's taking her to the hospital, but he needs some vehicles moved so he can get out."

"I'll find Bailey, and we'll come help," Stuart told them.

The two hurried off. Stuart couldn't leave without Bailey. He turned back to the line of blue plastic outhouses, glanced at his watch, then frowned. Bailey should have been back by now.

As he made his way to the toilets, his heart began to pound. All of the doors were closed. He began trying them, starting with the first one and going down the line. Any with people in them, he yelled, "Who's in there?"

Several men answered and one woman. Not Bailey. With growing urgency, he hurried down the row. Not Bailey. Not Bailey. He reached the last one. Not Bailey.

He looked around for her. Had she gone back to the dining area a different way, and he'd just missed her? He knew she'd been getting antsy, so invested in having this end here today. Had she done something reckless?

Stuart ran back out to where they'd been sitting earlier, searching the diminishing partygoers. No Bailey. People were leaving now that they'd eaten. Only the diehards would stay for the free booze until it, too, was cut off.

He looked around, aware that dusk was gathering and feeling his anxiety growing. Where was she? His heart had known even before he had started checking the toilets. She could have used going to the restroom as a ruse, daring the killer to finally make his move.

Still, he went back along the row of toilets, looking for a sign of a struggle, trying to think like the killer, because he didn't want to believe Bailey had gone rogue. If the killer had grabbed her here, wouldn't someone have noticed?

He hurried to the last stall and looked into the thick stand of cottonwoods. Golden leaves cascaded down in the breeze, ghostlike in the last of the daylight. He could smell the river but couldn't see it. He looked down at the bed of leaves on the ground. There was no way to track her. Except for her phone.

He looked on his phone and then at the last outhouse in the row. The phone was inside there. As soon as the person came out, he checked and knew at once. It had been dropped down into the toilet hole. He swore.

Stuart thought he was being so careful, hardly letting her out of his sight. But he knew in his gut, in his heart. The killer had her—just as she'd known the man would come for her. Why hadn't she called for help? What had happened after she'd disappeared around the corner along the row of portable toilets? Was it possible she'd dropped her phone into the hole so he couldn't follow her? Not even Bailey would do that to throw him off her trail.

His mind raced as he felt seconds ticking by. *Think.* Where would the killer take her? He tried to remember who of the four men Bailey had suspected were still at the party. He'd seen all four of them just minutes ago, hadn't he?

Through the low limbs of the cottonwoods, he could see nothing but darkness. If he was right and this was where she'd been grabbed, then where could he take her and not be seen? Not to get his valeted vehicle. He'd head for the river and the county road, where he'd either stashed another vehicle, or…

Or someone was picking him up.

The accomplice.

Making a quick call to the deputies he had standing by, he told them to stop any vehicle leaving the barbecue. Then he rushed back to the party to look one more time for Bailey. He felt as if he'd just missed her by a few minutes. But she was nowhere in sight. Because she was no longer here.

He was more convinced than ever that the killer would have taken her into the trees toward the river. But before he could move, he heard his name called and turned to see Holden rushing toward him. "If this is about Tilly—"

"No," Holden said, sounding winded. Or scared. Stuart's pulse jumped. "I saw her."

"Bailey?" he asked hopefully, but the rancher shook his head.

"The woman who told me that one of our horses was out at the last barbecue," Holden said, catching his breath. "I just saw her getting in her pickup and remembered. It was Norma, Norma Jones."

Stuart stared at him. That wasn't possible. Ralph Jones was the man? "Was Ralph with her?" he asked, already knowing the answer.

"She was by herself and seemed to be in a hurry. Where's Bailey?"

"Ralph Jones has her," he said, even though he was having trouble imagining that Ralph was the man. But how else could he explain it? Unless someone else had told Norma to notify Holden about the horse twelve years ago.

Stuart couldn't take the chance. "Don't let anyone else out on the road, and if you see Norma, don't let her leave. Or Ralph either." Stuart turned and ran toward the stable, where a saddled horse was waiting for just this occurrence. They had tried to think of everything, knowing if the man wanted to get to Bailey, he would.

As he swung up into the saddle and spurred the horse toward the cottonwoods, he notified his deputies. "Stop Norma Jones and her husband, Ralph. Whatever you do, don't let them get away."

CHAPTER TWENTY-SEVEN

STUART RACED THE horse through the dark shadows beneath the thick stand of cottonwoods. He told himself that Ralph would head for the river. Once he'd heard that Norma was headed for the county road along the river, he knew where she was going and why. He told himself that Ralph wouldn't hurt Bailey. Not yet.

He could feel darkness close in around him the moment he left the ranch and lights behind. Bailey was out here somewhere, probably already drugged. Norma would be coming down the county road to pick the two of them up. If he didn't stop them before that, he had no idea where they were taking Bailey.

Somewhere close? He still couldn't get his head around Norma being a part of this, let alone Ralph. But like most places, the Powder River Basin had an ugly underbelly. Most people never saw it, never knew anything about the evil in even their closest neighbors. But Bailey did.

Ahead he could see the river winding north to dump into the Yellowstone. Past it were more cottonwoods and finally the county road. His radio squawked, and he brought his horse up short to answer it.

"We have Norma," his deputy said.

"Is Bailey—"

"Sorry, Norma's alone. She said she and Ralph got into an argument, and she left him back at the barbecue. What do you want us to do with her?"

His mind raced. Had she been a decoy? Had he been wrong about her leaving to pick up Ralph and Bailey down the road? Wouldn't they have had a backup plan in case something like this happened? "Take her in for questioning. Don't let her out of your sight. On the way to town, watch the road. I don't believe he's back at the ranch. If he has Bailey..." He couldn't finish. "Keep her from making a phone call."

He was breathing hard as he looked through the trees, not knowing where to go or what to do. What if he was wrong and they hadn't come this way? Ralph could have her in a building on the ranch. All of the hands were busy. He could have already killed her.

Stuart heard the rustle of leaves over his pounding heart. He started to turn, saw the limb before it struck him, but only got a glimpse of Ralph. The blow doubled him over. He was going for his gun when he was hit again, this time in his side, hard enough to break his ribs and knock him off the horse.

The horse kept going as he tumbled to the ground. Desperately he tried to catch his breath and get his gun from his holster as a large dark shadow loomed over him. Ralph still held the limb in his hands as he advanced.

Stuart rolled to the side, coming up with his gun. He fired off two shots, both dead center. Ralph stumbled back, dropping the limb as he seemed about to collapse to the ground. But before the sheriff could get to his feet, the man had staggered upright, picking up a large rock as he did. Holding the rock over his head with both hands, his muscles bulging with the effort, his face red and twisted in a macabre grimace, Ralph lunged at him.

There was that instant when Stuart felt himself in his nightmare, that panic from being backed up against a wall with no way out. Only this time he wasn't wounded and bleeding to death, but he was injured and having trouble breathing, and the fear was the same. He didn't want to die here today.

He raised his police service revolver and fired again, four more shots that riddled the big man's body and his already drenched bloody shirt. He pulled the trigger yet again. The click of the empty chamber was so loud it startled him.

The report of the gunfire still hung for a moment in the air before everything went silent. Nothing moved—including Ralph Jones.

It felt as if time was suspended. Stuart could hear the rustle of the leaves overhead, smell the river, feel the warm earth beneath him along with the pain. At least a couple of his ribs were broken. One might have pierced his lung. He was having a hard time drawing breath.

But his gaze was on Ralph and his large, dark silhouette looming over him, not moving, the huge rock still balanced over his head. His gun empty, his chest heaving for air he couldn't seem to draw, Stuart crab-crawled backward until he collided with a tree trunk.

He was still fighting for breath, the empty gun in his hand, his heart lodged in his throat. He remembered the fear when he'd shot the woman who'd tried to kill him all those months ago. There'd been that irrational moment when he'd thought that someone so twisted, so malicious couldn't be killed by mere bullets. It was the same fleeting feeling he had before Ralph's legs gave out and he dropped the rock. It came down with him as he hit the ground.

Stuart leaned against the tree trunk, still fighting to breathe as he reloaded the gun, keeping his eye on Ralph as he did. He could see where Ralph's skull had collided with the rock when he fell. Yet Stuart still expected the big man to rise and lunge for him again. In his mind, this aberration had taken on superhuman powers that no mortal man could kill.

One day, he told himself, he would see Ralph Jones as nothing more than a sick, dangerous man with a wife who would do anything to keep him, including helping him rape and kill. But not today. Ralph Jones was a monster who'd haunted Bailey's nightmares and maybe always would. Stuart knew monsters were real. He'd known it since he was a kid. He'd seen a monster hide behind a kind-looking face, a sweet smile and even a piece of fudge, all of it making them even more frightening and evil.

Holstering his gun, Stuart pushed himself up, cradling his ribs with one arm, as he called out Bailey's name, fearing there would be no answer.

"Bailey!" This time his voice was a little louder, though it hurt his chest to call out. He heard a faint sound. The rustle of leaves. A small whimper like an animal caught in a trap. He moved toward the sound, terrified of what he would find.

She lay in beneath a tree some yards away. She was so still that for a painful heartbeat, he thought she was dead. But then she blinked up at him, a tear leaking out of one eye and sat up. He fell to his knees next to her, and pulled her close as he repeated, "It's over. It's finally over."

BAILEY DIDN'T REALIZE she was crying until Stuart fell to the ground next to her and kissed away her tears. Feeling was coming slowly back to her extremities. She tried to form the words but couldn't as she heard sirens in the distance. She looked into Stuart's eyes from where her head rested in his lap, felt her lips move but wasn't sure anything had come out. *Tell me he's dead.*

At first, she thought the movement she saw out of the corner of her eye was a deputy coming to help. But as the man came out of the trees, she saw his face, one side caved in. She opened her mouth. The sound less like a scream, more like a whine. Ralph was moving slowly, dragging one leg along with a tree limb. She could see his black crocodile boots, smell him.

Stuart was holding his ribs as if he was having trouble breathing. He was telling her that everything was going to be all right as she tried to warn him it wasn't over. She opened her mouth, but a whine came out of lips that felt numb and unmoving.

Ralph lifted the limb. The front of him was covered in blood, and his face— Her hand went to Stuart's holster and the gun. She pulled the weapon, drawing it out, startling Stuart as Ralph lunged forward using the tree limb for support. He was only feet away when he started to swing the limb. She saw his boots. buckaroo boots, shiny black crocodile dress boots, remembering the last time she saw them and the man coming at her.

Bailey raised the gun and fired and fired and fired until it merely clicked as it ran out of ammunition.

"He's dead," Stuart said as he joined her standing over Ralph's body and eased the gun from her hand. "He's dead, Bailey."

She finally heard the words she'd wanted to hear for twelve years. She began to cry as she saw the beams of flashlights and heard help coming through the trees.

CHAPTER TWENTY-EIGHT

AN INVESTIGATOR FROM the state crime team sat in on the interrogation of Norma Jones along with the county prosecutor and the sheriff. She'd declined having a lawyer present, saying that they were all crooks.

Stuart sat across from her, unable not to think of his mother. On the surface, Norma appeared to be a nice older woman who loved to cook and clean and make her famous fudge at Christmas. But under that facade lay something dark and dangerous.

Her husband, Ralph, had been a large, quiet man who had blended into the ranching community seamlessly. He'd headed up the fight against coalbed methane drilling, starting Dirty Business, the underground group. He attended church religiously with his wife at the community hall down the road from his ranch. He didn't look or act like a killer. Instead, the sheriff thought most people saw Ralph as harmless—including Bailey.

"You know what this is about, right, Norma?" Stuart asked, the video camera running. He was still having trouble breathing although his cracked ribs were taped. Fortunately they weren't broken and hadn't punctured a lung as he'd feared.

"Ralph," Norma said, nodding. She sat up straight, meeting their gazes, as if only too ready to help them. She hadn't cried when she'd heard that her husband was dead. She'd looked a little surprised, his deputy had said, but nothing more. She'd been shocked, though, to hear that she was being arrested, saying it wasn't her, it was Ralph and his lust for Bailey McKenna.

Now she folded her hands in her lap and looked the sheriff in the eye. "We are respectable people. Ralph was a good man. He wasn't perfect. Few men are. But I had dedicated my life to him—just as I promised his mother I would do. Truth is, he would have never looked twice at me if his mother hadn't encouraged him to marry me. She knew I would do anything to make him happy. He didn't cuss, and he rarely complained. I made a home for him, kept the cleanest house, lay with him whenever he asked, ignored his wandering eye." Her chin came up, her back ramrod straight. "I was raised to stand by my husband."

"Even help him kill?" the sheriff asked.

Norma waved that away and turned to the state crime investigator. "Did you know I make the best peanut butter fudge in the entire Powder River Basin and have for years? Ralph loved my fudge. I started making it just for him because it gave me such pleasure." She smiled as if remembering.

"You know Ralph gave women your fudge as small presents," Stuart said.

"Yes," she said with a sigh. "I knew. It was harmless."

"Like it was with Willow Branson?"

"I wouldn't know about that. Bailey though, she doesn't like my peanut butter fudge," Norma said, as if that told them everything there was to know about Bailey.

"Whose idea was it to kill her?" Stuart asked.

She drew herself up, chin rising again. "Something had to be done to end the spell that woman had on my husband. Ralph didn't want to be this way. He would cry, get down on his hands and knees, and beg me to help him. I had to help. There was no other way to get it out of his system."

"You know he raped those women," the state crime investigator said.

Norma pursed her lips. "Had to be done. Only way. If just killing them would have done it, I'd have taken care of it myself. But Ralph said this way, he could kill the horrible compulsion in him."

The room went deathly quiet for a few moments.

"Why brand them?" the sheriff finally asked.

"To mark them like the harlots they are."

"But why with a horseshoe brand?"

She seemed to think about that for a moment, frowning as she did. "I told you, didn't I, that we had tiny horseshoes as decorations at our wedding for luck and happiness?"

"But why brand these women with it?"

Her frown deepened. "I don't know. I guess because I still had one in my wood-burning craft kit. I wanted them marked. I told Ralph it was no different than branding cattle. Why does it matter? It's over." She started to get up, brushing off her dress skirt as she rose. "I need to see to my chores."

"You can't leave, Norma," the sheriff said. "You helped your husband assault and kill one woman and assault and attempt to kill the other. If Bailey hadn't gotten away, you and your husband would have killed her. Instead, you helped him not only commit these crimes, but also cover them up."

"He was my husband," she said, her voice steely. "A good woman does whatever she has to do to protect her husband and help him..." Her voice broke. "No matter what he needs, no matter what he does. I tried to save him from Bailey McKenna."

"Why her?" Stuart asked.

Norma frowned again, her lips pursing. "You never met Ralph's mother, did you, Sheriff? She and Ralph were very close. Ralph was her baby boy. He cried like one when she died. It had been just the two of them after her husband died young. Ralph had been the only child after a half-dozen miscarriages. She called him her miracle baby." She looked at the sheriff, locking her gaze with his. "I always thought it was odd how much Ralph's mother resembled Bailey." He felt the hair quill on the back of his neck. "I think he missed his mother."

Stuart turned to the state crime investigator. "If you wouldn't mind reading Norma her rights," he said quietly. "Then she is all yours." He rose and walked out of the room. Behind him, he could hear her Miranda rights being read and Norma's confusion as she was handcuffed and taken away.

Moving quickly down the hall, he shoved open the door and stepped outside to throw up in the grass, grabbing his side in pain. His stomach roiled, but the queasiness passed. He'd been planning to walk away from this job and would have if not for Bailey. He'd had no business working this case. He'd been too close to it from the start, not to mention where his head had been. He'd almost gotten her killed.

He wiped his mouth and took a large gulp of fresh air.

He felt sick to his stomach, shaken still. Not that he hadn't been from the moment he saw Willow Branson lying face down in the river. Just as Ralph had said, she'd looked so much like Bailey.

Stuart breathed deeply, his skin crawling from what Norma had said back in the interrogation room, and what she hadn't. Bailey was right. We didn't know our neighbors. We had no idea what goes on behind closed doors. Everyone had a secret, some more than others. Some worse than others.

Stuart Layton certainly had secrets. From the time he was but a child, he'd known to keep quiet about what went on behind his closed doors. He'd grown up scared of what kind of man he was. Worse, what he might be capable of doing. His greatest fear had always been what he would do if the truth came out about the woman who'd raised him.

His father had been sheriff, a man sworn to protect, and yet he hadn't protected Stuart from the woman who should have loved him. His childhood had been a horror show of frightening memories right up until the night his mother disappeared.

At the sudden touch of a hand on his shoulder, he started and turned quickly to find the county prosecutor looking much like Stuart felt. Ashen. But concern for him was written all over her face.

"That was ugly," the prosecutor said. "You going to be all right?"

That was a question Stuart had been asking himself for months. "I have no idea."

BAILEY FELT NUMB as she sat on the sheriff's front porch, watching the day fade. Stuart's house sat on a slight hill with a view of the Powder River now snaking its way north, bordered by golden-leafed cottonwoods cutting through the river bottom. Overhead, the sky darkened into her favorite clear, deep blue, while to the west, the sun's prism of pinks and reds and oranges rimmed the purples of the mountains. She could feel dusk begin to settle in around her. She liked this time of day, always had.

It was over. After twelve long years, her search was over. So why did she feel empty inside, hollowed out? Her attacker was dead. She'd shot him, seen him die. His accomplice would soon be on her way to prison. She thought of Norma's fudge and felt sick to her stomach.

She'd been wrong about more than how she would feel when *he* was dead. She'd eliminated Ralph from the list, but now couldn't remember why. It had to be more than the feeling that Ralph was harmless, always so polite and nice, the first one to help anyone in trouble—just like his wife had been when Bailey was growing up.

That's when she remembered. Ralph had an alibi. Norma had told her that she'd had to leave the barbecue early because she was sick. Several others from the barbecue had verified it. As far as anyone knew, she and Ralph had left together. Bailey had never verified if anyone had seen Ralph right before or when they were leaving. Norma had lied and somehow gotten him off the ranch without anyone seeing Ralph injured and bleeding.

Everyone in the Powder River Basin must be as shocked as she'd been. She'd been taken to the house, her father standing guard over nosy neighbors and will-wishing friends. Until she'd sneaked out and come here, where she felt more at home than she did at the massive home her father had built on the ranch. Her father would never understand that—she didn't herself.

At the sound of a vehicle, she squinted into the growing darkness to see Stuart's patrol SUV pull in. Just the sight of him as he stepped out made her feel better. He was still moving slowly because of his cracked ribs, but he smiled when he saw her as if he'd known this was where she'd come.

She saw then that he'd picked up a six-pack of beer. He pulled one loose and handed it to her before opening one for himself. They sat listening to the familiar sounds of Powder Crossing and the river that ran through it.

"I need to give you this back," Bailey said as she turned the engagement ring on her finger. Stuart started to object, but she stopped him. "It wasn't a real engagement." She pulled off the ring and held it out to him.

He stared at the ring in her hand but didn't move to take it. "Does it count that I wanted to believe it was real?" When she said nothing, he took the ring, studying it in his palm for a moment before he pocketed it.

HOLDEN HAD LIVED next to this river his whole life. He'd never doubted how important it was to their livelihood. But as he rode along its edge this morning, he couldn't imagine ever living anywhere that there wasn't flowing water. He'd watched this river make its way north for years. He'd heard every joke about the Powder.

He often thought of what his grandmother had told him when he was a boy: *It's unlucky to part company with someone near a stream.* Looking back, he knew he should have taken her words more seriously. It had been near a stream where he and Lottie had parted company. That certainly was unlucky.

But then again, his grandmother also said that if you were trying to get away from supernatural creatures, crossing running water was usually a good way to leave them behind. Lottie was the most beautiful creature he'd ever seen, but there was nothing supernatural going on there—unless it was love.

In the years since, he'd never questioned the power of free running water. He'd tried to live his life like a river that keeps flowing. But while a river didn't change its direction and just kept moving, he couldn't *not* look back. He had tried to forget the past and focus on the future. But when it came to Lottie, he'd failed. He couldn't forget her.

Which was why he was riding his horse over to their spot on the creek this morning. Bailey was safe, her attacker and Willow's killer dead, his accomplice in jail. Tilly was fine. Her contractions had been a false alarm, so that excitement too had passed. He'd put off trying to see Charlotte for as long as he could. Heart on his sleeve, he rode into the cool shadows of the cottonwoods and saw her.

She sat on her favorite large boulder, her knees pulled up to her chest, her gaze on the water running past. Her horse was tied to a tree back on Stafford Ranch property. It whinnied as if glad to see his mare, and Lottie looked up.

His throat tightened as he ground-tied his horse and made his way toward her on the rocks in the creek. She hadn't moved. She didn't even appear to be breathing as he neared.

He remembered all the other times, the good and the bad. The times they made love along the grassy shore. Also how she would threaten him with her whip or her rifle, both times still sitting on her horse, he noted.

Words failed him as he looked into her beautiful green eyes. As they filled with tears, he reached for her, dragging her from the rock into his arms. She melted against him, her arms going around his neck. They held each other like that for a long time.

Holden could hear the water, smell the fallen dried leaves of the cottonwoods, feel Lottie in his arms. A flock of geese cut a V in the brilliant blue of the Montana sky overhead, honking as they passed.

"You came home," he whispered, drawing back just enough to look into her eyes. She held his gaze and nodded. "Promise you'll never leave again."

Her smile filled his heart like helium. She buried her face in his shoulder, and he pulled her closer. Lottie had come home. He felt such a surge of hope, the future suddenly looking brighter. Anything was possible.

HOLLY JO HAD known that Tana wouldn't ride the bus long. Especially after she got a boyfriend with a driver's license and his father's old pickup.

But that was all right, because Holly Jo and Gus were talking again. As if it had happened overnight, Gus had shot up a few inches, which had made him as tall or taller than the other boys his age. He looked stronger, too, since he'd been working with his dad.

But the real change in Gus was because of what happened at school. She'd heard about it from Tana.

"Apparently Gus overheard Buck saying something rude about you, Holly Jo. Gus just walked up to Buck and punched him in the face, knocking him to the floor. Then Gus stood over him and said, 'If you ever say something like that about Holly Jo again, I'll kick your butt.'"

Holly Jo pretended to be embarrassed by the whole thing. But she couldn't help being proud of her old friend for sticking up for her. It changed how the other kids saw Gus as well. It gave him a kind of cred. He began making more friends. Even Buck and his friends gave him a wide berth as if Gus had earned their respect.

She and Gus had started sitting together on the bus. They'd become friends again. He came over to the ranch, where they rode horses together. She taught him a couple of tricks. The one thing she realized when she and Gus hung out together was that she wasn't ready to grow up. Not yet. Her life after being kidnapped had changed too fast. She didn't like the person she'd become with Buck. She hadn't been ready.

Nor had she been sure how she felt about Holden adopting her. But after the adoption had gone through, she found herself excited about it. She was now legally Holly Jo McKenna. She and Holden had agreed that she could still call him HH, even though sometimes she liked the idea of calling him Dad, since she'd never had one before. Maybe one day she would. She didn't think he would mind.

STUART AND BAILEY had said that they loved each other sitting in his patrol SUV at the barbecue, but that now seemed like a very long time ago. Stuart knew that people often did things they later regretted when they were under duress. His declaration had been heartfelt. He couldn't swear that Bailey's had.

As they sat on the porch, quietly letting darkness settle around them, they sipped their beers without talking. He thought of this woman he'd fallen in love with. She'd been wild in her youth, too pretty for her own good, and too smart. While she seemed to have curbed that wildness, there was still an intensity about her, a drive, as well as a wounded part of her that often came out as anger against the world. He'd seen it all up close and doubted finding her attacker had instantly changed that. It would take time, especially after twelve years.

Now at least he thought he understood the dark side of her. He knew what she had to be angry about. From the outside, Bailey had seemed to have it all. Her father was a wealthy, powerful man who owned a huge ranch in the Powder River Basin. Bailey was his only daughter. Growing up, he doubted she had wanted for anything.

Stuart, on the other hand, had lived a very modest existence and still did. He'd envied ranch kids born to land, money, prestige. It made him wonder what had been so awful about growing up on the McKenna Ranch that had made Bailey angry about her life. If anyone should be angry, it was him, raised by a hard, uninvolved father and a dangerous mother.

Just the thought of his mother reminded him of the book Bailey said she'd written. Now she would have her ending. He shouldn't have been surprised that she'd become a writer. All those years of devouring books, her interest in what made people tick from the time she was small, her need to dig deeper. It had always been there. It was a huge part of the woman he'd fallen in love with.

A breeze stirred the nearby trees, scattering dried leaves across the yard. Bailey put down her beer. He felt her gaze on him even before she stood and took his hand. He could feel her trembling. From the cold fall night? Or from fear?

She drew him up from the porch until they stood only

a breath apart. He saw her swallow, felt the push-pull of her emotions as he had for longer than he could remember.

"Would you want to make love with me?" Her voice broke.

"I never thought you'd ask," he said, grinning as he dragged her to him, squeezing her tight, and winced as he felt his cracked ribs complain.

"Oh, I forgot. Maybe we should wait until—"

"They'll be fine." He smiled at her and saw her fear. "We'll both be fine."

"I want this so badly, but—"

She didn't have to tell him that she felt damaged. He planned to do his damnedest to make her never feel like that again. "Bailey, you trust me?" She nodded and forced a smile, and he kissed her. "We have all night."

CHAPTER TWENTY-NINE

BAILEY FEARED THAT even though she loved Stuart, she couldn't do this. Just the thought brought back the horror of the masked man standing over her, the pain of being violated and scarred forever, and worst, a fear he would come for her again.

But Stuart didn't lead her to his bedroom as she'd anticipated. Once inside the house, he stopped in the kitchen to turn on the radio. Then he pulled her into a slow dance. They'd never danced together. The thought made her laugh to herself. They'd never even had a real date. She would have said that she hardly knew the sheriff, but that would have been a lie.

Surprisingly, they danced well together—as if they'd been doing it for years. As they moved to the music, he bent his head to the side of her neck. His breath against her sensitive skin behind her ear sent a shiver of desire through her. He pulled her closer, her breasts pressing against his hard chest. She could tell he was in pain. What had she been thinking even suggesting that they make love with him hurt?

She'd just wanted to get it over with. Just do it, even if it was trauma, telling herself it would be better the next time. If there was a next time.

The song ended, but another came on. Stuart didn't seem to be in any hurry as he kissed her softly on the mouth, tracing his tongue across her lips. She found herself beginning to relax a little. The kiss became more passionate as they danced.

Her breasts felt heavy, the nipples hard and aching for his touch. Breaking off the kiss, he began to trail kisses slowly down her throat, releasing button after button as he went. She felt her desire for this man burn hotter along with her fear.

He reached her bra and drew down the right side to lathe her nipple with his tongue before nipping at the hard point. She groaned his name and pressed against his mouth, heat rushing to her center.

But as he started to do the same with her left breast, she grabbed his hand to stop him. Their gazes locked, hers filling with tears. The brand on her breast was faint. *He* hadn't been able to hold the iron to it long enough to go through the second or third layer of skin.

But it was still scarred. A constant reminder and why she hadn't been with a man in all this time. She hadn't wanted Stuart to see her like this.

He took her hand, pressed it to his lips, his gaze never breaking with hers. When he released it, he opened his shirt. She hadn't really ever seen how scarred his chest and torso were before that moment. He'd always hurried to cover up—just as she did. Emotion weakened her knees and made her eyes fill as she leaned toward him and began to kiss his scars. He let out a soft moan as the music played and she kissed her way across his broad chest, lathing his nipple as he'd done to hers.

After a moment, she drew back and, heart pounding, let him remove her shirt and bra. She couldn't look at him at first, but then he cupped her left breast and kissed her scar as she had his. Tears filled her eyes.

When he lifted his head, he smiled and said, "You're beautiful, Bailey McKenna, scars and all."

She laughed. "You too, Stuart Layton, scars and all."

Then he kissed her, drawing her to him, into his strong arms. His body felt warm against hers. Hadn't she dreamed of this on all those nights when she'd come to him and he'd waited patiently, knowing she needed him, but unsure why?

Bailey barely remembered them taking off the rest of their clothes, leaving a trail of garments through the house as they fell into his bed. But she would always remember the gentle way he touched her, finding those sensitive spots that made her moan and writhe, wanting him like she'd never thought possible.

"Stuart," she'd pleaded at one point, gathering up a handful of his hair to pull him up to her mouth so she could kiss him. He'd given her so much pleasure, but now she wanted him inside her. "Please."

He had gently lowered himself on her, flesh to flesh, heart to heart. When he'd entered her, she'd felt both desire and relief. He made love to her, so different from her other nightmare memory that she felt it begin to fade. Stuart's love would heal her, already had, she thought as he made her come yet again before letting himself go. They'd been breathing hard, looking into each other's eyes and laughing. They done it. They'd found their way to each other against the odds.

She was smiling, cuddled against him, finally in that safe place she'd longed for. She wondered if he would resign as sheriff now or stay. She thought about her book. She could finally write that last chapter.

One day Stuart would ask her about his mother. Or maybe he'd wait until the book was published and read about it then. There'd been too many secrets, but some of them would be coming to light. She would weather that storm when it hit.

When she woke the next morning, she found him beside the bed on one knee. "Marry me, Bailey. I love you. You love me. We were made for each other."

She'd nodded, smiling at him as he put the ring back on her finger before he crawled into bed, promising to love, honor and cherish her. Then he set about showing her exactly how he planned to do all three.

CJ HAD CONVINCED himself that his mother wouldn't be coming back to the jail. Charlotte Stafford was no fool. Once Oakley told her about her visit to her brother, her mother would know for certain he couldn't change.

That's why he was so surprised when he was told he had a visitor and found his mother patiently waiting in the booth behind the Plexiglass partition. He sat down, picked up the phone, and saw that he was shaking. She'd offered him a chance to start over, to erase what he'd done, to change. He hadn't realized how badly he'd want to try until that moment.

"You came back," he said, unable to keep the surprise out of his voice any more than he could the fear of why she'd come. Would she be so cruel as to offer him a way out and then take it back? That would have been something he might have done. The thought didn't help.

"Have you had time to think over what we talked about?" she asked.

"I've done nothing but," he said honestly.

"I believe in second chances," she said. "Holden and I… well, we're going to be seeing each other."

He nodded. He'd wondered about her change of heart. He should have known it was Holden McKenna's doing. He ground his teeth for a moment, having spent his life hating the man for hurting his mother, and worse, hating her for having a weak spot for the man even after he had broken her heart.

"You've always been in love with him," he managed to say now that he knew where her generosity had come from. She was telling him that if he didn't accept this and Holden, he could rot in jail the rest of his life.

"How do you feel about that?" She studied him with eyes so much like his own.

He knew he had to be honest. If he too readily accepted this turn of events, she'd know he was lying. "I can't say I've ever liked him, but then again, he broke my mother's heart by marrying someone else." He met her gaze. "But if you can forgive him—"

"Forgiveness is a two-way street. I hurt him deeply too. I'm hoping our love, which has lasted all these years despite our…past, is strong enough to put all of that behind us."

"Are you talking marriage?" he asked, having trouble

even saying the words. "Where would you live? What would happen to the Stafford Ranch?"

He saw her expression and realized that he'd said too much.

"We aren't to that point. We haven't discussed any of this."

His greatest fear was that the Stafford Ranch would be gobbled up by the McKenna Ranch, and Holden would take everything. CJ had dreamed of the day when he would run the ranch. That dream popped like a bubble. If the ranch was gone, what was there for him if he got off and was released? What was the point?

"What are you offering me?" he asked, unable to keep his anger or his frustration out of his voice.

"Your brothers, Brand and Ryder, have been running the ranch," she said. "You would work with them, the three of you. I wouldn't take the ranch away from my children."

Work with Brand and Ryder? She had to be kidding. He'd run that ranch when they were still in diapers. "I see." He did see. He wouldn't go to prison, because his life would be a prison of its own.

He smiled. He knew exactly what he wanted to say. *I do believe in second chances. But I'm going to have to pass. I've hired a lawyer. He's probably not as good as one you could hire for me. Also, I wouldn't have your clout behind me. But I think I'm going to take my chances.*

Fortunately, he was too smart to say any of that. "Whatever you're offering me, Mother, I'd like to take it. I want a future." He was already thinking of the things he'd do if he was free. Going back to work the ranch wasn't one of them. "Thank you."

His mother smiled.